But I Already Said Goodbye

Wendy Thacher Jensen

Black Rose Writing | Texas

ISBN: 978-1-68513-193-7
PUBLISHED BY BLACK ROSE WRITING
www.blackrosewriting.com

Printed in the United States of America
Suggested Retail Price (SRP) $21.95

But I Already Said Goodbye is printed in Garamond Premier Pro

*As a planet-friendly publisher, Black Rose Writing does its best to eliminate unnecessary waste to reduce paper usage and energy costs, while never compromising the reading experience. As a result, the final word count vs. page count may not meet common expectations.

ACKNOWLEDGMENTS

For Jim LaVeck, who gave me the idea for this book, and gave so generously of his time for its development. For Jenny Stein, who made the manuscript oh so much better, and for Vic Boynton, who has always held my heart in her hands and who made this book possible in so many ways. For Maggie Jensen, for her beautiful and evocative cover design, and who listened to my ideas and gave me the courage to keep going. For James Jensen, who gave me the loving understanding I needed, when I needed it. For Jim Jensen, who gave me a safe place from which to create this story. For Christina Chambreau, Jennifer Ericsson, Barbara Malcolmson-Baily, Chanelle Moore, and my Writer's Night Out group from the New Hampshire Writer's Project (NHWP), for their fearless reading and honest reactions. For Masheri Chappelle of the NHWP who made a beautiful trailer and coached me during a reading of the book at the Hatbox Theater and a Literature Out Loud webinar. And finally, for the advocates at the Crisis Center of Central New Hampshire, who tirelessly help those in need 24 hours a day. Thank you all!

Praise for
But I Already Said Goodbye

"...it is beautifully written, and could change hearts and minds if picked up by the right readers."
–Tamira Thayne of FreedomChaser Books

"If we were granted access to the innermost thoughts and feelings of a young person subjected to sexual violation, how might we ourselves be changed? How can trust so profoundly betrayed become whole again? This groundbreaking novel sensitively depicts a harrowing yet hopeful quest for healing that begins in desolate isolation and ends with the creation of healthy community. The author challenges us to grow in empathy and understanding, not just for fellow humans, but also our fellow animals subjected to exploitation and abuse. With hard won insight derived from personal experience, Wendy Jensen shows how all forms of violence are similarly destructive, similarly wrong, and that each time we make a decision to stand up for the rights of others, we strengthen our connection to the best parts of ourselves."
–James LaVeck, Filmmaker, Co-founder of Tribe of Heart

"This is a heart wrenching, moving, and important book - ultimately, uplifting and hopeful. There were many poignant moments - the reality of animal abuse, and the painful reality and unfolding impact of domestic abuse were vivid and real. I was particularly moved reading Amber's emotional journey, navigating her way through the dark, treacherous terrain of her lived experience. As a survivor of sexual violence, although a different experience, these sections resonated, remembering my journey, 'moving through the dark, to get to the light.' This book offers hope to everyone - and the gift, that with support and love, we can create space within us to live whole."
–Janet Goldblatt Holmes, Writing Workshop Coordinator for *The Stories We Tell* **of the Voices and Faces Project**

"*But I Already Said Goodbye* delivers a smashing blow to the solar plexus as readers unravel the horrifying reality behind the narrator's fragile world. This is a novel about speaking the truth and finding the courage to soar."
–Ian M. Rogers, author of *MFA Thesis Novel*

"Amber's story spoke to me in so many ways. As a survivor of childhood sexual assault, and only recently speaking about it, I have learned every day is an opportunity to grow stronger and learn from my experience. As Amber says, 'My need to be heard had become larger than my wish to remain hidden.' I know I will read this book over and over because it is so genuine and beautifully written."
–Tina Smith, survivor

"From our own Crisis Center Advocate, Wendy Jensen, a novel worthy of the *New York Times* best seller list. Beautifully written with a soft spoken, gentle voice concerning two harsh, clandestine atrocities. Proud of you!"
–Paula Czech, author of *The Black Leather Satchel*

"Wendy Thacher Jensen's inspiring novel *But I Already Said Goodbye* takes the reader on a challenging but fulfilling journey of discovery, awareness, and compassion."
–Kim Stallwood, animal rights author & independent scholar

"This book tells a difficult story in a way that is believable and healing. The synopsis caused me to believe that Amber was in a relationship of imbalanced power with an older man. However, it is not a consensual relationship and is far worse than I imagined. Without giving the plot away, I have never read a book that puts words to the experience Amber is having with such realism. Her growth alongside people who spend their lives caring for and protecting animals, causes her to learn gradually how to set boundaries and care for herself. Difficult story to read, but one that needed to be written and available. A tender cat rescue, beautiful New Mexico scenery, and caring friends for Amber bring much-needed space and light to the story."
–Jill Bergkamp, educator

"This was a difficult book to review. There were ugly, sad parts. But, there were parts and animals to save Amber and help her heal from abuse. Tom was the shining light as well as the one-eyed savior."
–Edna Gadoury

More from
Wendy Thacher Jensen

Practical Handbook
of
Veterinary
Homeopathy

Healing Our

Companion Animals

from the Inside Out

"This is...an excellent way to come to an understanding
of what homeopathic medicine is about, how it is
understood, and how it is used in clinical practice.
Highly recommended."
–Richard H. Pitcairn, DVM, PhD,
author of *Dr. Pitcairn's Complete Guide to
Natural Health for Dogs & Cats*

Wendy Thacher Jensen, D.V.M.

But I Already
Said Goodbye

"I had wished for him then, that this world not overwhelm or harm him, little realizing that the greatest places of pain are found within."
—*The Curiosity*, Stephen P. Kiernan

"When fear and shame are comrades, tongues lie still."
—*Quarantine*, Jim Crace

CHAPTER 1

I managed to smile and look my interviewer in the eyes, though my fingers were twisted tightly together in my lap.

"So, why do you want to work here?"

I took a deep breath, only making my trembling more obvious. "I've been a vegetarian since I was nine years old, and it just seemed like I'd fit in."

"Good for you! So, you're already used to the jokes about how delicious meat is ..."

"Yes, and how grateful the animals are to die for a good cause ..."

"Yes! Hah! You've met those people, too. There's a lot of them out there. We need more like you! You said you graduated a couple years ago? Working full time at the shelter where you volunteered during high school? Awesome. I bet you saw a lot there and—"

She was interrupted when a small woman with bright red hair stuck her head into the room. "We need all hands on deck. It's that hoarder, Gloria, remember? She's been threatened with eviction and has agreed to give up her cats. We gotta jump on it."

My interviewer sat up straight and dropped her pen. "Marlene, wait, this is Amber. She can help." She turned back to me, her fingers raised to her lips. "Do you have time? Or do you have to be somewhere?"

I took a breath and nodded. Marlene, already half out of the door, turned back, took my hand and shook it briefly. She held on for a moment and looked into my eyes, then let go and turned away. "Well, all right then, follow me." She disappeared into the hallway, moving fast.

I ran down the hall to where Marlene was already opening the door to a small room filled with plastic animal carriers and empty cages. She looked up. "Amber, is it? If you are looking for a cushy job cuddling kittens, today will cure you of that. Here, grab some of these and we'll head out there. I'll take you in my car." We picked up two carriers in each hand and brought them out to the parking lot, loading them into an old rusted Toyota.

The Helping All Animals offices were in an old converted brick warehouse. It sat at the end of a quiet street, where the asphalt gave way to dirt. The road dwindled into a cow path as it continued on towards distant hills covered in pale green New Mexico scrub. The warehouse's faded bricks lifted above a crumbling parking lot, which radiated heat into our faces as Marlene slammed the car door. We headed back inside for one more load, and then the car was full.

Marlene rolled down the front windows, handing me a towel to cover the hot vinyl. "Here, don't burn yourself," she murmured, tucking another cloth underneath her legs where her denim shorts ended. The cages rattled as she maneuvered the car over the potholes at the entrance to the lot, and Jim Croce's voice crooned out of the radio. We turned onto the main road out of town, passing a billboard featuring President Reagan's smiling face. I leaned back and relaxed with the music, the knot in my stomach easing as I stretched out my legs.

"Gloria lives near the border, practically in Texas," Marlene commented as she accelerated onto the highway and maneuvered around a tractor trailer belching smoke. Bits of white fluff swept over the windshield, and I looked up as we passed to see hundreds of chickens crowded into cages on the flatbed. One small yellow foot protruded through wire mesh, toes flexing and extending as if trying to reach solid ground.

"Sounds like she has dozens of cats. Just got out of hand," Marlene muttered, almost to herself, pushing her dark-framed glasses higher on her nose. She explained that cats can have multiple litters a year. "Most people are surprised by how fast the kittens pile up." Finally the neighbors had complained, tired of waking to tomcat screams outside their bedroom windows and finding kittens playing under their parked cars. "After a while it's not cute anymore." She strummed her hands on the steering wheel, then closed her window and adjusted the air conditioning.

I cranked my window shut as well.

"So, I heard you worked at a shelter? Just so you know, we don't euthanize animals here. We do need a kennel worker, though. Got any other skills?"

"Well, I wrote some for the high school paper ... s ..."

"What do you mean?" she asked.

"I went to a couple different schools, and I worked for both papers." I was frantically reading my application over in my mind's eye, unprepared for interviewing without it.

"That could come in handy, too. You good with animals?" She reached up to scratch her nose and glanced over at me. "You all right?"

I tried to relax my shoulders, easing my elbows down towards the seat. "Yes, I'm fine, and I'm good with animals. Sometimes I would assist the vet when he visited the shelter. And I was the official dog-walker." No reaction from Marlene. I turned away, grimaced, and slumped further down into my seat.

"Why did you leave?"

I squirmed in my seat, pulling my shirt away from the moist skin on my stomach. I looked at Marlene, but then turned my eyes away again, uncomfortable with staring at her profile. "I want to do more for the animals. Adopting is important, but if I could prevent them from becoming homeless in the first place ..." I trailed off.

"Yeah. I know what you mean. Why do people let them breed and breed?"

We drove on in silence. I counted the telephone poles flashing by and watched the heat waves rippling on the highway ahead. I breathed in and held it for a moment. Here I was, sitting in a strange car with a woman I had just met, speeding to an unknown house to collect cats. My comfortable, familiar routine suddenly seemed very far away.

After several miles, we left the highway and made a few turns past small homes with cacti in their window boxes. Marlene sighed heavily as she pulled up to a tiny neglected yard, where a few women were carrying small cages out through a tattered screen door. Long ago, someone had cared enough to hang shutters at each window, but most of them were now lying in the dried weeds, paint long since peeled away. Marlene opened her door. "Lisa, how's it going?"

"Better for them, now," said a plump woman with a brown ponytail, clumps of fur sticking to her faded pink T-shirt. She held up her plastic carrier and grinned at the two little tabbies inside.

Marlene and I carried some empty cages across the yard and maneuvered them inside. The living room was tiny and overflowing with boxes, old broken TVs, discarded mail, and newspapers with headlines going back to Nixon. It smelled overwhelmingly of cat urine. Gloria sat in a wheelchair, in the only cleared spot in the living room, distractedly stroking three long-haired cats huddled on her lap. Dressed in a shabby bathrobe whose faded purple flowers mocked the seriousness of the situation, she looked sad and lost. About a dozen other cats fled as we crossed the room, disappearing silently around boxes and ripped-up furniture.

"What am I going to do? I can't live on the street! My babies need me," Gloria cried, a tear sliding down her wrinkled cheek.

Lisa went to her and patted her thin shoulder. Marlene, settling her cages down on a stack of newspapers, muttered quietly, "Lisa is our people person. Her heart is big enough to hold even the most guilty conscience."

"You're doing the right thing, ma'am," said Lisa, looking earnestly into Gloria's eyes while she held her bony hand. "We've come to help. We're just going to collect your babies and get them to a safe place so you can keep your home." Gloria's shoulders relaxed slightly with relief, then tightened again as she saw Marlene wrestle two of the friendlier animals into a carrier. They kept turning back, pushing away from the doorway of the carrier, their matted fur catching on the hinges. I went over to help, Gloria's wails rising behind me.

"What's going to happen to them? Where are you taking them?" she cried. "Maybelline! Sammy! Who else do you have in there?" Marlene frowned and turned away, lifting the carrier over a pile of old magazines and heading for the screen door.

Lisa knelt down, talking quietly to Gloria about finding homes through the local shelter, and spaying her cats so that they didn't have to keep having kittens. "They'll be in good hands."

We worked through the rest of the day, wearing surgical masks in the basement, where the smell made our eyes water. Most of the cats were harmless, but a few of the larger, more frightened tomcats had to be dragged out from underneath couches and piles of boxes, hissing and screaming until they scrambled into the backs of their carriers. Their business was one of survival, far from the pampered Persians in those cat food commercials. No crystal bowls for them.

The kittens were the easy part. Pretend-fierce, tiny bottlebrush tails pointing straight up, backs hunched, they skittered sideways away from us. Their hisses were almost inaudible, the barest puffs of air as they warned the lumbering humans away. They ran crazily in between the towers of magazines, zipping around the corners with their little paws scrabbling madly on the floor, sliding into the feet of a would-be rescuer, tumbling head over heels, only to zip off again. It was all a big game to them. We collected them gently, loading the carriers back into the cars, windows open to let out the heat and the smell.

Marlene settled a carrier into the back seat and took off her glasses, rubbing the lenses with the hem of her T-shirt. "I saw another kitten in that back room near the green couch. Can you get her, Amber?"

"Sure." I turned back to the house, crunching through the dead grass. Gloria, her lap now empty, twisted a tattered lace handkerchief around her fingers. She smiled weakly at me as I passed by her wheelchair. In the back room, I squeezed in between two stacks of sagging cardboard boxes and knelt to peer under a dirty couch crammed behind them. Just then, I felt small feet walking across my calves. I turned to gather up the tiny black kitten who was staring at me with bright green eyes. Watching her play-biting my knuckles, I mused that it was a blessing that she didn't know. She didn't know that there are not enough homes. She might land in paradise, no kittens of her own to worry over, living as queen of the household, lolling on her favorite perch and a soft cozy blanket, eating regular meals and nestling into a loving lap. But what about the sick ones, the ugly ones, or the old and lame ones? Who would care for them?

I tucked my heart away, knowing that safety and a good meal awaited her at the shelter. Hope was better than her present uncertain future.

The morning passed quickly, a growing number of meowing faces staring out of the carriers, eyes wide with fear. Two mothers were nursing litters. They were headed for the special room at the shelter where foster volunteers came to take them home until the nurslings were old enough for adoption.

· · ·

"The last room," said Marlene. Sweaty and tired, we put the last of our empty carriers down and closed the basement door behind us to prevent last-minute escapes. We lifted boxes and peered around paper piles, kneeling to look under tables, alert for any remaining signs of life. Then I saw him, wedged far back underneath a filthy ragged couch, panting, his ears pressed flat against his skull. He was big, gray and long haired, with a scar across his nose and one missing eye. His large jowls marked him as an older tom, and as he lifted his lip in a silent snarl, I could see that whatever had scarred his face and ruined his eye had also broken a few teeth.

I sat back on my heels. "I found another one," I said, "and he's big."

Marlene stood up and took a few steps away, her hand pressed to the small of her back. She stopped and turned back toward me, but she was already shaking her head, saying, "Nobody will want him, you know. He'll just be euthanized at the shelter. Probably on the first day. We could pretend we didn't see him." She pushed her glasses further up on her nose, wiped her hand across her forehead, and rubbed it on her shirt.

Something turned over in my stomach. "I'll take him," I said. Marlene frowned. I stared down at the couch, avoiding her eyes. She huffed in exasperation. Then she sighed a long, weary, exhausted breath, slapping her fingers back into the handle of a carrier. She pushed sweaty hair off her cheek and glared at me again. We looked at each other, listening to the snarls coming from underneath the stained couch. I waited for the trembling to ease, deep inside of me. Then I jumped as Marlene abruptly started for the door, stepping awkwardly over a pile of rusted saucepans.

"Okay, kid, but we've gotta get the rabies pole so we don't get killed by that little terror."

I breathed out in relief and followed her back outside.

At her car she set down the empty carrier and pulled out a long metal pole with a thick wire loop at the end. Holding it level between her hands, she twisted a collar at the mid-point and then showed me how the loop was now easy to pull open. "They call it a rabies pole because it'll keep you safe, even from crazed dogs." She pulled on the loop to make it bigger. "Get the loop around his neck and then pull on this knob here at the other end to tighten it down." She pulled and the loop shrank back down.

"The stick part keeps the animal from getting at your hand. Some people call them vicious, but I call them terrified. Biting makes sense if you think you are fighting for your life." She twisted the collar again. "This locks it down again. Here." She thumped the hot metal into my hand. "Try it on that fence post."

I twisted the collar and put the loop in place, then pulled it tight and locked it again.

Marlene nodded, "That's it. Do it a few times." She watched, hands on her hips, nodding. "With the cat, if you can include a foreleg in the noose, it hurts less, and you won't choke him. It's kinder, but not always possible. Work fast."

I gripped the pole tightly as we returned to the back room of the house.

The gray cat was silent when I peered under the couch, meeting my gaze with one bright yellow eye. This fellow was not going to come easily. I slowly snaked the pole under the couch, the metal slipping in my sweaty hands as it caught on ripped fabric hanging near the cat's face. He snarled and hissed, not the tiny puff of the kittens, but a loud scratchy grating, punctured by hair-raising screams as the pole approached his head. Each attempt to close the noose sent him whirling around with razor-sharp claws, despite the cramped space beneath the couch. I jerked back time and again, startled by the power and speed in his small frame. He was fighting so hard I feared he would hurt himself, breaking another tooth or even his leg in the metal snare.

"You know what, Amber," Marlene said, "He's too wild. Let him be."

But I kept working, sweat dripping down my face and stinging my eyes, until finally I got the noose in place, locking it down carefully. I admired the sturdy tom's defiance. He didn't find it necessary to be nice, soft, or pleasing. As I began to pull on the pole, his mouth opened wide and his whiskers trembled with another grating hiss. Then my vision flickered, darkening around the edges, and for a moment I was the one trapped.

"There you are, Amber," he snarled, "What are you doing under the bed?" His face was so close, mouth open, sweat glistening in his day-old stubble. His panting breath gathered over my nose as he pulled me out, my knees scraping against the dusty floorboards and my ponytail coming loose. He smiled as he stroked my hair with one hand, the other gripped tightly around my arm. "Such a good girl. My special girl." His voice was husky, barely a whisper, yet my chest was tight with the worry that someone might hear. I held still as his hands moved lower. Then I faded away into a dark quiet corner of my mind.

I rubbed my eyes and shook the memory away, grimacing. I had to focus on the gray cat right now. It was like catching a tiger by the tail. I dragged him out with the pole, as he screamed and twisted, finally depositing him into the waiting carrier. When we slammed the door on him and Marlene unlocked and removed the snare, he struck out one final time, lightning-quick, then settled, rumbling, against the back of the cage. He was breathing fast, trembling, suddenly looking very small and frightened. Eleven pounds can hold a lot of fierceness.

"You did it! You got him!" Marlene cried, peering into the cage and clapping me on the back. She rubbed her mouth and then grinned. "I really wasn't sure we could do this." She paused, thinking, "You really sure you want him? He might be better off in a barn-type living situation. If he likes horses."

"I'm sure," I said, "I want him." I picked some fur out of the wire loop, watching it drift down and land on the arm of the couch. The room was still hot, but I had gotten used to the smell.

"Well, okay then," Marlene picked the cat up and maneuvered him around a tilted stack of cardboard boxes. "You should feel pretty good about what you just did. I didn't think you were up to it."

"I do feel good," I said quietly, following her to the front room and back to the car.

I stared into the back seat at the rows of cages. Once the engine had started, all the cats quieted down, staring out mutely. Some were shivering, despite the heat. The tom managed to look more fierce than frightened, staring back with that almost glowing yellow eye. How had he survived in that mess of a house? Somehow he must have scavenged enough food to survive, because he wasn't thin, just lean and wiry.

"He healed all on his own," said Marlene, glancing at my face as she drove. "A vet would have made him look better." She explained how a surgeon working to heal his wounds would have carefully sewed his lids shut over the missing eye, allowing his fur to regrow and his face to look more normal. This cat's eye socket simply sank blackly into his skull. I looked out at the passing fields, imagining healing, without medical attention, from such a desperate injury. Why had he stayed when there was no one to help him?

Marlene's sudden question broke into my thoughts, "Do you have a place you can keep him?"

"Yeah – I don't think my housemates will mind." I turned back to the window, breathing deeply. The moving air felt good on my face.

The Rolling Stones sang "Angie" from the radio as we accelerated onto the highway. I drew in a deep breath, letting their mournful images of loss and despair dilute my own distress over what I had seen today in that destroyed house. My tension eased as the sweat prickled and dried on my arms and legs. I pulled my shirt away from my back where it had torn during the struggle with the cat. Just like Angie and Mick, we had done the best we could.

• • •

I sat up straighter when I saw the red brick walls at the end of the block. Lisa and the others were already there, carrying cages with meowing faces pressed to their metal door grates.

"Here we are. The kennels are around the back. We'll get them settled in and have our vet take a look." Marlene parked and got out, taking two carriers and leaving the door open.

I caught the gray cat's eye. "You wait. You get to come with me," I whispered.

After we finished unloading everyone else, Marlene reached for the last carrier. She ignored the tom's glare and handed me his cage. "Good work with that pole. I'll see you in the morning. You can bring the carrier back then. Bring him in to the vet hospital yourself, so they'll know he's yours." Turning away, she said over her shoulder, "Wear clothes you don't care about and report to the kennel."

"Thanks!" I wanted to hug her, but just headed tiredly to my car. The cat felt heavier than I remembered.

• • •

It hadn't taken Tom long to settle in. The veterinarian at HAA got rid of his fleas and treated him for worms. He said that Tom was healthy enough to neuter, and that without the desire to mate, he'd be a better house cat. The surgery was over quickly, and my fierce new friend recovered without incident.

Once home, I let him come out of the carrier on his own, which he did willingly—for food. The first time, he glared at me somberly, examining his surroundings carefully before bending down to eat. He used his litter box studiously, never spraying like some tomcats do. After a few days, I let him out of my bedroom and he cautiously explored the house, tail lifting when I spoke to him. That was a good sign. The day I found him lying on my bed when I came home, I knew that he was going to be okay.

It wasn't long before he allowed my touch, leaning his head down and closing his eye as if accepting a benediction. Soon he became the darling of the house. We made quite a pair, the two of us, watching *Star Trek* reruns and eating popcorn. I kept his box clean, scooping it daily and scrubbing it out periodically, and I also offered to brush him, which he always politely refused. But food was second to nothing, even cuddles. He never refused a meal.

• • •

"That summer went by fast, didn't it, Tom?" I turned from the flyspecked living room window and leaned down to gather him into my arms. Together we watched the sun disappear behind the hills, the last few shadows merging into the coming darkness. "You were one tough customer. Remember those days?"

Better if he didn't, I thought. Some things were best forgotten. We settled onto the soft worn couch and I flicked on the lamp, opening my latest book, *The Hobbit*. I admired Bilbo's bravery, heading out into the unknown even though he had a perfectly safe, cozy home tucked away underground. I crossed my legs up onto the couch and rested the book in my lap, next to Tom. His body vibrated against my leg, his purr louder than words. "Tom, maybe I should have named you Bilbo, for your bravery. But you would never have left Bag End. This I'm sure of. You would have known a good thing when you had it."

Tom purred with a scratchy burbly sound, standing up to push vigorously against my hand, arching his back as I massaged the strong muscles along his spine. "You big moog," I said, smiling. He was my only friend in this quiet almost-deserted neighborhood. "I can't believe how fat you've gotten."

I laughed as he flopped over to present his soft round belly for a rub. "Good thing you didn't have that belly when you were a tomcat. Would have seriously gotten in the way."

My fingers sank into his warm fur. "We're two peas in a pod, Tom." Like me, he didn't fit into the normal postcard family picture. He wasn't beautiful—indeed he was kind of ugly with his missing eye and formerly nasty attitude. I wasn't ugly exactly, but inside of me I carried my own private flaws.

I leaned over and buried my face in his fur. "You didn't need anyone back then, did you, Tom? Not even me. I'm lucky you didn't scratch my face right off."

Tom responded by squiggling around until his belly fur tickled the inside of my nose. I sneezed and he barely moved, staring up at me and blinking slowly, forepaws tucked loosely against his chest. I gently rubbed his cheek near his missing eye and he lifted up his chin for a scratch. I smiled. "You don't care about being pretty, do you? You don't even bother pretending." Tom's bad places were obvious and unashamed, and yet here he was, surviving in spite of it all.

I reveled in the ferocity of his emotions, from his hair-raising snarls and hisses to the loud purrs now used to describe his life. I soaked up his stoutheartedness and celebrated his orneriness, even though it had almost led to his destruction. How easily could he have ended up in the wrong hands, punished for a growl, or even killed for his defiance? I wished I was as brave as Tom, but defiance in my own life would surely only make everything so much worse.

CHAPTER 2

I found my footing quickly that first summer, surrounded by people I admired. They all worked hard to improve the lives of animals, from mice in laboratories to horses on farms. HAA worked with the media, taught classes, petitioned the courts, and put on rallies and demonstrations. We studied laboratory inspection reports obtained from Freedom of Information Act requests to uncover violations of the Animal Welfare Act. Armed with this data, we held scientists accountable. We brought cruelties out into the open, revealing them to our readers, publicizing the truth about how animals in our region of New Mexico were being treated.

HAA's magazine was full of uplifting success stories as well. Sometimes there were before and after photos of rescued animals. I was always amazed at the transformation from ugly and forlorn—heart-wrenching, really—to fat and happy, beautiful.

At first, I was assigned all the dirty jobs, like cleaning out the encrusted refrigerator and scrubbing runs and cages. Then after a new girl was hired, I graduated to walking and feeding the dogs. When large-scale rescue operations needed more hands, I always joined in.

One day we rescued over one hundred rabbits from a filthy neglected backyard breeding operation. The cages, made of open wire mesh stapled to wooden supports, were crammed full of gray, white, brown, and bicolored rabbits. Their foot pads were universally raw from living on feces-encrusted urine-soaked cage bottoms.

I partnered with Lisa, methodically moving from one sagging cage to the next, gently pulling the frightened animals out and putting them into plastic carriers and crates. We developed a rhythm, one guarding the door and holding the carrier open while the other gathered up each rabbit, one at a time. Some had enough fight left to kick up their heels irritably once they reached the solid footing inside the crates. Others simply accepted our touch quietly, almost listlessly. Many had moisture under their tails, revealing weeping raw ulcers from constant urine exposure. Others had wounds infested with maggots, hidden by layers of soft silky fur.

"Sometimes I really wonder how these people can keep going. Is all they see their own bottom line?" I asked Lisa as we tucked a struggling gray lop-eared rabbit in with a smaller white one.

"They wear blinders, I think," said Lisa. "Because look, if you keep your distance, you can't see their injuries. They look great from afar. Beautiful coats. That's how the breeders keep going."

"Yeah, and rabbits are so quiet," I agreed. "No barking to bother the neighbors." I looked at the next cage, where a tiny white bunny was tucked close in against a large fawn-colored one. Their noses wiggled, and I wondered if they could smell anything but the huge piles of excrement built up under their cage. Both jerked a little as I reached in, but they had nowhere to go. We tucked them together into the next carrier, where they quickly snuggled close, heads touching.

Lisa frowned, helping guide the next rabbit into another carrier. "Be careful with this one. She's hurt pretty badly."

I held the door open and watched her tenderly laying the miniature rabbit into the soft rags.

"Just because they can't make noise, doesn't mean they don't hurt," I said.

Lisa straightened up from the carrier and frowned, nodding sadly. She touched my shoulder and then turned to the next cage.

It was a long day.

• • •

I offered to write up a news story about the operation. Marlene demurred, but I wrote something anyway, and the next day she agreed to read it.

"Hey kid, this is not a bad start. Let me run it by Andy so he can give you some tips."

• • •

Andy turned out to be a very approachable editor. I took his many suggestions seriously. After several drafts, each of which he reviewed for me in detail, he finally accepted a small piece describing the now happy lives of some of those rescued rabbits. I found solace in writing up what I had seen, heard, smelled, and touched during the rescue. The injustice was real. I was sure that by knowing the details, my readers would see that nonhuman animals deserve the same as us, a chance to live their lives without fear, and to have their needs met. To me, that was worth fighting for.

From that point on, Marlene allowed me to divide my time between the kennels and the magazine, until the kennel staff added someone else. Then I was moved into writing and research full time, complete with my very own typewriter-equipped cubicle. For the first time in my life, what I did mattered to more than just one animal at a time, and I liked that.

• • •

"How's it going?" my housemate asked as I tossed my keys onto the small table near the door. She had the TV news on, but no sound. Reagan was shaking the hand of someone wearing a crisp Army dress uniform.

"Good enough, I guess," I said, thinking that men always looked a little funny all dressed up, like kids whose mothers had buttoned their shirts too tightly. Tom was twining around my feet, ignoring the President. Dinner was more important. I rubbed his ears and his purr got louder. He ran ahead of me to the kitchen.

We ate together, leftovers for me and canned food for him. I paged through *Watership Down*, my latest novel. The rabbits entranced me with their very own culture and language, struggling together to find safety. I smoothed my finger down the red crocheted hearts on the bookmark, smiling, then closed the book and stretched luxuriously. "You have it better than those rabbits, for sure, Tom." He was studiously wiping down his whiskers at my feet, next to his polished-clean dinner bowl. I picked up the novel and headed to the bathroom, Tom making a noise under his breath as he trailed me, still licking his lips. He jumped up heavily to the counter while I stared at myself in the mirror. He patted his reflection with a big furry paw, then sat back and watched my hands move as I finished preparing for bed.

"What a pair we make, huh, Tom? Not exactly movie star material. But at least I have two eyes." I examined my face with its stubby nose covered in freckles, and eyes that weren't exactly brown or green. "Leaf moldy brown," as my father liked to say. Mousy hair that I only paid attention to once a day when I braided it back out of the way. I scrubbed soap over my cheeks, enjoying the feel of the water sluicing over my skin, taking away the cares of the day. "Makeup really doesn't seem worth the effort, right, Tom? Silk purse out of a sow's ear, right? Can't be done. Besides, I think the pig deserves to keep her ears." I chuckled at my joke as Tom dabbled his paw in the sink, chasing the last drops down the drain. And besides, I thought, I didn't really want to stand out in a crowd.

"You put the drops to bed, then I'll put you to bed. Come on, you big oaf." I lifted him up to my shoulder, the book under my other arm, and retreated to my room for the night. "Hey you, don't get my shirt wet."

I grabbed an extra blanket and we snuggled together, letting the warm darkness wash over us and the quiet of the house settle into our bones. My neck and shoulder muscles finally eased from their usual daytime tightness, melting into the pillow. Today, at least, had been pretty peaceful. At work and at home. My housemates and I rarely had company over, and I liked it that way. Sometimes Mike showed up, but I didn't really have a choice about that. And they seemed to like him well enough.

Freed of the responsibilities of the kennel, I was glad to be a full-time researcher and writer. It had taken awhile, but the nightmare of high school was finally in the rearview mirror, though it still haunted me sometimes.

Wending down the crowded hallway, I looked up reflexively as a loud voice shouted a greeting, then jumped and almost dropped my books as the reply boomed right into my ear. Voices raised in crowds always sounded angry to me, the speaker out for revenge. Locker doors banged, metal on metal, driving thoughts from my head. I had to squirm past a large group blocking the hallway to my next class, clutching my books to my chest, trying to avoid notice. Hands and arms flew out of the crowd unpredictably, waving in the air, conjuring their stories to each other amidst sudden, shocking laughter. If I could avoid touch, it was better. I needed space between me and the almost menacing groups of classmates. It was a minefield that I had to navigate every day.

My previous shelter job, and now my new one, paid enough so that I could afford a room in a house at the edge of town, instead of living at home. Space to myself, finally. I also had wheels. After I graduated, my dad let me have the old car. So far, it was still running. Each night, I came home and locked the front door, relieved by the solid "chunk" of the deadbolt. And with Tom by my side, life was even better.

• • •

Meanwhile, along with my confidence, my voice on the page was getting stronger. I began to speak more forcefully, calling out the bad guys and telling people about the terrible things they had done. Not everybody appreciated the information, however.

"Amber, you really touched a nerve," said Marlene one bright morning, sunbeams streaming across our cubicles. A newspaper rustled in her hand. "Thank goodness for Freedom of Information Act requests."

"What? Let me see." I put down my pencil and took the proffered page.

"Letters to the editor, first one at the top of the page."

I sat back down and cleared a spot on my desk. It was written by the scientist at the local laboratory who had starved the rats under his care. Without the FOIA request, we would never have known that he didn't provide food over a long holiday weekend. His experiment had probably ended, so why spend extra money when the rats were just going to be killed the following week? Why should he care?

I smoothed the paper out on my desk. "*Miss Amber needs to take stock of her own life before she points the finger at somebody else,*" he wrote. My heart sank, and I drew in a breath. The spotlight had found me, picking me out of my dark corner. The letter continued, "*Where does she think the milk came from that she pours onto her cereal every morning? And those cosmetics and cleaning solutions she uses without a second thought? Scientists in laboratories carefully proved the safety of these products, following government-regulated animal testing protocols. While she's busy pointing the finger at honest hardworking professionals and ruining the reputations of conscientious researchers, she should do a little soul-searching of her own. The worst kind of hypocrite is the one who bites the hand that feeds her.*"

Marlene was still watching me over the partition. "Don't worry about it, kid. If you don't get 'em mad, then you're not doing any good."

I nodded, moving my hand slowly across the folds of the page.

She gazed at me for a minute longer. "His nasty accusations present an educational opportunity. Why don't you write back about Revlon no longer blinding rabbits in their product safety testing, and also about cruelty-free cleaning products?" Her voice seemed oddly grating and extra loud, competing with the clacking of typewriter keys from a nearby cubicle.

"Good idea," I said woodenly, folding up the paper and tucking it away in a drawer. When I first saw pictures of Revlon's wooden restraint boxes used for Draize testing, it took me a moment to realize that the fluffy whiteness at the end was a rabbit's head. Completely defenseless against the chemical eye drops. So easy for the lab technicians. No fuss.

Sleep took a long time to come that night.

• • •

Anger. I'd seen it before, of course, in other people, but I wasn't usually the cause. I was a peaceful person who preferred to work out compromises rather than argue. But now, I was telling the world (or at least my corner of

Albuquerque) what they really didn't want to know. It seemed to have become my job to point out situations that demanded change.

For a while after that first vitriolic letter, I was especially careful, waiting for company before walking out to my car at night, having the landlord replace the dead lightbulb on our porch, and keeping the deadbolt locked at home. By speaking loudly, which I had never done before, I felt as if I had stepped into an unwelcome and unfriendly limelight. My preferred voice was low and quiet, and I typically reacted only to conversations around me, either agreeing or staying silent. But each time I put pen to paper, or rather cranked another sheet of paper into the typewriter, the wrongness of it all and the subject's suffering would rise before me, clear as day, and equivocation became impossible. I had to tell the truth. At the completion of every article, the rush of what felt almost like righteous anger would fade, tides returning to the sea, leaving me wondering where those words had come from.

Then one day a part of me came unraveled, and my newfound confidence was badly shaken.

CHAPTER 3

Marlene sent me to a lecture given by a local community college professor. Sponsored by a local bird protection organization, the speaker had done an in-depth investigation of chicken slaughterhouse conditions. The weather was pleasant, so I walked the few miles from home. I sat in the middle school gymnasium on a creaky folding metal chair, surrounded by women wearing gauzy flowing skirts and jelly shoes. I watched the professor fielding questions at the front of the room. I admired anyone who could stand in front of a crowd and speak the truth. Speaking was much harder than hiding behind the written word.

The professor addressed cruelty issues occurring right in our own town. She talked about how impossible it was to honor and respect our fellow animals while simultaneously eating them and taking their eggs. She said that many people are more ready at first to give up eating cows, instead of chickens. "They tell me, 'But they are only chickens, right? They really don't matter that much, do they?' Well, what do you all think? Do chickens care about sunshine and dust baths and clean food and water and being with their families?"

The audience consisted of like-minded people. A chorus of yes's rang out, the woman next to me lifting a fist and shaking it, smiling.

"Yes, they do! So, let's talk about what happens to these birds. This film is all about what the industry doesn't want the public to know."

She said it better than I've heard it said before. I looked at her, nice suit and subtly effective makeup, her clear voice ringing out so confidently. She hardly needed a microphone. I could never be like her.

I was eleven the day I tried to make myself pretty. It was after school, when Dad said he'd be home later than usual. Seated in front of Mom's mirror, I pulled open the drawer and looked at her little plastic dishes of eye shadow and gold tubes of lipstick. Did Dad ever look in here? I wondered. Her things were untouched, almost a shrine, even though she had left us seven long years ago.

I soberly regarded my face and then pulled the top off one tube, twisting the bottom until a vivid red cylinder emerged, the wedge shape glistening. Its fruity sweet scent reminded me of Mom, and my stomach contracted slightly. I touched the waxy smoothness with my finger, picturing the closeness of her lips pressed just there, where the cylinder flattened near its end. I imagined it gliding slowly over her lips, spreading color in its path like a tiny paint roller.

I smiled a big fake smile, like I had seen her do, and placed the red tip onto my lips. Paint-by-numbers, right? Stay between the lines. I stretched my lip before the lipstick arrived, moving the tip slowly from one side to the other, and again on my lower lip. Then I sat back and looked at the results. My mouth was startlingly bright, glaring out from my pale face. The shape was wrong. I scratched with my fingernail to remove the red from where it had strayed at the edges, then returned the tube to its gold case, watching it disappear into the opening like a gopher into a burrow.

Next I selected blue eye shadow, and dabbed the miniature applicator into the center of the powdery square. Blue had been one of Mom's favorites. Leaning close into the mirror, I wiped the applicator across one eyelid, from the inner corner to the outer. The streak of color seemed just right. I moved to the other lid, but the streak faltered and swerved, as if my hand could only travel smoothly in one direction. I added more powder to the other side, but it went too far and I ran out of space.

I gave up on the shadow and tried the mascara, pulling it out from its tube with a wet sucking sound. The miniature brush was covered in sticky dark clumps. My hand trembled as I combed the brush through my lashes, spreading color across the fine hairs. When I finished, I gazed into the mirror silently. I took a deep breath, almost a sigh, and something hurt, deep inside my chest.

I scrubbed my face until it turned red, but the shadows remained.

The film footage was taken from inside a chicken slaughterhouse. The white birds, disheveled and dirty, were hung by their feet on a conveyor belt, then electrocuted by the water bath. A few souls with the will to struggle flapped around so much that they never touched the water. These hardy individuals, fully conscious and absolutely terrified, hung upside down, exhausted, as the conveyor belt carried them inexorably to the whirring razor-sharp blade, which finally ended their misery. Lots of blood, lots of manure into the scalding water bath which peeled away what was left of their feathers.

The presenter was talking. My body was rigid, frozen in place. Thankfully, she kept the lights down. "Most people don't really care about chickens," she said. "They are considered only as food, and there are a whole lot of hungry people. But meat costs money to produce, so speed is important to the company. The bird, instead of a living being in his or her own right, becomes just a commodity." She turned back to the film.

We forget, I thought. We forget that they feel, they think, they experience pain and terror and misery not only in the crowded sunless growing sheds, but in the trucks that take them to the slaughterhouse. Their last experience, of hanging helplessly upside-down by their legs while their companions are killed right in front of them, one by one, was so nightmarish that I couldn't begin to imagine it. Prey animals will flee or fight for their lives if they have to, just like any of us, but they aren't meant to be tortured before finally meeting their end. No one is.

My chair was uncomfortable, creaking every time I uncrossed and crossed my legs, and yet I had to move. I wriggled around, trying to ease the sudden ache in my back, my eyes never leaving the screen. My unrest went deeper as the flickering movie reels inexorably advanced the film, along with the conveyor belt. I was mesmerized, almost feeling the knife myself, feathers peeling off my skin with the scalding water bath, steam filling my throat until I had to get outside. But I was too embarrassed to move, not wanting to disturb the lady next to me, big curls teased up on her head, eyes riveted on the screen.

The movie clip was silent, but I imagined the noise of flesh being sliced, machinery humming and the wet slaps of the stunned birds' naked flesh against the metal bins. Five billion birds per year. Five billion.

Finally it ended, the credits followed by the blinding white square before the whirring projector was silenced. I stood up quickly, wanting to reach the door before the room lights came on and trapped me in my seat. The audience was totally silent, almost breathing together, a sigh of ... perhaps relief? Shock? Anger? I didn't want to hear what other people had to say. I didn't want to hear their murmured platitudes, or even words of dismay. It's not okay, it will never be okay. I wanted to be alone, suddenly, desperately, stumbling past knees covered in denim or cotton skirts, trying to remember the quickest way out. Wasn't there a fire exit back here? No. I turned and rushed along the wall, towards the front of the room, waiting for someone behind me to yell, "Stop! Where are you going?" and then I'd have to explain myself, I'd have to turn and talk, to ask a normal question, "Where is the door?" and find some way to explain my urgency, some way to make them understand I didn't belong here, I didn't need to see any more suffering, please just let me go.

There, finally, was a door. I pressed hard on the big metal hinged handle, hoping to make it outside before the loud clanking sounds turned any faces my way. It closed behind me. I sucked in a big gulp of the familiar dusty air, then took another deep breath, diluting the perfume scents from the crowd that had seeped into my lungs. I turned towards home, my heart still thumping. What was the matter with me? Surely I could handle these horrors, certainly I had examined and written about far worse.

I found the sidewalk and kept walking, staring down at my feet as they carried me away, left foot and then right foot, laces flipping with the motion of my sneakers. I concentrated on getting more distance between me and the school, like an escaping convict trying to blend into her surroundings. Thankfully, no one called out behind me, no one ran up behind me to grab my arm. I kept walking, slowly becoming aware of the solid feel of the concrete, and how my jeans whispered gently around my ankles. My breath slowed, losing its jagged edges.

The wind sighed through the nearby trees as I turned onto my street, calmer now. Almost home. I was going to be okay. A dust devil suddenly appeared on the sidewalk, lifting just ahead of my feet, whirling and turning before the wind died and brushed the bits of dirt and sand back into the cracks.

At my porch, I fumbled with the lock until I could twist the deadbolt and step into my own living room. I locked the door behind me and stood in the semi-darkness, feeling my chest rise with its next breath. "Hello?" The house was empty. Tom's glad cry eased my clinging panic and we sank together into the soft, welcoming sofa. I wrapped my legs in my warm blanket and covered my eyes in the quiet, until the darkness finally slowed my thumping heart. If not for Tom, nudging my hands through the blanket, insistent upon his dinner, I might have stayed curled up forever.

CHAPTER 4

The next morning at work I dove into my pile of newspapers, eager for distraction. Three hours later, a timid knock came behind me. Surrounded by bits of newspapers piled into discards, not-yet-read's, and could-be-of-interest's, I turned and saw one of the front desk people grinning at me. I grimaced and rubbed my neck. It felt stiff, as if I hadn't moved in hours.

"Hi! Some of us are getting lunch at the burrito place, if you want to come."

"Me?" I stood up slowly and rubbed my eyes, glad for a break. My stomach growled. "I'll be there in a sec."

"'Kay!" She disappeared down the hall.

I blinked and felt myself returning to my own skin. While skimming over articles on pet care, how to handle wildlife in your backyard, how to bag the biggest deer, and Princess Diana's shaggy pony, I had briefly escaped my own dark places. Lunch with my co-workers would bring me the rest of the way back to a lighter, more carefree world, I hoped. Perhaps we all enjoyed the break, laughing about things that didn't matter, unimportant stories that didn't echo with other pained darknesses.

I felt safe with this crowd. Lunch times hadn't always been easy for me in school. We'd moved so often that I was perpetually the new girl. As I grabbed my wallet from a desk drawer, I thought about how much better things were for me now.

It was the first day of sixth grade. The heavy plastic tray shook in my hand and my glass hit my plate with a loud clinking sound. I was looking out over the lunch room, searching for a free seat, but I didn't want anybody to know that I was looking. Everybody arrived already knowing where to sit, their names invisibly imprinted at their places. Looking around was a mark of the odd person out. Everybody but me sat relaxed, hands energetically emphasizing their conversations or draped loosely over their neighbors' shoulders. "She is MINE. These are MY friends."

As a newcomer, I belonged nowhere. I tried to seem nonchalant, but only felt more desperate and exposed. The dangers of choosing wrong were great. A pained look and a possessive hand placed over the seat sent me down along the aisle, already marked by the first refusal. Face reddened and hands trembling, I had no hope of appearing confident the second time around. If I took an unclaimed seat that was too near a large group, the expanding circle of popularity, which never included me, quickly sent me off on my search yet again. Feigning ignorance of social groupings didn't protect me, as there was always somebody bold enough to ask me to move over and make room for their friends (it always hurt no matter how politely the request was made). I counted myself lucky if I could simply be ignored, except for the occasional glances that seemed to say, "Who are you and why are you listening in?" It was easier to eat alone, outside, in a deserted courtyard. I could breathe there. It was comfortable enough even on cold days, if I wore my coat and ate quickly.

I tucked my wallet into my pocket and left my cubicle, joining Chris, one of the other researchers. He was tall and gangly, and not much older than me, I guessed. He was good-looking in an artistic way, thin with fluffy dark hair that tumbled over his cheeks. Marlene and some others joined us as we walked, their light chatter soothing me. A few talked about a successful campaign which improved the living conditions of baby dairy calves, known by the public as veal calves. Having the bad luck of being born male, they were taken from their mothers and chained into individual narrow stalls, where they were fed milk replacement solutions, until being killed for people to eat. Meat eaters liked the pale flesh of young animals whose muscles had never walked, never run, only stood up and lay down again, until their slaughter a few months later. The anemia of a young animal fed only an iron-poor liquid diet when other calves their age would already be eating hay and grains also created soft flesh, tender on the plate. That way the farmer could make some money on calves who couldn't go into the milking herd.

What separated them from us? Why was it considered acceptable to remove these babies from their mothers, who called for them for days, sometimes, lowing sadly, their milk-laden teats instead returned to the automated metal milking machines? I touched my face, remembering my own mother's kiss.

I turned to match the flow of bodies across the parking lot, looking ahead to the sidewalk, where the path naturally narrowed between a hedge and the road. I was suddenly reminded of the steel chute used to funnel large groups of semi-wild cows or horses into a single line, making it easier to separate and treat each one individually. Used to running wild on the range, moving with their families and friends, did they feel exposed and vulnerable when their sister or brother suddenly dropped behind, sheared away by steel fencing? Instead of comforting rough familiar fur and steamy hot breath mixing with their own, they felt only cold walls, while the yells and thumping from men made their hearts race and their hooves fly, fly on, in hopes of an opening ahead. Behind were galloping frenzied bodies pushing them forward into something completely unknown.

I shook my head as I stepped onto the sidewalk, joining a woman with a tie-dyed bandanna. I had just missed the empty space, where I may have been forced to walk alone, neither belonging to the group ahead, nor to the group behind. We flowed together with the crowd. I took a deep breath of hot heavy sunlit air and asked how HAA had convinced the farmers to change their policies on the calves.

"One of our researchers spent months investigating other operations," my sidewalk partner explained. "She discovered that calves raised with the freedom to move around, instead of being tied up in, you know, those little crates, were healthier. More to the point, they gained more weight and suffered from less disease. Her facts and figures convinced the local farmers that the change would not only help the calves, but the bottom line as well."

The smell of car exhaust accompanied us as we tramped down the uneven sidewalk. We stopped at a small restaurant about three blocks from the offices, waiting for the rest of our group. The windows were decorated with sparkly green cactus cut-outs.

I glanced over at Chris, but he was frowning down at a weed in the crack of the sidewalk, scuffing at it with his sneaker and twisting his tie-dye T-shirt. He turned to Carter, the mail room guy, who was heavyset, dressed in ripped jeans and an Oxford button-down shirt. They shook hands, pantomiming happiness and exaggerated relief.

"Yay, got those crazy activists off our back, and all it cost us was a few feet of fencing," said Carter.

Chris dramatically wiped his brow and said, "Yep! Who knew all they wanted was fatter calves for us, so we could make more money! Wahoo!"

Carter laughed and grabbed the door, disappearing inside. For a moment I felt lost, unmoored. Cigarette smoke smells spilled out from inside.

Marlene grabbed the door just before it finished closing and held it for me, shaking her head. I moved quickly, grateful for the opening. A decision made. As we stepped out of the bright sunshine, she turned towards me, studying my expression. "They are right, you know. The calves are still slaughtered." She smiled sadly, then lifted her head. "These boys give me hope for the future of the movement. We could be dreaming bigger."

"You mean, abolishing veal entirely?" I asked.

"That's what I mean," she said.

I imagined an end to the killing, and a tight spot relaxed in my chest. A bigger pen sounded good, but it was such a tiny change against the enormity of the calves' deaths. Would a jury find a murderer any less guilty if he laid his victim in perfumed satin sheets before killing her? I didn't think so.

Inside the restaurant it was small, crowded, and very loud. I followed Marlene to the window booths, where Chris sat with a group, dipping a corn chip into salsa. Marlene grabbed two chairs.

"Should we start another table?" I asked.

"Nah," she said, "They'll make room. Come on." We looked for an opening.

I jumped when she yelled over the noise of the crowd, "Hey everybody, let us in! I've got Amber, and remember, she handles one mean rabies pole!" The chorus of cheers was friendly and enthusiastic. The noise and attention were slightly overwhelming, but I belonged here. These were my friends.

• • •

The meal was good, served efficiently by the harried wait staff. "Hey Amber, where are you from?" Chris said, wiping taco sauce off his upper lip with a paper napkin. He had a small scar on one cheek, which only added to his charm. I'd heard him joke about getting hurt in a basketball accident, which always got some laughs. He glanced down at my hands. I quickly stopped twisting my fingers together and tucked my hands under the table. My cheeks burned while I tried to smile up at him.

"Tennessee, Texas, Arizona ..." I felt that familiar panic creep in, and I hoped it wasn't showing on my face. I was a fake, without the easy answer most people gave. No common ground to hang a hat on, no unfolding memories of a place that noted and welcomed my changes from toddler to child to teenager, just a constant newness. Here comes the strange new girl. Again.

"Wow. You've certainly been around. I'm a local yokel myself." Chris took his last bite of taco and wiped his hands on a napkin as the waiter brought out checks. Chris slipped his wallet out of his back pocket. I sat back and listened to the chatter of our group. My panic eased, though I felt distant, observing, almost floating above, and yet, marveling at myself. I was here, in the "in" crowd. I had made it through the chute to the other side. I held my breath for a moment and blinked, wondering how long it would last.

CHAPTER 5

"His fur is like mink, Amber. You take such good care of him," Lisa said. Tom never took long to claim Lisa's lap. She grabbed a handful of popcorn from the bowl on my coffee table and wriggled her other hand into his fur. We had become friends after the rabbit operation, meeting for lunch and talking over work projects. I could relax around Lisa. Her sorrow for the animals didn't translate to hatred for the ones who abused them.

I rubbed his ears. "Tom, you remember when Lisa came over that first time? You liked her right away. You sure have good taste in women."

Lisa smiled down at Tom, gently smoothing the fur down his back. He closed his eye and raised his head with every stroke. Lisa looked up at me and wrinkled her brow. "What is it?"

"He sure loves that, Lisa. You know just how to touch him. Unlike some people ..."

"Like who?" she asked.

I mumbled something about my housemates' friends. Lisa opened her mouth to say more, but I jumped up to load the VCR and bustled around the room looking for the remote. "It was just here, why can't my roomies leave it on the coffee table where it'd be obvious ..."

Lisa, looking thoughtful, gently lifted Tom's rear and pulled out the remote from underneath him. "This what you're looking for?"

"Yeah." I settled back down beside them, taking the remote and starting up the movie.

"This cat of yours is quite something. If I didn't know any better, I'd say he was a re-incarnated old soul. His job in life is to look after you." She offered me the bowl of popcorn, gazing at me again and saying that this movie would be good for me. "Pure silliness is just the ticket for us today."

I agreed. It was a relief to stop worrying about work for a change. *Monty Python and The Holy Grail* would be a well-deserved break from reality. We laughed uproariously at the crudely made attack rabbit, our concerns forgotten in the stark contrast between the delicate white bunny hopping in the peaceful glen to the blood-covered ravenous attack thing killing the medieval knights.

"This might be even better than the three stooges." I groaned and put my hands over my stomach, my belly hurting from popcorn or laughing, I couldn't be sure which. "Revenge of the killer bunny."

"Yeah, it's so ridiculous, you just have to go with it. I give up! I surrender to the Knights of Ni!" She held her white napkin up in the air.

I pulled her arm down, grinning. "But I do wonder sometimes, do these guys, the actors, ever do anything serious in their lives?"

"I don't know. Maybe it doesn't matter," she said, "Maybe this is just as important. Their genius is to make us forget all our troubles, if only for an hour or so."

I didn't know, but it certainly felt good, like some inner muscles, way too tense, finally took a big sigh and relaxed, for the first time in years. A bigger space was opening up inside me. I picked up the empty popcorn bowl and carried it into the kitchen, pausing to gaze out at the hills, their green subtly changing from vibrant summer colors to more muted fall tones. Space. Felt good.

Then I put my hand on my stomach, and realized there still was a small hard knot, almost burning. The blood in the show was purely theatrical, smeared across the knights' armor and the white fur of the obviously fake stuffed rabbit. But somewhere deep inside, this pretend violence called to me, in a way I could not understand. I had held a sword before, on a field trip, as a child. The weight of it had been satisfying, and I remembered desperately wanting to swing it wildly, spinning around in a circle. Cutting away whatever, whomever stood close enough. I imagined the screams and knew that finally I would have space. That my skin could finally breathe. I shuddered, feeling again the burning, deep inside, that had nothing to do with popcorn and laughter.

"So what'cha thinkin'?" Lisa had come up behind me, sharing the view.

I jumped a bit, then shoved my hands into my jeans pockets and stared at the clouds catching the lowering rays of the sun. Pink and gold and blue all in one small puff of water vapor. "Well, that attack rabbit stole my heart," I said. "I was thinking about the Draize test for cosmetic product safety."

Lisa looked somber. "Yeah. They used rabbits because they're so sweet and easy to handle. At least Revlon stopped it, but the other companies ..."

"He's like all the Draize rabbits finally getting revenge."

Lisa clapped her hands together. "Yes! A bloody I'm-going-to-eat-your-heart-out Easter bunny!" We laughed again, smiling at each other happily.

Lisa sighed deeply, and said, "I'm glad to hear you laughing, Amber. I was worried that this work might get you down too much. We can't let the bastards get to us, you know." She reached out to hug me.

I pulled away and tucked my hands casually back into my pockets, biting my lip. "Yeah, sure, I know, I'm good ... So, wanna do another movie again sometime?"

"Sure, sure," she said, glancing again at my face.

CHAPTER 6

"Hey kid, I need a hand. Can you spare an hour?" Marlene peered over my cubicle wall, tapping her fingers along the top. A young boy had called about a Canada goose he had in his house. He thought she might be starved, too small to keep up with the migrating flocks. We both thought something might be wrong since he was able to catch her.

I stood up and stretched. "Sure, Marlene, I would love to get outside. Is it still raining?"

"Don't worry, you won't melt." She handed me a map with scrawled directions.

• • •

"So you said Canada geese are your favorite birds?" asked Marlene as we drove through the suburbs, looking for the turn onto Howard Avenue. "Any experience handling them?"

"My aunt kept geese, and she taught me a lot. But there's something about the wild ones that always gets me. I like their honking as they fly, heading south." Every fall their cries pulled at my heart, opening up folded places deep inside and blessing the darkness within, somehow.

"Yeah, they get to go someplace better," said Marlene, quietly, almost to herself.

I agreed, wondering if she wanted to follow their calls, drifting behind their wing beats and watching the land change beneath her as she headed for a fresh start in a warmer place. A place where everything could start anew, a safe place where she could rest her weary wings and bask in the soft sunlight, without worries about raising her babies. I rubbed my arms reflexively, wondering what it would be like to simply lift powerful wings and rise out of the here and now, drifting over trees and valleys and mountains to places where nobody could find you.

The traffic slowed to a stop and Marlene jiggled the gear stick. "God, the traffic always builds up here, no matter what time it is. What, is there a party somewhere? Yard sale?" The rain flicked on the windshield, the wipers smearing it away. She paused and glowered at a stain on her shirt. "You know, it's probably just that she's molting, now that I think of it. Happens about this time every summer, and they really can't fly until those big wing feathers come in." She gestured angrily at a driver. "Come on, what's so complicated about a four-way stop. It's called taking turns, you dimwit!"

Our turn came and she gunned the car across the intersection. I stared down at the map crinkling on my lap, bracing myself with my other hand. "Looks like it's the third right."

The boy lived in a ranch house by the lake. Geese were scattered about the yard, grazing or resting in the long grass with their glossy black heads held straight up like signposts. They watched us as we walked up the front path, and a large gander honked loudly, tilting his bill down as if warning us away. He stood his ground as we came closer.

We sought the shelter of the porch and knocked, watching the rain bead on the gander's feathers and roll down to the ground around his feet. When the teenager let us in, he took us downstairs to the dark basement where a goose huddled, twine tied tightly around her leg and attached to a cinder block. While I looked her all over, Marlene asked him, "You just walk right up to her, or did you have to trick her somehow?"

"Naw, she was in a group near the shore where I was fishin,' and when she came near to steal my bait, I grabbed her. I tied her leg to keep her from pooping all over the basement. She's pretty small, huh?" He hooked his thumbs in his pockets and grinned, sucking on his teeth.

"Yeah," said Marlene, "I bet she's one of the new babies from this year." She turned towards me, smiling, "All okay?"

I nodded.

She turned back to him. "You know, she's just getting her growth in, while the adults are molting. I don't think you have to worry about her. Amber, need some help?"

"Just have to get this twine off," I said. It had cut into her leg, but the wound was not yet festering. Anger rose inside me, and I thought of the knights' swords. But not now. It was not the time for anger. This youngster needed my help. I teased the twine from the raw areas, holding the goose gently between my knees. She was quiet, bright eyes staring all around, bill slightly open as she panted in the warm basement. She didn't belong here, wounded or not. She was small, but strong and healthy. She belonged outside with her family. "I won't tell," I mouthed silently, then suddenly the twine came free and I scooped her up into my arms.

"Let's get her back outside." I carried her up the steps and set her down on the grass. She ran, wings outstretched, as if to regather her freedom. She joined the group, greeted by a clamor of honking.

The kid laughed. "I guess she's okay, then? That's good."

I crossed my arms over my chest and watched the goose until I lost her in the feathered crowd. Dimly I heard Marlene thanking him for caring. Would the goose tell her mother about the dark place, about her pain and fear? Would she warn them to stay away, to fly far from those strange bare-skinned beings? Would she remember the one who had held her gently and pulled the rope from her leg before setting her free?

"What's the matter?" Marlene said as we headed back to the office. "She's free, isn't she?"

"Yeah, that's a good thing," I said, trying to make my voice match my words. I sat quietly, staring out at the fence posts flickering by. Far away in a field, a tiny tractor puffed black smoke as it maneuvered through a gate.

"Nothing to be sad about, Amber. You should feel good about this." Marlene paused for a moment. "Was her leg okay?"

I looked down at my lap. "There was a wound ..."

"Why didn't you say something? We could have brought her to our vet." She eased up on the gas pedal and the car slowed.

"Nah, it wasn't that bad." I pictured the goose in a cage under bright examination room lights and felt sick to my stomach.

Marlene seemed hurt that I hadn't asked for her opinion. "Well, you should have showed it to me or something, so we could have decided together." I glanced over, watching her grab a bit of her hair and chew on the ends. She slumped down in her seat. After a while, her mood softened a bit. "I'm glad that kid cared, that's something." She turned a crooked smile briefly in my direction. "You did great in there. I guess your aunt really taught you a lot."

"Thanks." I could still feel the powerful muscles along the goose's wings, stretched tightly as iron bands across the bones beneath. The soft down cradling her breast as I lifted her into my arms. And the ugly painful wound encircling her leg. I stared down at my hands. "Yeah, I guess she did."

My mother's hands always knew what to do. They could craft delicate embroidered bookmarks, tend freshly scraped knees, lift a tear from my cheek, and in the next breath envelop me in a celebratory bear hug, "You did it, Amber, you went down the slide all by yourself!" Those hands made the world a safe place, allowing me the freedom to explore, yet opening wide for me when it was time to come home. But no longer. When I concentrate, I can still feel her deep within me, telling me how special I am, and how strong. But most days, I just feel empty.

CHAPTER 7

It was my first protest. We converged on the show tent at the fairgrounds by one's and two's, knowing that the police were alert for any disruption. I watched the proud smiling children, just a few years younger than I, leading their beautiful young animals around the ring. Horns and hooves polished to a high shine, coats glossy from careful bathing and brushing, the calves bounced excitedly when they could, surprised by all the new sounds and smells. The children calmed their animals, talking softly and caressing the broad furry cheeks. These farm kids raised their animals from birth, tending to their every need, training them to accept and even seek human interaction.

$\bullet \quad \bullet \quad \bullet$

I had asked Marlene about 4-H, the program for kids aspiring to be farmers, the day before the protest. We sat in the lunch room eating our sandwiches. "Don't these kids love their animals and take good care of them?" I asked, taking another bite of my sandwich.

Marlene made a face, putting down her drink. "Sure they do. But then it's over, after the animal gets enough muscle on him to sell." She folded her arms around herself, as if she was cold. "4-H says it teaches young people to be proud of their pampered animals. But it's all a mirage, because after a certain age, their milk, wool and ultimately the meat of their bodies are what everyone is after. It's called a life lesson, because to be good at 'animal husbandry,'" she made quotes in the air with her fingers, "means maximizing cash value, and hardening oneself to the betrayal at the auction block. There's a tradition of paying these kids extra high prices for the first animal they raise and sell, as if that fixes everything."

"So the animals learn to trust these kids, and then they're sold. That's harsh." My bite of sandwich made a lump in my throat.

"Yeah, well, that's why we'll be there, to make it more obvious. We think it stinks."

. . .

We all met in one section of the bleachers. On a signal, we pulled our outer shirts over our heads to reveal white T-shirts imprinted with the blood-red slogan, "Meat is Murder." I wanted to hide, to run, to do anything but stand up in public and reveal my own outrage at the betrayal of these animals, and these children. I felt far removed from my own skin, almost floating above the crowd as I stood there with my friends. There were gasps from the crowd. Silent, we stood in the stands until uniformed officers led us away, one by one.

Waiting for my turn, I felt a flicker of pride through my fear. I was standing up for something I believed in, and it felt good, it felt right. Grabbed by the arm, I turned and looked into the ring one more time, and saw tears in the eyes of a rosy-cheeked girl with braids. Her calf pulled impatiently on his halter. He wanted to be in his warm cozy stall, filled with sweet straw. "See what you did?" said the police officer, an angry young man, stiff in his spotless uniform.

. . .

Chris collected us from the police station after HAA posted our bail, and I was the last one left. He was angry. "Those calves, they still die, you know, just like the veal calves do." He was holding tightly to the steering wheel and popping the clutch too roughly. Our bodies jerked forwards and backwards as the engine shifted and revved. "Really, we didn't do them any damned good at all."

I remembered the metal chain with the number 871 hanging on Marlene's bulletin board. She had told me it reminded her of whom we were fighting for. "It's true, Chris. Maybe the veal calves can move around more now, but—"

"Well, woohoo, so what, they get to stretch their legs before they're rounded up and killed and eaten, just like the 4-H calves? What did we really accomplish? Better conditions at the concentration camp? Making little kids cry when they feel bad enough already?"

"Yes, but at least this time, we aren't talking about bigger pens. We made a statement—"

"Meat is murder, yes, I know," his voice was loud, and the hot breeze from the highway rippled through his hair. I eased myself closer to the door of the old Chevrolet.

He continued, "Don't you feel so helpless sometimes? Meat is murder, and that's exactly what's going to happen to those calves. Period."

I sat silently, my stomach tight, then whispered, "What can we do?"

He sighed and dropped a hand into his lap, turning briefly to look at me. "Well, there are other places they could go."

"There are? Like sanctuaries? Does HAA have money—"

"I know, I know, there are no funds for that. Money makes the world go 'round. But those calves—they are on an assembly line that's still running, and it makes me crazy. I want to put up a road block and stop those fucking trucks." He lifted his hand and rubbed hard at his eyes. His cheek was bright red, making the scar stand out, a small crescent moon next to his wispy beard. "They trust people, those calves, you know? They think people care ... Oh, Amber ..."

It seemed like a long time until the lights of my house showed up, shining brightly through the trees. "I wish we could have saved them, too. I'm sorry—" I reached out for his shoulder, then pulled my hand away quickly when he grabbed at the gear stick, downshifting before the turn into my driveway. The headlights caught the fluttering leaves of the aspen in the yard, and as we stopped, sparkling bits of dust floated up from the tires. I could still smell the fairgrounds on our clothes—dust, manure, and sweet hay.

"Amber ..." he turned to look at me. "It's just that we could do more, you know? We are only pretending to do good. We're not doing anything real."

I nodded and thanked him for the ride, reaching for the door handle, "See you tomorrow." I waited, listening carefully to his breathing.

"I'm going to be looking for something else to do, I think." The car engine hummed quietly, idling, and I saw Tom in the window, waiting.

I took a deep breath, "Where would you go?"

"I don't know yet, maybe a group that saves old-growth forests or something. I could get myself chained to a tree. More effective than wearing a chicken suit in front of McDonald's." He laughed, but his eyes were still sad.

I stared at him a moment longer, and he turned away, gazing out into the darkness, "I'll see ya, Amber. You did good. Keep it up."

I slid out of the car, suddenly wanting to be alone, to touch Tom and feel his purr deep within. I waved as Chris backed out of the driveway and accelerated down the road, then stepped up to my door and pulled my keys out of my jeans pocket.

•　•　•

That night, HAA employees gathered together again for Italian food at Antonio's. I looked forward to these dinners. The conversations drifted over me, lulling me into a new sense of belonging. I didn't have to defend my choice of a salad over a steak to these people. Their own plates were already heaped with vegetarian selections. And there was always a seat saved, just for me.

There were so many of us that we filled a corner with our enthusiasm. The candles set on each table invited close conversation, gently lighting up my friend's faces. Good smells came from the kitchen, luscious sauces and fresh-baked bread. I sat down next to Lisa, who turned and said, "Wow, Amber, that was pretty wild, huh? Getting arrested and everything?"

"I was pretty nervous. I've never actually tried to draw the attention of law enforcement before, you know?" Others nodded their heads, understanding. Chris had not joined us. "I hope we made some people think."

She touched my arm, nodding. "There was a short piece in the paper about what we did, so maybe that woke up a few people," she said, "Maybe they'll think about the issues we raised. Letting kids love somebody, then taking their friends away again. Just isn't right."

As our food arrived, I leaned close to Lisa, telling her what the cop had said, and that he had seemed angry.

She slowly picked up her fork and slipped it into her beans, "Scary, isn't it?" When I nodded, mute, she looked at my face and said, "Well, don't let it get to you. You're standing up against a horrendous wrong. It's like they are all sleepwalking, and only we can see the suffering."

I looked down at my food, "I know. The suffering of the animals, and also the kids. Both."

"Exactly!" she said, taking a sip of soda. "And the cops, well, all they see are the kids. But maybe after this demonstration they'll go home and think just a bit about the animals, because it's not like we were crazy shouting lunatics or anything. We made a good point."

· · ·

But what exactly had we done? Chris' tears—I thought about the tears of the girl with the braids. Was she crying for her ruined moment in the ring, or was she thinking of her calf? The little Jersey, lovingly raised from birth, taught to accept human touch, to wear a halter and follow her lead—he wasn't headed back to his cozy stall. His next stop was a truck, crammed in with other calves, headed to the slaughterhouse. Of what use was his training now? And the girl, what had she learned? Did the blue ribbon, fluttering from the empty halter, make her grief any less?

That night I lay awake, thinking of the little goose tied painfully in the dark, stinking basement, hearing her family honking outside. I imagined the

Jersey calf, pushed up the ramp into the truck, face spattered with manure. My sleep was restless, interrupted by a familiar nightmare.

Running, running, leaping up to fly as if my arms were wings, flapping frantically, but never escaping the reach of those long greedy arms. The strong grip on my ankles, the plummet back into a sweaty hairy embrace. Cigarette smoke breath.

Thankfully, I always woke up before the hard muscular arms closed around me, but I was trembling, breathing fast. Tom helped, purring in the crook of my legs. Touching his scarred head and hearing his rumbling calmed me and reassured me that all was well. If he was relaxed, then I could sleep again.

The nightmares were nothing new. They started after my mother died, but lately they crowded into my sleep as if they'd been waiting in line. Maybe I just needed to work harder, save more animals, be more effective, and be a bigger part of HAA's "lean, mean, fighting machine," as Marlene called it.

CHAPTER 8

Fall announced itself with a glorious change in the air, a wind that cooled the skin instead of simply raising dust storms and blowing tumbleweeds. The leaves finished falling and the nights found Tom and I snuggled in thick blankets.

Tonight the moon shone directly into my window, as it often did, reflecting off Tom's bright eye when my restlessness woke him. I pulled him close and tried again to sleep, but I was nervous about the coming day.

Maybe if I focused my thoughts on something I didn't need to control, it would calm the whirling in my head, putting the brakes on the turning spinning merry-go-'round. A sudden gust outside sent leaf shadows whirling and dancing across the wall over my bed. The wind. I loved it so. I took a deep breath as if I could capture its power and draw it deep into my body. I imagined the tumbling blowing air as a great beast spread out all across the lands and oceans, one part moving and another part reacting, all interconnected. I stroked Tom's fur until I drifted off in spite of myself.

Later I woke to the sun in my eyes, and Tom staring at me. "I know, I know, I have to get ready."

He grumbled and left the bed.

Today was my first solo outreach effort. I took a quick shower, fed Tom, and loaded my stuff into the car. The local elementary school was just across town, where a teacher had invited me to teach her kids about helping animals. I'd tell them how to keep their dogs and cats safe, and how to help during a visit to the veterinarian. I'd talk about spaying and neutering to reduce unwanted litters, and then I'd hand out some yummy vegetarian recipes. Lisa, a former elementary school teacher, had told me that kids are more open to change. When they are given a peek behind the fairytale of happy farmed animals rollicking in their barnyard, the kids ask questions and want to know more. They can handle the truth behind their hamburgers and hot dogs.

• • •

Later that day, I was typing up my report for the latest newsletter on my battered blue metal Brother typewriter, struggling to get the correction paper out from where I had dropped it down onto the type bar levers. The talk with the kids had gone well. The students had been enthusiastic about helping animals. Perhaps I had planted a seed or two. I enjoyed hearing about their favorite dogs and cats at home. Excitement and love shone out of their little faces, so pure and unconscious it made my heart catch.

Remembering, I felt a darkness deep inside of me, a tiny spot of fear, as if their pure unguarded feelings were a target, somehow. I shook my head as I scrabbled inside the typewriter. "You don't make sense," I muttered to myself, "Probably just jealous."

"Amber, you finished yet?" I looked up and saw Chris. He stepped into my cubicle and laid a book on my desk, then leaned over and rubbed my shoulders. It felt good. Since the ride home from the 4-H protest, we had become close, spending our spare time together. I was always glad to see him, knowing that at any moment, he might be off on another adventure.

I looked at the battered paperback. "*Carrie.* Stephen King. You like it?" I asked, rolling my shoulders happily, my fear forgotten.

"Well, it gives me nightmares, but otherwise I like it. Reading about violence that isn't real. I don't know, somehow it helps."

I shook my head, thinking about nightmares. "Sometimes his books seem too real. A bullied high school girl and her blown-out-of-proportion bloody revenge." I shivered dramatically.

"Yeah, well, good for her, standing up for herself. I think Carrie is cool. She doesn't take any guff. How soon can you leave?"

I felt a quiver deep in my stomach, a small falling away, as quiet as a fawn in the forest. But I smiled up at him anyway. "Not finished yet, I gotta correct a few more typos, and then I still have my conclusion."

"Well, if you wanna join us for dinner tonight, I can wait a bit and we can go together."

I glanced up, leaned back in my seat, and pushed the hair off my forehead. "I don't want to hold you up, really. Maybe I can meet you there."

He smirked at me, raising his hand towards my face, then dropped it and tucked it back into his jeans pocket. I held back a sudden urge to grab that hand and kiss it. He told me where they were meeting, and turned to go.

I waved, then turned back to my desk and looked for the little white square. It was sticking up in between the "H" and the "Y." I pulled it out, and then noticed black ink smudged across my fingers. Grimacing, I sought out the closest mirror, which was in the bathroom. Sure enough, there was a matching black smudge on my forehead. I rubbed at it angrily, only making the smear larger. Why hadn't he told me? Suddenly I felt stupid. "Amber, you are no swan," I said to myself. But only after checking that the bathroom stalls were all empty.

The story *The Ugly Duckling* always gave me a funny feeling growing up. This baby bird, treated badly just because he was different, grows up into an amazing and beautiful swan. The message was, "Don't worry if you feel different from all the others. You are special in your own way." I knew, even as a child, that I was supposed to be relieved and happy at the end, celebrating the new life of this poor ugly baby. But what bothered me was how the real ducklings got off scot-free. They hounded this baby, treating him so badly that he left the family, left the relative security of the barnyard for an uncertain future on his own. And he was just a young bird, still flightless. The bullies got away with it. True to life, but it didn't make for a pleasing story.

The rest of the story I liked better. He survived. Despite his miserable beginnings, he proved himself strong and capable. I could identify with that—working hard and not whining or lamenting your losses.

I used to daydream about looking into a mirror one day and finding myself beautiful, talented, and powerful, able to fly with the other swans and leave the nasty ducks behind. I laughed, quietly. Maybe I had found some swans here at HAA. Maybe someday I would fit in. I grimaced at myself in the mirror, tucked my hair behind my ears, and left the bathroom, my footsteps the only sound in the deserted warehouse.

I finished up my article and settled it on top of the pile on the magazine editor's desk, then returned to fine-tune another article on painful laboratory experiments being carried out on dogs. The three pages were covered with red felt-tip pen editing marks. One after another, I made each correction. It was like meditation, focusing minutely on word choices and phrasing, getting the feel of the sentences just right. For a time, I forgot all the frustrations of the day.

There. All typed up again, and much better this time. I looked up at the clock and realized that it had been another hour. Surely they had all eaten by then. Oh well. Who needed more cigarette smoke? I turned in my second article, packed up, and went home. I'd tell Chris I wasn't feeling well or something. Would be sort of true. I just wanted to curl up in my room right now and be left alone. Tom would understand, but I didn't want to explain myself to anybody else. I might mess up their nice day.

It took a hard scrub with hot soapy water before my face was ready for my pillow that night.

CHAPTER 9

Finally Friday afternoon, and I was heading into the weekend with my work caught up. Nothing hanging over my head. Chris was coming over later, continuing our Friday night tradition of spaghetti with homemade sauce. But before then, I had time to relax and unwind.

Tom was pleased to see me, as always. I looked down at him, standing near me on the couch. "Hello, handsome." He gazed up into my eyes, his paws working away at the cushion, a habit left over from kittenhood. "Dreaming of your mama, Tom?" I gave him a quick pat and then walked down the hall, hearing a thump behind me as he left the couch to keep an eye on me. I rummaged through my storage chest and pulled out my old photo album, wanting to see my mother's face again. Most of the sequins had fallen off the cover, leaving small lumps of Elmer's glue behind.

Returning to the couch, Tom in tow, I pushed away my housemate's jacket and sat down, inviting Tom to snuggle close against me. I opened the thick cardboard cover and smiled, looking at a little face with small light-brown braids sticking out, not quite long enough to touch her shoulders. Ribbons tied at the ends. I had loved those blue ribbons.

"Here, Tom, that's me again, before you met me. We were camping in the mesa. See my big smile? I adored camping." There I was again, face smeared with chocolate, holding a coat hanger with a marshmallow perched precariously at its tip. My T-shirt, smudged with ashes, had a big yellow peace sign on it. I turned the page. "That's my best friend from when we lived in Tennessee." Tom purred and snuggled tighter against my leg, curling into his "I'm happy" ball.

Young faces, covered in freckles, so serious, the camera catching us looking over our shoulders. Were we telling secrets? Figuring out how to catch the most beautiful butterflies? Photographs capture the image, but the feelings sometimes leak away.

Another page. Most of the pictures were just me, here in front of yet another house, there dressed for another day at a different school with my pink backpack. I'd hide a favorite stuffed animal in there, usually a horse, imagining him life-sized and clumping behind me down the new schoolroom halls. He helped me find the cubby for my blue metal lunchbox. He knew the apple inside was for him. "Later. Wait until lunchtime, silly," I'd tell him, and he would snort. He followed me to my seat, his warm hay-scented breath on my neck as I bent over my assignment. He kept me company and reminded me to smile when meeting new friends. Dad used to tell me that if I smiled more, people would like me better. I think that's true. "Do you think so, Tom?" He tightened his paws around his nose, curling more tightly into sleep.

Here, a picture of a yellow house, with a graceful maple tree in the front yard. I remembered the tree, but not the house. Was that the one with the little understair closet that was such a good hiding place? I wasn't sure. But I did remember coming home to the sight of boxes piled in the driveway, again. My stomach sinking, I ran inside to find my father wrapping plates in brown paper and settling them into a box on the kitchen floor. "Daddy, what's wrong!"

He smiled at me and held his arms out. I dropped my backpack and buried my face in his shirt. His arms closed around me and I remember with piercing clarity wanting to stay there forever. No new schools, no new lunch lines, no new teachers. Just a warm safe hug.

"What's the matter, little pea?"

I sniffled, "Is it because of me?"

"What do you mean?"

I pulled my face away from his chest and rubbed my eyes. "The smiles. I didn't smile enough, that was it, wasn't it?" I buried my face back into his shirt, the stripes blurring together, blues into greens into reds.

He held me tighter, and I felt his chest lift in a sigh, "Aw, honey, it's not that. There's this guy that promised me a good job in his new company. It'll be good for us, and you'll even have a yard with a swing."

A swing one time, a nearby horse farm the next time, his promises would always distract me from the sadness of leaving. I hugged him again, feeling safe and protected, and then helped pack up my toys. I knew the drill.

I got pretty good at leaving. Always in search of a better boss, more interesting work, or higher wages, my dad never seemed to settle for what he had. Nothing made him happy for long. He'd get that look in his eye, and I'd know that we were in for another change. It would happen every couple of years. Just enough time to get to know the neighborhood, all the open fields and nearby forests, the fun places for biking. Friends at school were temporary, so it didn't matter so much if they liked other people more than me. It would soon be moving time again, time to pack my things away into boxes, adjust to a new home and a new school. Would there be a lawn with a flower bed? I could never be sure, since nobody ever asked my opinion.

My favorite things would ride near me in my suitcase. A little ragged corduroy horse accompanied me for many years, along with Tigee, a threadbare tiger hand puppet. They each carried a little piece of me, quietly and unobtrusively, tucked into the corner between my socks and my hair brush. Out they'd come, the first to arrive in a new room or motel, staking their claim and making the strangeness familiar somehow.

"Here, Tom, here I am on my banana seat bicycle." Once I was old enough to wander on my own, I discovered that nature always welcomed me in my explorations. Which trees were the best for climbing? Where were the meadows that had escaped the mowers long enough to harbor small growing things and tiny fascinating animals? Each place had unique wonders for a small girl who was happier wandering alone outside than being home. The deserts had long-tailed lizards, the blue of their tails an unbelievable richness not found elsewhere, except in the deep summer sky just before a storm. Lizards with the longest tails were difficult to find, because the tail was the first to go if a predator tried to grab them up for lunch. The longest tail I ever found was on a lizard hiding inside a soda can, seeking the sweet drops left behind. The little brown horned lizards, easier to catch, sat in funny awkward poses on my palm, looking back at me as I studied them, before I set them down and they trundled away through the grass.

I fingered a picture cut out from a magazine and glued into the scrapbook. "Look here, Tom, that's a praying mantis. See how his arms are lifted up, like he's talking to God?" Praying mantises made interesting playmates. I'd catch them and keep them for a while in shoeboxes. They would eat whatever small bug I could catch for them, their upraised arms, serenely prayerful, transforming in a flash into powerful vises gripping the small insect bodies. They took their time dining, not noticing me watching over the lip of the box. "Grasshopper brains, Tom, that's what they liked the best."

I stared out the front window, past the scraggly aspens at the edge of the curb. The sun was dropping towards the distant hills, glowing brightly beneath low purple-edged clouds. No longer wandering the mesas in my free time, I now explored when I ran, breathing fast to bring some life into my soul, wondering what the next years would bring. But some things don't change, no matter how far you run. Some people just follow you.

I turned the page. "There's my mother, Tom. Isn't she beautiful?" We were standing together, my hand tightly clasped in hers, gazing solemnly into the camera. Had Dad just told us to pipe down? Mom and I would sometimes get loud, crazy, pretending to be small animals with high piping voices, having tea parties or planning exciting adventures. But something about our voices would always irritate Dad if he was home, and he would come storming out of the bedroom, making up some chore that needed to be tended to, right now. His rage confused and scared me, but I was protected by the circle of my mother's arms.

"Oh, hush, honey," she'd say, "You'll scare Amber."

"I really don't care. If she hasn't picked up her toys by bedtime, then I'll break them all."

Mom sighed and turned to me. "Wait for me in the front yard, and we'll throw a Frisbee, okay?"

I jumped up and grabbed my new yellow disc before rushing out the door.

"Here, Tom, see? It was my favorite Frisbee. I learned to throw pretty good. I wonder if I still have that disc." I turned the page. "Oh, here are my stuffed animals all lined up on my bed. My favorite was Lilac, the purple unicorn. And the little teddy bear with the funny hat. See him there?" I pointed, then felt vaguely silly, sitting there with Tom. I hoped that nobody was home and listening. I had loved those toys, but not as much as my little striped real-life cat, Roxie. I paged through the album, stopping at the photo of Roxie, clutched in my arms. "You aren't jealous, are you, Tom? After all, she's prettier than you." My grin in that picture was as wide as the ocean. Roxie wanted to be put down, but she had paused to look up at the camera, as if asking for help.

"And here's me and my kite, Tom. That one really could fly. Cut my fingers once on the string when it was really windy. I thought we were both about to fly away to Oz or something." I laughed, remembering the throbbing, the powerful straining of the faraway kite traveling all the way down through the string and into my hands, like a kiss from God. I had held so tightly, clinging to my very own bit of wildness.

I reached the back of the album, where I had tucked old photographs from my babyhood and before. "Here's my dad when he was a teenager, Tom. He's so skinny! And look at that hair!" I laughed at the upswept style that made him look so rakish. His smile dared the camera to turn away. I never really saw him smile much when I was growing up, except perhaps when he settled down for a smoke at the end of the day, and Mom would bring him his favorite TV dinner and a drink. The ice cubes would clink as he drank, staring out at the trees in the yard. He enjoyed watching the birds. He would set up feeders and little feathered jewels would come flitting into the yard. Mom kept them filled with seed all year.

"Oh, here, Tom, here's my Mom when she was young. I think this is a date they went on, probably before I was around." The grainy black-and-white photo showed my mother wearing a light-colored dress, smiling up at

Dad, who had his arm around her. Their hands were linked and my mother's hair was curled into big waves, falling softly down past her shoulders.

Mom had gotten sick soon after they were married, with something in her stomach that required surgery, and even a blood transfusion. Dad was frightened of losing her, he told me, and he visited every day while she was in the hospital. That's why they waited a few years before having me. She recovered slowly. We would joke about it, saying that I was a good luck baby. "When you came," Mom would say, "the sun returned."

Dad would humph and say, "Yeah, the early morning sunshine, when we could have been sleeping."

"Here I am as a baby, Tom. Aren't I cute?" Dad had given me some photos after Mom died. He said they made him sad. Here he was, leaning up against a car shiny with chrome, his hand curled over the tail fin, with Brylcreemed hair and a goofy grin. I'd never seen such lightness in his face, except in those old photos. "I wonder whether he ever thought about getting remarried, Tom. Maybe a new wife would make him happy." Life laid heavily on his shoulders now. Lately I could hardly believe that his thick, dejected body had ever been that buoyant and carefree.

One night, when I was about six years old, I caught him crying, which scared me. I had needed help with my lettering. I was learning cursive, and the loops and whorls were very confusing.

I ran down the hall into Dad's office and stormed over to his desk when I saw him hold a handkerchief up to his eyes, dabbing almost angrily. "Boy, you sure can make a lot of noise for such a little bitty thing," he said, tucking the handkerchief away into his pocket and glaring in my direction.

I stood in front of his desk and stared, homework forgotten in my hand. He looked back at me, the anger leaking away and leaving him sad, almost deflated. Smaller, somehow. And tired. So tired.

"Whatcha' got there, Am'?"

"Daddy, are you sad?"

He took a deep breath, "Well, yes, I suppose I am, little pea. I miss your momma."

"Yeah, me too," and my lips quivered. His embrace was warm and fatherly, soothing my fears. We sat together silently for a while, then I laid my crumpled paper down on his desk. He curled his big hand around mine to make the letters, and we laughed at the awkwardness of it. "Q just doesn't make sense!" I insisted.

"I know. But you gotta keep trying. See how it goes up, then down, then whirls around?"

"It's dancing!" I wiggled in his lap and threw my hands in the air. "Like a ballerina!" But then he got angry. The change was sudden, like a freak thunderstorm. He pushed me off his lap roughly, telling me I almost put the pencil in his eye and why couldn't I be more careful. I grabbed my paper and ran out, staying in my room until he called me out for dinner. He was silent for the whole meal.

I shifted the album in my lap and turned a page. "Look, Tom," I said, "here's some of my writing from when I was little. So scrawly and funny! When Dad'd help me, my hand would disappear into his fist, with the pencil sticking out the other side." I took Tom's furry paw in my hand and gently closed my fingers around his toes. His purr got louder, like I was part of a pleasant dream. I opened my hand and looked at the tufts of fur sticking out between his toes. "His hands aren't quite as furry as your paws, though, Tom."

I set his foot down gently on my lap. His toes curled up, claws forming a small hooked circle, then they relaxed again, the sharp tips disappearing into gray fur. "Sometimes I wished he had smaller hands, though, Tom. Like when he broke my favorite sparkly pencil because I left it on his recliner. I guess it made a hole when he sat on it."

I closed my eyes, breathing slowly, fingers resting in the softness of Tom's belly. "Some days it felt like I had two daddies, but I really only wanted just one."

•   •   •

A bang on the front door sent Tom scurrying under the couch. We weren't used to visitors, but he was the only one who could fit under there, so I let him be and answered the door, my own heart pounding. Chris grinned at me through the screen, holding bread aloft like a prize, and my heart calmed a bit as I fumbled with the door. The bread's paper wrapper crackled as he moved past me into the living room, bringing with him the smells of rain and shampoo. I closed the door and hugged him, his damp hair brushing my cheek. I felt the bones of his spine through his thin jacket.

"Amber! I missed you yesterday."

"It took me so long to finish up, I figured you'd all be finished eating by then."

"What were you working on?" he asked.

"It's the dog experiments going on at that lab in Albuquerque, where they do heart surgery and then make them run on treadmills afterwards. I was way past my deadline."

He pulled at his ear, the way he did when he was thinking. "Well," he said, "I cried in the restaurant. I embarrassed myself."

I laughed, "Come on into the kitchen, and I'll get the water on."

"Where should I put this?" he said, hardly needing to ask as he headed into the kitchen, waving the bread over his shoulder.

"Counter, and the cutting board's ready for you." I listened to tires on the wet road outside before I joined him, adjusting to a new person in my space. Felt different in here, as it always did when he came. A small invasion. But good.

I started work on the sauce, settling a pan of chopped onion and garlic onto the stove, and soon the aroma filled the kitchen, steam from the boiling pasta coating the windows. I rinsed off a tomato for the salad and set it on the cutting board, water drops rolling off the bright red skin.

"Thin slices? Or chunks?" I asked Chris.

"Chunks, definitely," he nodded, slicing the bread, his tongue stuck out slightly between his teeth. Bits of broken off crust followed the track of the knife as it slid through the loaf.

"Got some garlic? I could put it in the bread." He pulled open the fridge and stood staring inside, Tom joining him.

"Got some, but I'd rather—"

"Found it! I'm gonna do my masterly chef imitation." He pounced on the garlic as Tom raced out of the kitchen, whiskers flaring. Chris peeled a few cloves and began chopping. "Bonzai!" His hands flew into the air and suddenly I realized I wasn't the only nervous one. I laughed, relieved, thinking that chopped garlic chunks inside the bread were a small price to pay for friendly company.

Dinner was good, interrupted only briefly by two of my housemates. They joined us with bowls of Ramen noodles, but it wasn't long before they left for their rooms, complaining about long hard days. We were alone again.

Chris and I sat contently on the couch, rubbing our stomachs and groaning eloquently about how much we had eaten. We found a vampire movie and laughed over the melodramatic lighting and the fanged villain, so intense and serious.

I touched his arm and said, "Do you remember *Dark Shadows*, with Barnabas, the vampire who loved his family?" Imagine being a vampire and yet still caring about people. Who thinks of these things?

"Do ya think he ever said, 'Ah, to heck with it all, I'm hungry,' before biting into his father's neck?" said Chris, licking his finger and rubbing it over his lower lip.

"Nah, he's got a bunch of people in the town he can kill."

"Well, I'm certainly not hungry anymore," Chris murmured, stroking Tom's back. After a few visits, Tom had decided that Chris was actually a very nice person. Now, his favorite place was insinuated between us on the couch.

"Actually, that vampire reminds me of that new guy at work, kind of dark and creepy-looking," Chris shuddered dramatically.

"You silly! He's not creepy! He's got a big heart. Do you know how many dogs he has at home?"

"Nah—"

"Six! And he cooks for them, imagine that! You know, he wants to be a chef some day. I think his dogs are stand-ins for future customers."

Chris leaned back and scratched his neck. "Wow, that's great. That's a lot of work. So, he's got aspirations outside of HAA? Hey are you gonna stay with them forever, like Marlene? I think she has a secret apartment behind that back office or something."

I imagined us leaving HAA together, heading off on some adventure. But would he even want me to come? "Well, I don't know. Seems like it'd be fun to work in an art gallery or something. Or maybe a library." I touched the soft fur on Tom's sides, moving my fingers in small circles.

"Yeah, no blood, sweat, or tears," he said quietly, smiling and touching my cheek, "It does get old some days."

I held my breath until his hand moved down to rub the top of Tom's head.

The three of us sat companionably on the couch, watching a commercial about butter, with dancing cartoon cows. I thought of the calves in the show ring at last summer's protest, when the rays of the sun lit up the fur around their ears, making large double halos.

Chris was reading my mind, "Remember those cops at the 4-H fairgrounds? They thought they were so tough. Shit. I laughed at them in their little golf carts." He hadn't mentioned the protest again since driving me home from the police station.

"Well, I was scared of them. Some of those farm kids might have been their nieces or nephews."

He straightened, started to speak, then closed his mouth, nostrils flaring.

"It's just that—" I began, "We don't—"

"Those kids were doing what their parents told them to do, I know," His voice was loud. He kept his gaze on the TV screen. "But they're all in it together. Betraying the animals who trusted them the most. They taught those calves that they were safe. That trust was violated."

I sat quietly, my neck hurting and a headache beginning behind my right eye. Then I touched his lips gently. "I know. We did all we could and it wasn't enough. But you care."

He took my hand, his fingers strangely cold, then reached out with his other hand and tucked my hair behind my ear, trailing his finger lightly down my neck. I held still, barely breathing. "Yeah, life sucks sometimes," he said, watching my face.

My whole body felt rigid, braced against any feeling. The throbbing behind my eye became a tunneling, a pushing, a burrowing animal seeking release.

"Well," he said, releasing my hand and leaning back, glancing at the TV, "If I had a million dollars, I would close down those fairgrounds, let all the animals go or something, or turn the fairgrounds into one big sanctuary."

I rubbed at my eyes, breathing in a deep breath. "Yeah, well someone would have to feed them. Why not you?"

He laughed and leaned over Tom to pull me close. Tom wriggled out and gave us both an indignant glare.

"Look," I said, "he's mad."

"I know." He came close and kissed me, and suddenly the world shifted and the garlic on his breath tasted like cigarettes. Deep inside I sank far away, while my outer shell received his kiss and even responded, hungrily. His lips touched mine as if through cotton, barely felt. Part of me floated above the couch, as if I was watching two strangers from a distance. The kiss and his warm arm on my back were separate from my inner self, strange and muted. I pulled away and smiled distractedly, watching for Chris' reaction. He sighed and leaned back.

"Well, that was nice. We'll have to do it again sometime."

I searched his face and saw only contentment. "Yes," I sighed, hugely.

"Wow, that one came from the ends of your toes, I think," he said, grinning at me and wriggling deeper into the couch. Then he lifted his hand and traced down the seam of my jeans. I felt numb, waiting, caught between wanting more and frightened by the intensity within my body. I couldn't tell if it was desire or fear, because they both felt the same—tight muscles, wide eyes, a pulling in the skin that was everywhere and yet nowhere all at once. I struggled to control my breathing and reached out carefully for the old afghan I kept nearby.

We sat together, not touching or speaking, and watched the rest of the show. I was grateful for the reprieve, unknowingly given.

CHAPTER 10

The winter was going by quickly, and my hands were full writing articles and researching alternatives to animal experiments. I was continually amazed at how researchers simply followed the "traditional" models. The mouse model for obesity and aging. The rhesus monkey model for AIDS drugs. Taking out the pancreas in dogs to clumsily mimic naturally-occurring diabetes. But if the goal is to help humans, then the best model is a human patient. Human data is directly applicable to humans, without concern for differing physiologies. For example, a drug that causes sedation in dogs causes excitement in cats. How helpful is data on one species, if it can't be extrapolated, and if that species doesn't naturally get the same disease? I searched for scientific studies using human tissue and clinical research to develop treatments. After such intense mental focus, I was always glad to get home to relax and not think. But today I had brought some work home.

I enjoyed Chris' visits, but tonight it was just me and Tom. Nobody to care for, nobody to cook for. A sandwich would be just the thing.

I was standing in front of the opened fridge when the front door rattled. My stomach sank. I knew who it was.

"Hey hon', you home?" Rough, guttural voice. "Can I come in?" He wasn't really asking.

I let him in, closing the door behind him, staring at my hand on the knob. My nails really needed cutting. They were getting long.

"Sorry about the other night," he said, reaching out his large hand to squeeze my shoulder. Our last phone call had ended with angry words. Mostly of him yelling, calling me stupid. "I was just mad. My boss has been giving me a hard time." His face was relaxed, lips moist and reddened from the cold.

"Well, Mike, you know, rats feel, just like we do. They—"

"Amber, I really don't care about rats. I care more about people, and you should, too."

"But testing burn ointments on rats doesn't prove they help humans."

"Well, aren't you the smart one?" He smiled and lifted the paper bag in his hand. "All that thinking make you hungry?" The smell of the Chinese food, greasy in its folded cardboard boxes, made my stomach rumble.

We walked together into the kitchen. I tried again. "I just wanted to brag about my article, Mike. I worked hard on that. Took a lot of research."

"Yeah, that's good. Good for you," he said as he pulled takeout containers out of the bag and set them on the table. I sat down for a bite, and he moved a chair over and sat close, his arm lingering over my shoulders, his breath puffing into my ear. "Man, you smell so good. How come you always smell so good?"

"It's called shampoo. Ever heard of it?"

His laugh was loud, startling me into dropping my fork. "Hah! You are a clever one. What, don't you like my aftershave?" He leaned in close, nuzzling my neck, but all I could smell was cigarettes.

I scrunched up my face against the sandpaper feel of stubble, and picked up my fork and stirred the food around on my plate. Then I collected the loose papers from work and pushed them carefully away from a small droplet of soy sauce. I was writing a report on a local university research laboratory. Animals left without postoperative care, no pain medicine after major surgery, too many surgeries without enough recovery in between. This experiment used rats, who don't have as large a following as cats and dogs, but we care about all animals at HAA. And there are laws.

Mike's hand slid down my side, pausing on my breast before continuing down into my lap. His breathing quickened.

I leaned away from the table, appetite gone. I didn't want to drive him away, because I loved him, but his visits seemed more about him than me lately. I wished he'd come after dark instead, like he used to, so I wouldn't have to see his sad sick expression. "You gonna eat?" I asked.

He leaned away and spooned more meat into his bowl, then lifted a few forkfuls to his mouth, bits of rice falling off to lie in the folds of his shirt. "Mmm mmm those people sure can cook." He got up and opened the fridge. "Want one?"

"No, thanks."

He sat down, popped off the top of his beer, then drank deeply, throat working with each swallow. I watched him wipe off his lips as he set the bottle back down on the table, sighing. He smiled at me again, reaching out to rub my back, his hand large and warm. I felt the heat from it through the thin cotton of my T-shirt.

"Hey," I murmured, a heavy weight sinking into my chest, "what's up?"

But he didn't answer. He usually preferred silence. The atmosphere was thick with his need, and I thought of those rats, trapped in their clear Plexiglass containers, waiting for the next hand reaching in from above. Where would they go next? Into the anesthesia chamber, choking on the fumes that brought nausea and then blackness? If they were lucky, a maze with a bit of food reward at the end? Or more likely, a sharp needle stick before drugged oblivion? I shrugged off his hand, getting up for a glass of water.

Finished eating, we moved into the living room and switched on the TV, watching Mork and Mindy arguing. We laughed a bit, Mike louder than me. I brought him out another beer and watched him bring it to his lips, then wipe them with his other hand before taking another swallow. I brought some papers to the couch, hoping to look over an article copied from the *New England Journal of Medicine*, but I couldn't concentrate. My mind kept veering off and stopping as if hitting a blank wall. I gave up after reading the same sentence five times without understanding.

I needed something, or somebody. Tom, where was Tom? I cleared away the dishes while Mike had his usual after-dinner smoke. Wiping down the counter, I collected the bits of rice and stir-fry into my hand and shook them into the trash can. I wished Chris was here instead. I quickly buried that thought, feeling inconsiderate.

What would my next day at work bring, I wondered, trying to focus on something, anything else. What was my project? Charities, animal experiments ... mice ... The ash tray clinked. Break over. We settled on the couch to watch the last of the episode.

"You guys gonna eat this?" a voice called from the kitchen. We told her to help herself. "Thanks!" she hurried away, a book in one hand and a takeout container in the other. "Hey Mike, hey Amber! Good night!" she called cheerily as she headed down the hall. I lifted my hand in a wave, but it didn't matter. She was already gone.

• • •

Later, tired, in my bedroom, I stood in the darkness, wondering why I felt so wrong. I pulled off my clothes and slipped under the covers, willing sleep to come, or something that would numb my feelings more completely. I heard the floorboards creak as he came in from the hall, fingers fumbling on his clothes. Then a stifled vicious curse as he stubbed his toe on the dresser by the door. He approached slowly, and the street light filtering in through the blinds caught his eyes slanting away as if denying what was to come. If I closed my eyes it might go faster, but I never did, because a surprise, though rare, would make everything harder.

Beer on his breath, cigarette smoke stink in his clothes. The smell would linger in my room, my bed, my body. I thought of the shower longingly, knowing that just after the finish he would leave, a quick peck on the cheek and the same, "Gotta get home, see ya, Amber. Be good."

He rolled away, sighing. I had lightened his day. That was a good thing. I think. "'Bye, Mike," I mumbled into the pillow, feigning my usual sleepiness.

Be good. I wondered what that meant as I washed him off me in the steamy shower, wearily soaping myself clean, but not feeling any better. I lit a candle to chase away the smells, but it did nothing to ease the ache in my heart. Maybe there would come a time, someday, when he would just want to talk. Just tell me about his day, about his struggles with his boss, about his inner thoughts and feelings. I never saw his real smile, only his guilty greeting and a final twisted grimace at the end. Who was he really, inside? And what did it mean that we were still together?

Suddenly tears came, the heat of them surprising me. Where was my comfortable numbness? I didn't really want to feel, didn't want to acknowledge anything. Sleep kept me safe, kept me separate from what happened in that bed, what had been happening since before I could remember. It just was. And until now, I had kept the knowledge of his visits locked away in another part of my being, but the wall dividing my two realities was breaking down. This couldn't go on. I had to do something.

CHAPTER 11

As winter ended, the steady changes of the landscape foretold warmer temperatures. Almost in a day, bare branches transformed into frostings of pale green leaves or bursts of pink blossoms. But closely aligned with spring's burgeoning growth, the widening cracks in my inner walls admitted more light and air, leaving me increasingly uneasy. I sought refuge in my comfortable routine, up early for breakfast, a run down the road away from town, then a quick shower and a bowl of cereal, before heading into work. But routine didn't seem to work as well as it used to.

At HAA I checked my inbox slips for anything urgent, then we had our group meeting to review any ongoing cases. After that, back to the typewriter to write reports, then to the library for research for the next newsletter, then back to the office to type Freedom of Information Act requests. The FOIA required public laboratories to release records cataloging their use of funds in research. We could discover how many animals were used, what their protocol was for treating the animals humanely (or at least what the experimenters considered humane). We could also check for any violations or citations. HAA sought the truth, and I wrote about it, so the public would know that their taxes were needlessly harming animals. The experiments were more about big business than about helping anyone. It was exhausting, immersing myself in such extreme ugliness, but at least the busyness kept me from thinking too much.

Once a week we ate lunch as a group. I discovered that sushi is actually vegetarian, and refers to rice cooked with vinegar, with or without added raw fish. It was delicious with avocado and cucumber and carrots instead. Then, after lunch, back to work, the rest of the day spent calling other activists to coordinate protest efforts, unless we had our own active case.

The harder I worked, the more interesting the work became. I felt a satisfying sense of purpose in writing descriptions of the animals' plights and finding them printed in the HAA magazine. Writing gave me a focus, laying out the truth without any pulled punches. Each time I got the words just right, a little wrinkle inside me smoothed down—a small bumpy sore spot relaxing into knowingness. The right words were my solace for all the suffering. Abandoned kittens, discarded puppies, chained dogs, starved horses, all had their story to tell, and the telling made things just a bit better, each time.

· · ·

One morning, on my run, I heard a high-pitched wail that wasn't like any bird I knew. I stopped and looked around. The road was deserted except for a cardboard box, tilted crookedly at the edge of the road where the asphalt gave way to gravel. I walked back to the box, but all was silent. I pulled back the cardboard flap, and my heart rose into my throat. Four sets of eyes ringed by black clumps of discharge gazed up at me from four furry little faces. The kittens' tiny noses were sore and red from caked-on green mucus. The orange one opened her mouth to mew, blinking in the sunlight. Gasping, I gathered up the box and rushed to work early.

· · ·

The little orange kitten was the only one of the litter who survived. The vet said that fleas, intestinal parasites, starvation and exposure had weakened the rest, causing damage so great that even his expert help could not save them.

My newsletter piece was a small celebration for the one we saved. The little foundling recovered and put on weight in just two weeks. Her coat blossomed, lustrous stripes shining out of her formerly dull orange fur. She had lots of company in the wards, as spring was always a busy time in the shelter.

I came to see her during my break. There were lots of unwanted kittens mewing at their cage bars, but the orange foundling had attracted the attention of a little white-haired lady leaning on her cane. She was dabbing a lace-edged handkerchief to her nose.

"Hello, ma'am, are you all right?" I asked her.

The kitten squeaked and pressed herself to the front of the cage, her little tail upright and vibrating. Compared to the day she arrived, she was almost shining, with bright clear eyes and a glistening coat.

"Oh, thank you my dear, I'm fine, just missing my Morris." She tucked her handkerchief into her sleeve and smiled up at me.

"Morris was your ... ?"

"My old kitty. I lost him from the kidney disease just last month, and I've been so lonely without him. He'd been with me twenty years, ever since my husband died."

I touched her sleeve. "I'm so sorry." The kitten reached a white paw through the bars, stretching out so far that her face was pressed into the metal grate. Her voice was muffled as she waved her paw, blindly.

"Oh, isn't she just darling!" she said, "She looks a lot like Morris, actually."

"I think she likes you," I said, opening the cage carefully and collecting the kitten into my arms. She immediately began purring as the old woman stroked her head with one finger.

"Oh," she breathed, "so precious."

The paperwork went smoothly, and I volunteered to deliver the kitten to her new home the very next day.

• • •

The drive was peaceful, the kitten resting quietly in her carrier. Having survived near death, a quiet ride in a car was nothing for this tough little one. At a stoplight, I pulled down a corner of the box. She was nodding off, her tiny paws tucked underneath her, an adult in miniature. The cool air in the car swirled into her box and ruffled the fur inside her ears. She fluttered them, quick as bird's wings, without waking.

I rang the doorbell while I peered through the screen door. "Hello there! I've brought your kitten!"

"I'm coming, I'm coming, just takes me a bit," she said, her white hair tucked into a neat bun at the back of her head. Her light gray sweatshirt was plastered with small hand prints in various colors of paint, and "Montrose Elementary First Grade" was emblazoned across the bottom in sparkly blue. She held the door for me as I carried the kitten into the small living room and settled the box on the couch. The old lady sighed softly as she sank into the recliner behind me. I turned with the kitten in my hands, and the two looked at each other for a moment, the kitten sniffing the air, her whiskers trembling.

The lady drew in a breath and lifted her hands away, as if surprised, when I placed the kitten into her lap. Then her eyes sparkled and her lined face lifted into a smile of pure joy, like a mother's first smile at her newborn. As her gnarled fingers stroked gently down the kitten's back, a purr spilled out of the little chest, and the small whiskered face, clean now, lifted up and gazed at her benefactress.

• • •

I finished my newsletter story with the old lady's final words, "Thank you, my dear. You brought me my new friend." A new friend, I thought. It was me, I had saved this little one. The kitten had come a long way from a dirty-faced scrawny foundling to a plump little bundle with glistening fur. Now, she would finally be loved, the way she was meant to be.

I imagined readers wiping a tear from their eye after reading an article I had written, and resolving to adopt a kitten, save a stray, call their congressman about a local laboratory, or join a rally. Maybe they would think twice before ordering meat from a menu the next time. Maybe they would discover that they could still be beautiful, dressing up for that special occasion, without a fur coat.

It felt good to speak out and give a voice to the animals who had none. That day, I drove home feeling lighter, my heart lifted with an unfamiliar sense of peace and hope.

CHAPTER 12

My peace didn't last long.

"No! No!" It was dark when I woke, my own shouts ringing inside my head. I lay still, feeling Tom sleeping quietly at my side. Somehow I hadn't disturbed him. I was breathing too fast, and my pillow felt damp, as if I'd laid down just after a hard run. Shreds of dream clung to my mind, suffocating me. Suddenly I was struggling underneath something heavy, pressing me down into the bed. I couldn't breathe. I twisted my head back and forth and wrenched my arms out from the covers, startling Tom, who flew onto the floor with a squawk. I took a breath, the pressure lifting as my hands pulled the suddenly rough blanket away from my throat.

I strained to see into the darkness, but couldn't seem to open my lids. "No!" For a moment my panic returned, then I realized that the darkness was so absolute it made no difference whether my eyes were open or closed. The streetlight. It must have gone out. That was it. I relaxed slightly, coming more into the present, into my body there on my bed. I turned on the bedside lamp and lay squinting in the sudden glaring brightness, staring up at the cracks in the ceiling. "Tom, it's alright, I just had a dream." I heard his footsteps padding across the rug. "It's just me. I'm okay now, boy." He blinked at me from across the room.

After a moment I stood to get a glass of water, the coolness soothing as it trickled down my throat. When I returned to bed, I was still trembling.

Tom waited a while to return. He was a cautious one. He knew not to be around when things weren't safe.

· · ·

Saturday, and I wanted to be alone. I arose early, moving quietly so as not to wake anyone but Tom. I laced up my sneakers and stepped out onto the porch, zipping up my jacket. Out on the road the leaf coats of the trees were changing to a thicker, deeper green. The air was cold and crisp, smelling of rain to come. But it took most of my run to clear the sense of suffocating weight still clinging to my body.

In the shower afterwards, I listened for my housemates. I held my breath until I could escape safely into my room with a book and a banana grabbed from the kitchen. I was just in time, because before I turned the first page my housemates began moving around, chatting about their bosses, the latest news story, how President Reagan was doing after the assassination attempt. All things that seemed very far away and unimportant to Tom and I.

· · ·

An eruption of laughter from the kitchen made Tom's ears flicker. Footsteps came down the hall, and he jumped off the bed and looked up at the door. Someone knocked.

"Amber, ya gotta see this!"

I left my bed and picked up Tom, holding his suddenly wriggly body tightly against my sweatshirt as I opened the door. He squirmed harder. "Yeah, what is it?"

My housemate grinned over an old photo of a child, seated in Santa Claus' lap, mouth wide open in a silent scream. "I just found this in an old box of my mom's. Isn't it hilarious? That's me. Santa didn't have any ice cream that day."

I chuckled and let Tom down. He zipped out the door. "I guess ice cream is better than Santa. Don't let him out, okay?"

She agreed and I gently closed the door and curled up on my bed again, alone this time. I listened to the laughing voices and felt frozen inside. They all sounded so relaxed, happy, and intimate. I wrapped my blanket around myself and imagined holding my hands out to a cheery flickering flame. It felt good. But if I got too close, the fire might burn me. How to get warm? How to be around other people when I felt so sad inside? They didn't really want to know the darkness inside of me.

I leaned down and picked up the photo album from the floor near my bed. It was open to the picture of me, about four years old, in a puffy little pink party dress. I remembered that dress. I wore it to my mother's funeral. I thought if I wore my best dress, then I would feel happy again, but it hadn't worked.

My hands were grabbed suddenly, roughly, by the wrists, my fingers curled tightly together inside his huge fists. His hands were sweaty and warm. "Come on, girl, you gotta stay with me here. People want to see you." I didn't want to go. I didn't want to see my mother lying in a coffin with its frilly pink lace pillow. It just didn't seem right. I tried to pull away as Daddy bent to lift me right up. But just when his arm came around me, raising my dress higher on my tights, a voice stopped him.

"Oh, Holy Mother of God, my dear man, how are you managing?" It was our neighbor, the wrinkled old lady, with her black hat pinned carefully on top of her white head. She leaned down to greet me, admiring my pink dress. She touched my face, running her papery fingers over my cheek. "Your Mommy made that for you, I'd guess. What a wonderful Mommy she was." Her voice breaking, she straightened hurriedly and reached out to adjust my dad's collar. I slipped away, stepping quietly past all the legs until I found the hanging coats along the wall. I pushed between a soft brown wool coat and a long black leather one, tucking myself away, pulling my shoes in close, so that I could think and breathe and be untouched for just a little while. I needed to feel the outline of my skin separate from the world around me.

I shook off the memory and gathered up my book, reading until the house was quiet again. Tom scratched at the door and I let him back in. "Hi,

Tom, are they gone?" We walked over the creaking floorboards to the kitchen and warmed some leftover french fries for lunch.

Tom purred and stared at the french fry in my hand.

"No, you have your own food, silly. French fries are for girls, not cats."

Tom's stare did not waver, following my hand as it traveled upwards to my lips. I spluttered on the ketchup, laughing, "If I was a bird, you'd have me hypnotized, my little man cat!"

I spent the weekend reading and daydreaming about kittens and kites and Chris. Later, drifting into sleep, calm after tending to Tom and having some cereal for dinner, something happened. The room around me changed.

All sound ceased. Deadened, muffled, the world receded, the dimness making me smaller and smaller until I was a child again. The walls were further away, the ceiling higher. Cigarette smell from a looming shape, huge and menacing. I cried out, but there was no sound. There was a shaded figure, and his fingers, so large, had dark stains. If I lay still, barely breathing, like Bambi when his mother left him alone, maybe he would leave, or at least it wouldn't hurt. The only way out was down, further into the muffling darkness. A smothering, no emotion left, apart from an overwhelming fear too big to comprehend.

I thought I was going crazy, or maybe I was already nuts. I felt sick, down deep into my furthest insides. I sought sleep as a refuge. I didn't want to know any more.

I survived the night, though that really wasn't in doubt. I was safely locked in my own room, Tom purring by my side, after all, right? When I awoke the figure was gone, sounds had returned, and sunlight was creeping in under the curtains. I touched myself all over, wondering how my skin could still cover my bones. Surely my outline had been melted away, my body shrunk, my mind disintegrated into nothingness. But here I was, and it was time to get up and go back to work.

CHAPTER 13

I felt different, but my cubicle was unchanged, the same paper pile, typewriter, pencil holder, empty glass. I collapsed into my chair, glad for routine tasks to keep my mind focused outside of myself. I was so weary, deep down into my bones. The familiarity of this space felt as soothing as an old patched and well-loved comforter, pulled tightly around me to keep out the cold. The chair felt the same, with its little rip near where my leg touched on the right side, and the stain on the back from some old mishap. It creaked, just like before, when I leaned down to get another paper for the typewriter. The sameness reassured me that life went on, days marched by as they always had.

I cranked a fresh sheet of paper into my typewriter and pulled my stack of Freedom of Information Act replies closer to my right elbow. I ran my finger down the columns and started typing, "At Las Cruces laboratory, researchers killed 400 rabbits while searching for a link between blood cholesterol levels and diet." At my left elbow was an article detailing the history of cholesterol research from the past century. "Perhaps hoping to achieve the same success as Anitschkow's rabbit studies from the early 1900s, these researchers nevertheless ignored current medical opinion that herbivores are poor substitutes for human beings. The digestive system of a rabbit differs dramatically from ours ..." Then I compared the rabbit data with information obtained from studies on human volunteers. The morning passed fairly quickly.

Hunger pangs eventually interrupted my concentration. I considered ignoring the rules against eating at my desk, but decided that the limited privacy I sought was not worth the risk. Luckily, the lunch room was fairly deserted, and better yet, Lisa was already there, enjoying her last few potato chips. I brought my lunch over, settling into the chair closest to the wall, facing the door. She asked me how it was going.

"Fine, yeah, Lisa. I'm thinking about rabbits and cholesterol."

"Ah," she said, "sounds fascinating."

I chuckled. "Well, it kind of is, once you get into it. Amazing what you can find out when you know where to look. Like the way these rabbits, natural vegetarians, when forced to eat a high-cholesterol diet, get plaque accumulations in the aorta rather than the coronary arteries, like people do. Of course, then they get really sick with liver disease from the unnatural diet. The researchers are becoming experts at making rabbits sick, instead of helping sick humans." I took a big bite of my sandwich, looking down at the table.

"Well, I gotta go, but you keep up the good work, Amber." She picked up her plate and then paused, touching my hand. "Call me some time? You seem a little ... shellshocked or something."

"I will!" I smiled up at her, willing the darkness down, like stuffing dirty laundry into a sack. "Sorry, I'm distracted about my article. I'll see you soon!"

She smiled and moved away, stopping at the doorway and grinning at me. "What do you think? Can we take in a movie?"

I agreed and concentrated on finishing my lunch. Did she know how close I was to breaking apart? That day, I left a bit early, grabbing paperwork to continue at home. I had a meeting with a science teacher in the morning, and I wanted to be prepared and rested.

CHAPTER 14

"My sweet girl," he said, tenderly stroking my cheek with his roughened stained fingers. I tucked the ribbon from my braid back over my shoulder and smiled, glad for the attention, even as my belly sank into the sure knowledge of what happened next.

I shook my head, pulling my focus back to the present, and parked next to the pink and yellow merry-go-'round. It was covered with children whose excited voices carried clearly through my windows. The day was promising to be hot, a touch of summer come early, but that didn't slow the kids down. Their brightly colored T-shirts flashed in the sun as they raced from one end of the playground to the other, chasing a ball and laughing uproariously as it hit a tetherball post and flew back over their heads. It was recess, when their science teacher had agreed to speak with me about alternatives to hatching chicks in her classroom.

My preparation for this meeting had been rigorous. I had developed detailed lesson plans to teach children about the life cycle of chickens while supporting and nourishing the students' natural love for animals. Outwardly I was ready, but my stomach churned, and I desperately wished I could re-start the car and drive away, anywhere, away from this brick building with its windows plastered with bright paintings of hand prints and rising suns and rainbows.

I gathered up my cardboard box of materials and headed into the warm dim interior of the school. Room 114 wasn't far down the right-hand hallway. A large woman with close-cropped dark brown hair and red-framed glasses looked up from her desk and smiled, clearing a place for my box. We shook hands awkwardly.

"Please, pull up a chair, and thanks for coming."

"Thank you for having me. You have a beautiful classroom."

She thanked me. I looked at the rows of small desks, the posters of owls and other animals, and colorful watercolor paintings depicting the life cycle of the monarch butterfly. "Jimmy," "Maggie," "Brenda," the names were printed carefully along the bottom edge of each painting. I imagined the students, bending over their work, elbows splayed across the tabletop, some with tongues stuck out just a bit between their teeth, making their letters carefully with the small paintbrushes.

"So what do you have here for me?"

I pulled out my first photo, showing a contented mother hen with tiny fuzzy yellow heads peeking out from under her wings. Something about the delicate little balls of yellow fluff reminded me of the sweet softness of little blond-headed girls. "Did you know chickens can make over twenty different sounds and that each one has a unique meaning?"

She pushed her glasses up on her nose and bent over the photo, bemused, smiling. "Do they really?"

"Yes. One day, I visited some chickens on a local farm. I found the rooster in the side yard and offered him some bits of my apple. He looked over the apple I had laid on the ground, then straightened up as tall as he could get and made a loud 'tuck-tuck-tuck' sound. Hens came running from all over the yard. They hadn't made a move until he called them over." I described the maternal murmurs hens make over their eggs, talking to their babies even before they are hatched. "The babies know their mother's voice right from the very beginning." I showed her another photograph of little chicks clustered about their mother as she strolled through the grass.

"These are cute, but you said you had some ideas about teaching the basics of egg hatching?"

I took a breath, "If you want to have an egg hatch right in front of the children, then yes, an incubator in the classroom is the easiest choice. Or a video. But if you want the children to really understand what life is like for creatures who are different from us, how they communicate, how they eat, how they dust bathe, how they relate to each other, what things they love to do, how they cackle for joy after laying an egg; then visiting a farm or sanctuary is really the only way." I had rehearsed this line several times in front of a mirror, Tom listening seriously. Lisa had coached me as well.

She sat back in her chair, scratched behind one ear, then glanced at her watch.

I forged on, "The incubator gives the students only a tiny distorted bit of information and also teaches them it's okay for some newborns to die without ever seeing their mothers."

Her face twisted. "I usually don't have many that die, and anyway, I take them out before the children come in. Look I really have to get back to work. But thank you for coming, Miss ... ?"

"Amber."

"... Amber. Thank you for coming."

I held my seat for a moment longer, thinking quickly. "The chicks simply don't do well in an incubator. The lesson learned is not worth the suffering."

She turned away and started moving papers around her desk with jerky, erratic motions. Was she angry?

"I have information about ordering films showing chicks hatching, which you can even run in slow motion. I can leave it all for you. Thank you for caring." The meeting was over already.

Back in the car, I felt like a runner who had just finished a sprint. All the wind was pushed out of me. Who was I to think I could change anyone? I found a rock radio station and turned it up loud for the hot drive back. But even Elton John, singing about the blues, couldn't cheer me up. I had failed, and the ache inside me lasted for hours.

· · ·

Nearing the HAA offices, I turned off the radio, hoping to make a quiet entrance. I would rather have slunk home, but I had more work left, and the day was not yet over. Amazingly, there was a shady spot left in the parking lot. As I trudged into the building, I thought about the materials I had left on the teacher's desk. Were they in the trash can yet?

Lisa met me at the door, her eyes crinkling from her friendly smile. I smiled back, knowing she would ask about my meeting.

She saw through my forced smile. "That bad?" We turned towards the offices.

"Well, I wasn't exactly a star player."

"What did she say?"

"'Thank you, Miss Whatever-Your-Name-Is-Again, but I always hide the dead ones before the students arrive.' She considers herself a kind person."

Lisa's grin was sympathetic. "She just automatically hides the injustice from her students, and to her, that makes it all okay. But we know it doesn't."

I was silent. I didn't feel good. A ball was forming in my stomach, rising up and threatening my breathing. I knew if I stayed in the hall any longer, I might choke, or split apart into a thousand separate pieces. I needed to be alone, to wrap my arms around myself before everything came apart.

"Amber? You okay?" Lisa put her hand out to stop me as we turned the corner towards the cubicles.

I took a deep breath and told her I was fine. I must be fine. I could breathe, I could talk, I could keep going. For now. "I gotta get my article ready. See ya later." I turned away.

"Hey Amber!"

"Yeah," I said, slowing to glance at the floor at her feet. She had bright green shoelaces in her black canvas tennis shoes.

"Sometimes you just gotta accept that you did the best you could. We can't force it down their throats. But the important thing is that you care, and that you showed up for the animals."

Finally alone in my cubicle, I wasn't sure I was cut out for this work. It would be easier to not care. Just mechanically provide the alternative lesson plan, strewing papers about the schools like Johnny Appleseed, hoping that some day, my information might bear fruit and change some minds. I twisted my hands together, trying to soothe myself, savagely pinching the loose skin between my thumb and palm. The pain eased my distress somewhat, but I was still a failure. I didn't fight for those tiny chicks. I didn't fight for the children, earnestly working on their letters, unaware of the dead chicks hidden carelessly under papers in the trash bin by the teacher's desk.

· · ·

"Whatcha' doin'?" Lisa asked, her bright voice spilling out from the phone so that even Tom noticed. I had barely gotten home before the phone rang. My hands ached and I tucked the phone into my shoulder, grimacing. I must have had the steering wheel in a death grip.

"Just petting this here gentleman cat, who won't leave me alone," I reached down to Tom's uplifted head, and he butted me, hard. I winced.

"Well, he knows whose lap is the best, for sure."

"Yeah, well, he doesn't have a choice, really, right?"

There was a pause. "You okay?"

"Sure," I said, breathing out. "Sorry. I'm fine, just thinking I have the wrong line of work."

"What? You are smart, caring, conscientious, what more could HAA want?"

"Somebody more effective, maybe?"

"You don't think that most of us get frustrated sometimes?" Her tone was gentle. "Don't be too hard on yourself. We are doing agonizingly difficult work. Changing society always seems totally futile, until change actually happens." She sighed. "I remember one of my first interactions with a science teacher who couldn't comprehend teaching anatomy without killing animals. She treated me like I was a total nitwit, like I understood nothing about teaching or about children. God. I went home and cried." Lisa stopped, listening. I could almost feel her antennae pointed towards me, gauging my reaction.

I sank into the couch, inviting Tom up. The silence continued, but it felt soothing, like Lisa was there, touching me gently, just where it hurt. I rubbed Tom's belly as he purred. His silky fur soothed the sore skin on my palm. "I don't know, it seems like I'm not really the right person for this job. I don't fight hard enough."

"Amber. You are an amazing woman with a heart of gold. You are a warrior!"

"Yeah, right," I said, working to keep the derision out of my voice. I didn't want to hurt her feelings.

"Well, you give yourself some extra care tonight, okay?"

"I know, I know. Take care of myself first," I said wearily. I murmured thanks and got off the phone, mumbling something about my dinner and the oven. "Hey Tom, finally got her off my back," I said as I crunched through a hastily made salad and waited for the end of the commercial.

Tom was watching me.

"Okay, okay, I didn't really mean that, guy. Geez, just kidding." I needed something to take my mind off myself, my own miseries. I wished that *Star Trek* was still on. Captain Kirk, now there was a good man. He always tried to help, even if he did have to kiss all the pretty girls along the way. But at least everybody loved him. And he sure knew how to love himself.

CHAPTER 15

"It's not that horrible, really, just people sitting around talking about their struggles—"

"Oh, sounds really fun," I teased, not listening too closely. I had my hands in my pockets so Lisa wouldn't ask questions. The skin was healing rapidly, but there were still tender bruised places in the thinner areas of skin.

We were taking a walk during our lunch break, enjoying a perfect spring day. The trees were changing rapidly, encouraged by the recent warm spell. The purpleleaf plum trees along the road were in full glorious bloom, coaxed out of their closely held buds. It always seemed like magic, this transformation from bare branches to floating halos of pink petals in just two short weeks. We strolled as the gentle sun warmed our faces. The breeze had just the ghost of a bite, and I could feel the coolness rushing down into my chest as I took a deep breath. "The air is so wonderful today. It's cleaning all the office dust out of my lungs."

Lisa tried again, "No, really, these Alcoholics Anonymous groups provide a very real service. It's really hard to stop a habit in isolation. I've been sober for ten years now, but on bad days, I still really wouldn't mind just locking myself in my room with a six- or twelve-pack. Instead, I talk to people struggling with the same wish, and I don't feel so alone anymore."

I stopped and looked at her. "Lisa, I didn't know. I ..." I stumbled to a stop, embarrassed.

Lisa looked at me and grinned, then laid her hand gently on my shoulder. "No worries, it was a long time ago, just after my father died, and before I met Tony. I went through a bad time." She tilted her head to watch little birds flitting through the trees. The pin on her sweater, a cat's face with jewels for eyes, glinted in the sunlight for a moment. As we walked on, her hair fell forward to cover her face before she absently tucked it behind her ear. A small breeze rustled the branches and the birds made tiny chipping noises as we passed.

"Lisa."

"Yes, sweetie?" She looked up at me, her gaze warm and unguarded, as if nothing had changed.

I looked away and shoved my hands into my jeans pockets. "I just ... I was just thinking about how, growing up, my dad would always have a beer in his hand. It was like an extension of his arm." My stomach clenched, thinking of the six-pack cooling in my fridge. I felt Lisa's gaze still on my face, and turned away, heading back towards HAA. She followed. My mind was far away.

"So you know what it's like," she said.

"What?"

"Being around an alcoholic."

"Well, I don't know—"

"Yeah, with a beer always in his hand, that's what he was, Amber."

Something wriggled in my mind, then slid away quickly before I could examine it closely. We were silent, our shadows tucked around our feet as we stepped carefully over a recently-broken section of sidewalk. The weeds had already sprouted up between the cement pieces. I bent to pick a white clover flower and held it out to Lisa with a flourish. "For you, the belle of the ball."

She laughed, taking the flower and twirling it in her fingers as we walked. Then her smile faded. "You dealt with that, growing up. You know, there's a group called Al-Anon which is just for children of alcoholics, Amber. Or spouses—anyone who is dealing with people who use alcohol as a crutch."

"Well, I just figured that beer was one of the food groups. 'Specially for adults." Lisa's lop-sided grin calmed some of the whirling in my stomach. "No, I get it, Lisa, I'm glad you have that group. Does Tony go with you?"

She laughed, "Tony would never give up his beer," then she looked thoughtful, "but maybe he'd come, just to support me. It might be good for him to hear some of the newbies' stories. He'd understand better why I don't drink anymore."

I tried to imagine what it would be like, having someone love you that much. I thought of my mother. She would have done anything for me.

"We still on for tomorrow night, right, Amber?"

"Yup! Tony's cooking!"

"Good! I'll pick you up, because I'll be in the area dropping off something for Marlene."

Once back at the office, we headed to our desks. I sat back in my chair for a moment, thinking about my dad. Mom often tried to help him when he was storming around, flailing at the world and scaring me. She would sit down in the center of his storm and simply listen, really listen to his words and also the pain beneath the words. His circles would get smaller and smaller, a moon orbiting around a planet, whirling, whirling, until the orbit finally collapsed into the planet's larger gravity. When he finally let her hold him, the majesty of her calm always touched me, down to my very bones.

I didn't share Mom's patience. To me, his words were a storm of pollution, dirtying the room and poisoning the air. I wanted to run away, to find a safe place where I could be quiet and still, clean again. But Mom simply allowed the storm to blow itself out, without judgment, without blame, waiting for him to seek solace in her arms. One day, I asked her what was making Daddy so mad.

She smiled, but her eyes were sad. "I've known your daddy a long time, and his life has not been easy." She took my hand and kissed it, then tucked it up against her cheek. We called that a hand-ker-cheek kiss. "Honey, his daddy didn't understand him. He did things to him ..." Her voice got very small, and her eyes looked far away.

"What do you mean? Couldn't he just tell someone?"

"Well, he tried, honey, but it's hard explaining when you are still little. Then, when you get bigger, the time for explaining is over."

"But you always listen to me."

"That's true, and I always will, 'Ber." She hugged me close. Her blouse tickled my nose and I giggled. "Now let's go out and find those daisies you said were growing by the driveway."

When I drove home that afternoon, I imagined the soft touch of her blouse on my cheek, and her warm, strong arms holding me. Some days, I missed her so much, the wanting was like a hole, right down into my very center.

CHAPTER 16

The next morning came early, as if borrowing its time from the night. I woke tired, still reaching for something that I couldn't quite hold on to. I showered quickly after my run and grabbed some bread for the car ride. Work went smoothly, my tiredness releasing residual tension, making writing come more easily. My new piece on our McDonald's demonstration contained just the right balance of facts and a sober description of exactly what went into the creation of a Big Mac.

I was ready for Lisa by seven that night. I prepared myself to meet Tony. Only a good person would have merited Lisa, I thought, but part of me wondered. Did he know how important he was in her life?

I wasn't used to being a guest in someone else's house. It would be different, more exposed and personal than the restaurant gatherings I had learned to enjoy with my colleagues. I thought back to family dinners growing up. There were rigid rules and expectations. Boundaries off which we could all rebound, like aquarium glass walls, the real world just beyond our outstretched fingers. I sit here, and you sit there. I set the table, and you wash the dishes afterwards. Each person read their part in the play, Dad holding the orbital center as he reasserted his main character role, every night. Yet even as we played our parts, careful and controlled, Dad's emotions flowed off him like water over a dam, heedless of the drowning creatures downstream. We bowed our heads to reaffirm our status, pretending to thank an invisible God for our food.

I felt Lisa grinning at me from the driver's seat, and my mind returned to the present with a jolt. "Hey there, girl, glad you're coming!" Then she sniffed, "What's that, perfume? Not tryin' to take my man away, are you?"

I rubbed my eyes and shook my head, and a chuckle lifted me out of my thoughts. "Ha! It's soap! But anyway, I haven't even met him yet! You that worried?"

"I don't know, you're taller than me, you're skinny, and you exercise like a demon."

I took a breath. "But—"

"And you are definitely smarter. And a good writer."

"Lisa, don't forget about how well I can do the hula hoop."

"Oh yeah! I forgot that! Hey, really?"

I stretched up and stroked the roof of the car, watching the fabric smooth behind my fingers. "There is so much you don't know about me, Lisa. It's sad, really."

"Yeah, I know. I'll just have to spill my soup on you or something." We laughed uproariously, and something uncoiled from deep inside me that had been tight for so, so long.

"That McDonald's demonstration went well, don'tcha think?" Lisa asked, squinting in the sunlight streaming out from behind low-hanging clouds on the horizon. "Our handout had good details about the amount of corn required for flesh burgers versus what could be directly feeding people. 'Do the math.' Twelve pounds of grain to produce one pound of cow flesh. Goodness."

"The cow suits really got a lot of attention, too," I said, cracking my window and breathing in the sage smells from the nearby hills. I thought of the little boy who had stood and stared at the cows handing out fact sheets, his mouth hanging open while his mother pulled his arm. My eyes were buzzing and squinched from squinting at my typewriter page all day, and it felt good to gaze at the setting sun's light on the distant hills. The light changed so fast, I thought, while the world spun away into night.

"Mommy, do we eat cows?" the boy had asked. She picked him up and hurried into the restaurant, frowning. His little face looking back over her shoulder made me catch my breath, so pure, so curious, simply wanting the truth.

"So we heading over to Chris' place?" Lisa asked.

I reeled my thoughts back into the car again. "No, he has an interview with a science professor about teaching anatomy using human cadavers and models."

"Ah, too bad, but glad he got the interview," Lisa smiled and leaned back in her seat. "Good for him. I'll look forward to reading what he finds out. I hope Chris can convince the professor to stop those orders of cats from the shelter."

I breathed out sharply. "Can you even imagine, Lisa, that shelters would do something like that?" I clasped my hands tightly together where they rested in my lap. "To be taken from a place of safety? I wonder if the shelter where I worked sold their cats. Would they have even told me?"

"I doubt it. Wouldn't be something they'd want advertised."

I swallowed the bitter fluid rising from my stomach, a feeling of corruption reaching me even here, in the safety of my best friend's car. I stared out the window, letting the passing trees calm me, one, two, three ... avoiding thinking too hard about betrayal. I flipped through the radio stations until I found John Denver singing "Annie's Song." Speaking of betrayal. But at least he was asking for forgiveness. We sang along, and the sweetness of the music eased my tension. Eventually my stomach softened, leaving me feeling warm inside, more peaceful. Safe. Would be nice to feel this way all the time.

We parked and stepped out of the car, the night air a gentle touch on our skin. The light over the front door flickered with circling insects. As Lisa pushed open the door, I was met with the delicious smells of Italian cooking. A tall man with dark hair and just a hint of beard on his cheeks stood just inside, drying his hands on a towel slung over his shoulder. "Hi, I'm Tony—"

Lisa grabbed his sweater and pulled him to her, standing on her tiptoes to kiss him lightly on the nose. "Of course you are! I've talked Amber's ear off about you, you nut!"

I shook his hand, liking the warm solid feeling. Men's hands are so different than women's. Thicker, stiffer, like they could lift tree trunks and not get tired.

Tony took my frozen offering and turned the carton in his hands, studying the label. He pursed his lips, lifted his chin in the air and frowned seriously down at me. "A great selection, ma'am. Nondairy frozen dessert. It will go perfectly." Lisa punched him lightly in the stomach and he wheezed, laughing, then turned away, carrying the carton aloft.

We followed Tony into the living room, full of book-lined walls and cozy couches. "Sit any place. Wanna drink or something? Tony's made his special bean dip. Vegan, of course." Lisa grinned at him and gave him another quick kiss, her eyes sparkling. I had never seen her so happy. It gave me a warm feeling in the pit of my stomach. Tony left for the kitchen, smiling, saying something about checking the soup. He was tall and rangy, moving like an athlete. I remembered Lisa mentioning that he was a long-distance runner.

"That sounds yummy. And yes, Lisa, I'll have a soda. You have any dogs who live with you? Cats?"

"Tony's allergic. He gets bad asthmatic attacks. Soda? Okay, coming right up! Marlene and David will be here in a minute."

I settled into a soft armchair, thinking that Tom would have really liked it. I almost wished he was here, asking for my lap—my small security blanket. The books lining the walls included animal stories along with murder mysteries, which were Lisa's favorites. I stood to examine the pictures on the mantelpiece more closely. Lisa and Tony, smiling, with a waterfall behind them.

"That's from Niagara Falls, our first trip together. That's when Tony proposed. It was very romantic," Lisa smiled as she held out a glass mug, filled nearly to the top.

"Wow, I must rate, you frosted my mug first." I took a sip, shutting my eyes. The bubbles floated up from the soda and burst, tiny geysers on my cheeks and eyelids. I wiped my face and pointed at the photo next to the books, in a slim gold frame, "This a younger Tony?"

"Yeah, such a sweetie!" Lisa smirked, then got more serious. "You like him? Tony?"

"I hardly met the man, and you are already picking my brain?"

She sighed, "He's just so, I don't know—understanding. He doesn't expect me to be a certain way, you know? He just loves me for ... Oh God I sound like a Hallmark card."

"It's okay. Someone has to have the perfect life so they know what to write on the cards." I took another sip and licked my lips, tasting the sweetness left behind.

The doorbell rang and Marlene came in with David. Lisa greeted them, hugged Marlene briefly, then took her bowl of salad and closed the door behind them. "What would you guys like to drink? Oh, and David, this is Amber."

I shook his hand. He was thickset, with curly dark hair, and the lines on his face made him look older than Marlene.

Marlene pushed her glasses up her nose. "A beer would be fine for me, Lisa, but David'll have a seltzer, if you have one." She settled herself into the green velvet armchair by the windows and looked out at the little wooden bird feeder hanging above the bushes. "With lemon," she added, ignoring David's look. He took her sweater and hung it on the coat rack near the door, then sat across from her at the end of the blue corduroy couch.

"Got it!" Lisa disappeared into the kitchen.

I settled back down on the other end of the couch, watching David pick at the lint on his polo shirt. The silence felt strange, almost like a vacuum compared to the usual noisy restaurant crowds. "Marlene, how long have you been at HAA?" I asked.

Lisa brought David his drink. She handed another mug to Marlene, who took it without looking, then wiped one hand on her jeans. Lisa watched David as he took a sip.

"Too long," said Marlene. "I was one of the first employees, back when it started. I cleaned a lot of kennels." She glanced again at David, "That's where I met him."

David sipped slowly, then poked at his floating lemon slice.

"Really? I thought you used to work at an electronics store, David," Lisa said, straightening her pink apron. She looked from Marlene's face to David's fingers. He was holding the lemon beneath the bubbles at the surface of his seltzer.

"He wasn't working at HAA—" started Marlene.

"I can talk for myself, you know," muttered David.

Lisa drew in a breath, then Tony called and she disappeared back into the kitchen. There was a silence while Marlene turned back to the window. Three house sparrows were flitting around the feeder.

David looked over at me. "I met Marlene when she came to inspect my house. I wanted a dog from HAA, and they had to be sure I wouldn't torture it to death or anything."

Marlene shook her head. "Him."

"What?" said David.

"He's a him, not an it."

David sighed.

"Well, you got a really nice dog out of the deal," she paused, "and a wife."

"Yeah," he snorted, "I did, that's true. And the rest is history."

Lisa appeared with an armload of bright red cloth napkins and place settings, and began laying them out on the dining room table. David stood to help, taking the napkins and adding one to each setting. They murmured together, Lisa nodding and flashing a grin, briefly laying her hand on his arm before disappearing back into the kitchen. David sat back down on the sofa, smiling.

"It's ready, pick your seats," called Tony, setting out a plate of steaming bread. We all got up, carrying our drinks, and chose our places around the table, brightly lit with fluttering candles.

"That's Betty's spot," said Lisa, indicating the head of the table, "The rest are up for grabs."

A tiny old woman, with bright blue eyes and white hair gathered back into a small ponytail, was coming slowly down the stairs. Tony moved to stand close by, steadying her, his hand gently on her elbow. She looked up at him and smiled, "Thank you, my dear."

"Everybody, this is my Mom, Betty," said Lisa, "She's hard of hearing, but don't let that fool you. She loves company, and loves animals just as much as we do."

David sighed heavily as he pulled his chair away from the table.

Dinner was delicious, eggplant lasagna, salad, beets, and homemade brown bread. Betty ate appreciatively, watching as we joked together, her eyes flicking from one face to another. I wondered if her hearing was really as bad as Lisa had said.

This dinner differed from those I had had long ago. At first, I was unmoored, floating free, vaguely uneasy. Like a plow horse suddenly set adrift without her traces, I had no guidance. How should I act? Who did they need me to be?

I watched at first, tucking my outer edges in tightly to escape notice. But these were my friends, and they drew me out. Gentle questions, quick glances, and shared laughter gradually enveloped me. I had never felt this involved before, a part of a whole and yet still myself at the very core.

To be seen without being examined, without being evaluated, was like quenching a thirst I didn't know I had; a thirst that had lived in me always. For the first time in my life, I was sated, and my emotional needs were met. I drank greedily, still expecting a rebuff at every turn, but instead, receiving reciprocal attention and care. Such peace!

I spread margarine on a second thick slice of bread. "Lisa, this is a real treat."

"Don't thank me, Tony's the cook."

Tony looked at her and beamed. "Only when there's company. Anyone want more beets? I got more on the stove, just speak up."

"Well, I'm glad you are all here," Lisa smirked, "because when it's just me and my Mom, it's peanut butter and jelly."

"Oh, I get the picture!" said Marlene. She took a large forkful of lasagna, "Well, he can come visit me anytime he wants to try out a new recipe." She glanced over at David, who was chasing some last bits of salad around his bowl. He selected a cherry tomato and popped it into his mouth, chewing thoughtfully.

"Sure, like maybe prime rib?" said David.

Marlene's face darkened as she tucked her napkin underneath her plate. "Very funny, David, hah, hah." She looked up, "Is there more of that wine around here somewhere?" She rose and moved her chair out from the table, her movements jerky.

I sat very still, staring at the food left on my plate. With my fork, I pressed hard into a small chunk of beet, watching the red juice flow out around the prongs. My stomach roiled, and I slowly and carefully put down the fork.

Suddenly everyone was talking at once, too loudly. Tony and Lisa were both offering more wine to Marlene, from the sideboard near the table. Betty was asking what had happened, what had she missed, and Lisa told her that David had made a joke.

"What was it? Tell me, I don't want to be left out," said Betty.

Lisa looked at Tony and said, "I think, Mama, that it's time for dessert. Want apple pie or blueberry?"

Betty scanned our faces, finally settling on David's. She narrowed her eyes. "What was the joke?"

David pressed his lips together and fumbled with his napkin.

Tony looked at David, then at Lisa, then sighed, "David said that if I came over, I could cook steak for Marlene."

Lisa's eyes widened briefly, then she looked down at her napkin, smoothing it tightly over her lap.

Betty put her napkin down and looked at David, frowning, "But I don't think—"

David stood quickly, grabbing his plate with a loud jangling of silverware, and headed towards the kitchen. "Geez ..."

"It's okay, Betty," Tony said, "he was just trying to be funny."

Lisa put her hand on David's arm as he brushed by, "David—" He disappeared into the kitchen.

"Well, I don't think it was that funny. We don't eat animals around here, doesn't he know that?" Betty said.

"He knows that, Mama. It was just a—"

"I'll have the apple," said Betty, sitting back and folding her hands in her lap, her lips pressed tightly together.

I watched Tony rise and collect Betty's plate, his movements precise and measured. "I'll get you some, Ma." He followed David out, catching Lisa's eye on his way past, "Coming right up!"

We heard Tony talking sternly in the kitchen, telling David to lighten up. Lisa smiled at Betty and patted her arm.

Marlene returned to her chair, sipping from a full wine glass. She swirled the dark liquid, then set it down and glanced at her watch. "Sorry, guys, he just gets that way sometimes. Thinks he's funny."

"That's okay, Marlene, not your fault," Lisa said, "Who else for pie?"

David came out with a pie tin held aloft. "Apple, right, Betty?"

We cleared the table quickly and ate our dessert in silence. The candles lit our faces and glittered bright reflections off the silverware. I could still smell the bread, its aroma softening the sharper smells of wine and lasagna sauce.

Lisa clapped her hands, making us all jump. "Amber! I have a favor to ask. Would you be one of my bridesmaids for our wedding next fall?"

"What wedding?" asked Betty.

"Come on, Mama, you know Tony and I are getting married!"

"Oh, yes, and I'm even invited. Don't forget, something old, something new ..."

"Something borrowed, something blue. I know, Mom, I'll be wearing your veil from Grandma." She met my eyes, "You wouldn't believe how pretty it is. I'll show you guys later." Lisa gave her mother a kiss on the cheek, "More wine, Mama?"

Betty nodded, patting her daughter's hand and watching the deep red wine rise in her glass, "That's plenty, thank you. You will be a beautiful bride, my dear. This I know."

"Well, if I look anything like you did at your wedding, then I'll be as happy as a pig in mud." Lisa glanced at me, her eyes bright, "So, Amber, can you do it? Marlene is going to be my matron of honor."

I looked over at Marlene, who was studiously collecting the last bits of pie crumbs from her plate. She pressed her finger into the small pile, then popped it into her mouth. She met my eyes, then drew her finger out slowly, wiping it on her napkin. She took another large swallow of wine.

I watched her slump back in her chair. "Well, I've never done it before, but how hard could it be?" I said, "I can't think of a better reason to get fancied up than your wedding."

"I knew you'd say yes!" Lisa poked Tony in the chest, and he took her hand and grinned, raising his glass of wine towards me. "It's a good thing we started early, because it's taken us months to find a caterer willing and able to prepare a vegetarian feast."

Lisa added, "We've settled on this beautiful country club on the lake. You'll love it, Amber. Thanks so much for doing this!"

• • •

After dinner Lisa brought Marlene and I into her room. A deep blue silky material was laid out on her striped bedspread. Marlene fingered the material, nodding, "This is for the bridesmaid dresses. Nice, isn't it, Amber? Lisa will do us all proud."

Lisa opened a battered cardboard box and lifted out a lace veil, spreading it over the dress material on the bed.

A stuffed rabbit with huge floppy ears and worn gray plush fur was on a chair nearby. I picked up the rabbit, admiring his ears. "Lisa, who's this?" I asked.

"That's Brando. I was in love with Marlon Brando when I was growing up." She took the rabbit from me and placed him gently on the bed. "Do you like the dress material?"

"Well, I'm not really a dress person, but the material sure is pretty. I love the color. I hope I can do it justice."

Lisa snorted and glanced at Marlene, who had sat down on the bed and settled the bunny into her lap. "Don't worry, Amber, you'll look fantastic. I'm the one who has to worry," she patted her stomach, "especially if I keep eating like that."

"And the veil," I said, "well, it's really special."

Marlene got up, settled the bunny back on the bed, and gently lifted the veil, placing it on Lisa's head, pulling it down over her face. We stood quietly, Lisa beaming out from the delicate lacy material. There were tiny embroidered flowers in the lace, reminding me of dandelion seeds, blown from their stems and caught in the netting. Marlene drew in a breath, "It's beautiful, Lisa. As are you."

Lisa was quiet, looking down, a small smile on her lips.

I looked closely at the veil where it fanned out across Lisa's shoulders. "This is handmade, isn't it? It's gorgeous!" I said, admiring the tiny intricate knotted patterns.

"Yes, it's needle lace. My grandmother learned from her Mom, my great-grandmother, back when she was young. Just a needle and thread, can you believe it?"

"A labor of love, truly." I felt the edge of the veil between my fingers, imagining the needle's path, in and out of the web of lace, fingers working carefully to place each knot. Was she thinking of her future husband as she worked, imagining the moment when he lifted the veil and looked into the eyes of his new bride? So long ago. "I bet your Mom is happy about you continuing a family tradition. So, you gonna have a daughter any time soon?"

Lisa sniffed, lifting the veil to rub at her eyes, "Aack! Can't think about kids yet! My goodness. Do you really like the dress material, you guys?"

Marlene was staring at Lisa, her gaze loose and unfocused. "Lisa, I'm sorry about dinner. He just—"

"Don't worry about it. I was just thinking about how glad I am for friends like you, and for Tony. I'm really a lucky person. Things are good for me, and I'm not sure—"

"What's going on in here, a secret meeting?" David sauntered in, hands in his pockets. "Marlene, we really should go." He held a hand out to his wife, waiting, "I have some paperwork I've gotta finish before tomorrow. Come on, Marlene."

She blinked at David's words and shook her head slightly. "Yeah, right, coming. Lisa, these are just fine and it will be a beautiful ceremony." Marlene turned towards David but avoided his hand, looking back at Lisa as she tucked the veil back into its box. "See you at work."

They turned to the door, David giving a small wave. "Thanks for dinner."

"Sure, guys, and Marlene," said Lisa, "no worries."

We heard Tony's deep voice as he saw them out. I smoothed my hand over the soft material of the dress. "I'm glad to see you so happy, Lisa."

She put her hand on my arm. "I know, huh? I'm not sure I deserve it, but Amber, I'm glad you came."

CHAPTER 17

Finally the weekend, and I had plans. I was hiking up into the hills, and the weather looked like it was going to cooperate. Dry and not too warm. The map crinkled in the breeze from the windows as I accelerated onto the highway, feeling my spirits lift as the hills rose on the horizon. The warm air swirled around my hair and touched the corners of my eyes, pulling away some moisture, before I reached for my HAA baseball cap and tucked the stray strands underneath it. Had I remembered everything? Water, check, a couple of sandwiches, check, long-sleeved shirt, check, first aid kit, check. I was hiking by myself today. Lisa had a friend's wedding, "Groan! You should see the bridesmaid's dress. It makes me look like a stuffed pepper!" and Chris was taking a weekend class, "Calculators. You don't have to do it all by hand anymore, Amber!" Perhaps this trip was meant to be taken alone.

I turned the radio off when the station got too fuzzy, listening to the hum of my tires on the asphalt. I was glad the night was over. I had woken with every creak from the house. Every gust of wind sending dried leaves against my screen disturbed my sleep. It felt like most of the night I had lain awake, listening for ... what? Footsteps? A key in the lock? I wasn't sure.

Tom, on the other hand, had slept soundly, a bundle of gray fur snoring by my pillow. I poked him once, but he just turned over and resumed snoring.

The drive was two hours, and as the hills got closer, I could make out thick sections of sagebrush and a few scattered aspen trees. Three turns later and I was at the trailhead. I pulled off the road and slipped out of the car, unfolding gratefully and stomping the life back into my feet. I settled my pack on my shoulders, sipped from my canteen, and strode up the path.

The first part was steep, lifting up and away from the parking area. Just a few minutes later I could look directly down on my car. Nobody else had arrived yet, which meant more solitude for me. I turned away, stepping up the path, over boulders and loose shale. Dust puffed out with every footstep, coasting gently behind me to land in the path, erasing any sign that I'd been there. I squinted into the sun, estimating the time remaining. Several hours.

It felt good, striding higher into the thinning air, muscles responding to the work, breath reaching deeper into my chest. I was used to a faster pace, but the roads around my house were flat, and today I carried a pack. It was different work than running, more sustained, each step firmly connected to the land around me. I was surprised by a brown lizard who scurried across the path and into the shade of some rocks. He was fast! I grinned at a marmot's sudden squeal and stopped to offer him a bit of cracker from my pack. He sat up on his hindquarters, twitching his nose and working his yellow teeth together. I bent lower, and he disappeared underneath a boulder with a flip of his furry tail.

Steadily climbing, I reached the summit and worked my way along the ridge of the hills until I was ready to rest and eat my lunch. I took a deep breath and pulled off my pack, settling onto a dusty boulder, shaded by a grove of aspens. I rubbed at my shoulders, lifting my sweaty shirt off my skin, feeling the air slide over the dampness underneath. The aspens' gently rustling leaves signaled a breath of coolness from the desert air. A distant creaking sound alerted me to a hawk, hanging high and calling for somebody.

My sandwiches were warm now, along with my water, but they still tasted good. I finished the last crumb and bit into an apple, its juices running down my cheek until I dabbed at them with my sleeve. Then suddenly I was crying, the tears following the path of the apple juice, running down and making tiny droplets in the dust on my boots. I rubbed my sleeve across my eyes angrily, not wanting this here, not now. What was it? The call of the hawk? The solitude, not even Tom to touch me and make sure I was real?

I stood up, grabbed a rock at my feet and threw it as hard as I could, straight down the steep slope in front of my toes. "No!" It was a long time before I heard the faint sound of it landing, bouncing until it came to rest. I felt just a bit better. I scrabbled up a handful of pebbles and flung them into the void, listening to the clattering as they cascaded down. I dug at my feet for handful after handful, grunting with the effort of throwing them as far as I could without tumbling after them myself. "No!" I screamed, "No! No! No!" The only thing connecting me to that spot, the only thought keeping me from throwing myself off the ridge after the tumbling rocks, was a furry gray cat waiting for his dinner.

I turned back to the base of the boulder behind me again and again, scratching into the dirt for loose stones, hurling them as hard as I could into the dusty abyss, yelling my defiance until my voice cracked. Finally, I became aware of stinging pains in my fingers and looked down to see blood pooling around my nails. I felt like a swimmer surfacing after a dive under dark, salty water. I took a deep breath and dropped the last few pebbles onto my boots, vaguely ashamed at the damage I had caused. The sting, the hurt, and the shame eased my fury somewhat. Instead of threatening to obliterate me, the huge mess of feelings shrank just enough to fit inside my heart again, tucked away into a familiar shape. I could do this. I could go on.

I carefully settled back down on the boulder, watching the sun as it began its descent to the tops of the facing hills. Something clinked in my pocket as I shifted my position, and I gingerly reached in to find my keys.

"Mike, I got something for you."

"What is it, 'Ber?" He was waxing his truck, rubbing the polish until it shone.

I held up a key, smiling proudly, "I got a place. Well, really, just a room. This is for you, so you can come visit whenever."

"So you found a place? Will I like it alright?" He stopped waxing and held out his hand. The wind lifted his shirt, briefly showing a triangle of hairy stomach.

I put the shiny new key into his worn palm. "Sure, I think so. I share the kitchen and bath with two roommates, but we all kinda have different schedules, so I think it'll work out great."

He studied me for a moment, squeezing the key in his big fist and leaning back onto the truck door. "Really! Happened pretty quick, huh? That's great, Amber. Hey, ya gonna make me some dinner or somethin' sometime?"

"Well, I..." I faltered a bit, not quite knowing what to say. Why had I just handed over that key so quickly, anyway?

"Don't worry, I won't expect any three-course meals or anything. Not too often, anyways." He cackled and slapped me on the back, making my ponytail jump crazily.

I crossed my arms tightly, trying to smile.

"You must be doing good to get your own place. How many rooms you got?"

I thought of the bedroom and suddenly felt violently sick. "I gotta go," I mumbled, turning away and pulling out my car keys. I had to get out of there.

"What's the matter? Going so soon? Leaving me again? When can I come over?" The questions followed me like arrows.

I answered automatically as I bolted to the car, trying not to look like a fleeing animal. "Anytime." I had no other answer, at least not one I thought I was allowed to have. Any other answer would have felt wrong. Who was I to turn him away now, after so many years of accepting him into my bed?

I tucked away my keys, closed my pack and slung it over my shoulders, turning back down the path and blinking to clear my eyes. As the breeze gently pushed past my cheeks, it dried the wetness and I began to feel better. I lifted my canteen to my lips, the trickling warmish water bathing my tongue and easing some of my distress. The beauty of the descending sun's rays shimmering over the sagebrush on the peak of the next hill calmed me and let me know nothing had changed in the world around me. The only change happening was from deep within.

CHAPTER 18

I loved running in the cooler air that arrives with fall, hinting at the scent of crisp leaves. The geese were restless overhead, calling their goodbyes. I imagined Tony running, his loping stride quickly outdistancing mine. Maybe next time Lisa had me over I'd ask him about his favorite running spots.

At work I avoided one-on-one meetings and concentrated on getting the background research complete so that others could work at the front lines instead of me. The worst thing that happened that fall was that my house fridge broke, but the landlord brought over a new one. Nice having new things. But I didn't get to enjoy it long before Mike came over again for a late dinner. He arrived at my door with beer, stubbing out his cigarette in the dirt beside the front step. I stared down at the small pile, then followed him inside.

The bottles clanged together as he shoved them into the fridge. He marveled at how quiet it was.

"Yeah, Mike, I know, nice, isn't it?"

"Yeah, well, it's a lot nicer than mine, that's for sure. How much money is that landlord of yours making offa you?" He pulled a beer out of the six-pack and looked around for the opener.

I handed it to him. "Don't worry, it's just a room, it's not too much. You know, the rest of it is shared, the living room, the kitchen, the TV ... you ever seen Monty Python? There's a rerun on tonight." I checked the rice casserole cooking in the oven. It was done. I turned off the heat.

He settled into one of the padded metal chairs around the kitchen table and took a long swallow from his beer. "Those stupid actors with their fake English accents? I wonder how much they get paid to prance around like that?"

"They're not fake," I said, spooning rice into two bowls, "I think they're like the three stooges with a purpose. They have a mission, a plan, a reason for being—"

"Yeah, right, they got nothing on the stooges." The chair creaked as he twisted around. "Nobody home but you? Those housemates of yours sure work a lot. You get lonely? Good thing there's me." He smiled and scratched his neck, his fingers rasping on stubble.

I licked my lips, imagining I tasted dust from my hike. "*M.A.S.H.* it is, then." I looked at him, so relaxed, smiling at me with the skin crinkling around his eyes. "I'm working on this project about raising chicks. I'm collecting film references and some amazing photographs, and I think I could make a difference—"

"They are just a bunch of self-important stupid ninnies, in my book." He jerked upright and glanced at my face. "What's wrong, girl?" he said, touching my hair with his nicotine-stained fingers. His gentle touch awoke a yearning inside me, but then it twisted into something ugly and I wanted to cringe away. Caught in between, I couldn't move. Moving would have revealed more than I wanted him to see. The new space inside me was suddenly crushed, shrunken down to almost nothing. Where was Tom? I wanted him in my arms right now.

I quickly brushed my hand through my hair, smoothing down the strands that had caught on his calloused fingers. "Nothing. I'm fine. Here, you take these and I'll get us some salad. I'll bring it out. Go turn on the show."

I opened the fridge and took out the salad, settling it on the counter and lifting out servings for us both. Steam from the casserole rose towards the small window above the counter, obscuring my view of a bit of fluffy cloud.

I returned and handed Mike his plate, then settled beside him on the couch. He breathed into my ear, the warmth and moisture coagulating on my neck.

I shrunk away, dropping my napkin. "Oops, sorry, can you get it on? I think it's about to start," I said, "I don't know where the remote is lately."

"Sure, I got it, doll," he put his plate down and rose heavily, walking to the TV, leaning over to squint at the buttons, "Channel 3, right?" He pressed a button and the screen crackled to life, sparkling flashes of gray and white coalescing into a picture, while the familiar theme song played—"Suicide is Painless." Ironically cheerful music.

As Mike lowered himself next to me, I wanted to disappear. Leave my body behind and flick out of there, gone in an instant. Usually I could achieve this if I concentrated, but tonight my usual exit wasn't working so well, as if I was a firmly tethered balloon, fluttering, unable to lift up and away. No matter how hard I pulled on my string.

I watched Hawkeye teasing Radar, hearing myself laughing along with Mike, as if the sounds came from someone else. I mechanically spooned rice and broccoli into my mouth, watching him wipe the beer foam from his lips. His throat worked as he drank, his Adam's apple rising and falling with a wet sound. He rose heavily from the couch for seconds, and then thirds.

"Wanna beer? I'm having another one."

"No thanks, Mike, I'm good. You know, I'm not old enough yet."

"Yeah, yeah, well in the comfort of your own house, what're they gonna do? Come arrest you?" He put down his plate and started rubbing my shoulder.

Maybe if I just stayed awake, it would be better. If I stayed out of that bedroom ... I jumped up awkwardly, saying I wanted to wash the dishes.

He jerked around on the sofa. "The show's not over yet, Amber, where ya goin'? I'm not even finished eatin' yet."

"I got a lot to do tomorrow and don't want these dishes waiting for me."

"Aw, come on, this is the good part. Set a bit. It's only nine thirty."

I made various excuses to keep getting up, almost frantic with the need to move, to stay awake, aware, present. Did he sense my pulling away, my awakening disgust? So much to feel right now. My fault, this was all my fault.

I should have told him no right from the start, right from the very beginning. It's just that I never remembered being given a chance.

His next question stopped me in my tracks as I fumbled with the plates. "Ya got a boyfriend yet from that radical group of yours?"

"I got some friends, yeah, but nobody special." I thought of the feel of Chris' muscular back through his jacket, so different from Mike's fleshy ribs.

"A pretty girl like you? A shame." I heard satisfaction in his voice, and suddenly I was determined to stay awake all night if I had to. I couldn't ask him to leave without risking his anger, but I could stay here, in front of the TV, away from the dark bedroom and everything that came with it.

The night went slowly, the TV scenes flickering by, Mike looking at me more and more quizzically, finally realizing that something had changed. His movements became more uncertain, and watching this, I gripped more firmly to my new clarity. I wanted to do this. I could do this. Finally, he gathered his feet under him, then, sighing with effort, stood up, murmuring, "I'm tired, I gotta go, Amber, see ya later."

I was speechless, a hidden wail of shameful anguish wanting to keep him there, anything to have him stay and love me and appreciate me and tell me what a good person I was. Had he really called me pretty? I stood silently, unable to say goodbye, my breath caught between a gasp of fear and a whoop of excitement. Had I made him angry? At what cost?

The screen door banged, and it was over. I heard his truck start up, the tires crunching on gravel and then smoothing out on the road, accelerating away, quieter and quieter, until I could no longer hear any sounds. My world closed down to a small space in my head, and I stood still, wondering what had just happened. Then a small hard head rubbed against my leg. Tom. He knew. He knew everything was going to be all right.

I twisted the deadbolt on the front door, reassured by its firm chunking sound. Then I turned towards the bedroom, scooping up Tom on the way. He didn't mind that my hands were trembling. A hot bath. That's what I needed now. I set him down on the fluffy rug beside the tub, turned on the tap full blast, and poured in some bubble bath. I smiled at the lavender smell rising from the hot suds. It smelled like freedom.

CHAPTER 19

"God, grant me the serenity to accept the things I cannot change, courage to change the things I can, and wisdom to know the difference." The meeting had started. We sat somberly in a big circle, holding plates with homemade coffee cake and cookies, metal folding chairs creaking. I smiled at the woman on my left, but she avoided my eyes, her heavy mascara and curly brown hair protecting her face. A large woman across the circle beamed at me as if inviting acceptance. I wasn't ready to introduce myself, but I mumbled my name when my turn came. The books lining the wall behind us smelled musty, as if they had sat there forever, untouched.

I had seen the flier whenever I ran by the bulletin board outside the little church in town. Al-Anon. "Come talk about issues surrounding alcoholism," it said. I didn't think that was my problem, but Mike sure did drink a lot. I'm not sure I ever saw him without a beer in his hand, or reaching for one nearby. "Share your story and gain strength from others." Seemed like a good thing—to talk about the feelings whirling around in my head. "In my own head, I'm behind enemy lines," a friend had told me once, and I was sure ready to take off my combat fatigues.

The stories were fascinating—so different than what I had imagined. These people were actually looking at what was wrong in their lives and examining how they could make things better. Some had already made changes, helping not only their loved ones, but themselves, first fearlessly examining what was happening, what was there in front of them. Their eyes were wide open. I admired their bravery.

One girl, younger than I, talked about how her mother would come home and break out the beer, every Friday at five p.m., like clockwork. Her weekends were a blur growing up. She learned at seven years old to make macaroni and cheese for herself and her younger brother, also helping him with his homework, while her mother slept on the couch. "Joey didn't get why his mother slept all the time. He just kind of accepted it. Mom would pull herself together in time for work on Monday."

At least that mother kept it together during the week, I thought. Then I felt guilty. I picked at the crumbs left on my plate and avoided the facilitator's gaze. She was a ponytailed woman with lively brown eyes and a bright polka-dotted T-shirt.

Another woman, about forty-five years old, tired and already gray, patted her carefully arranged hairdo as she spoke. The dark bruises on the left side of her jaw, only partially hidden by makeup, almost glowed as she described nightly beatings after the flow of liquor began. She told us she'd escape into the bedroom, but her husband would find her there, angry that she had not made his life the way he had imagined it should be. Or maybe he had wanted steak instead of fried chicken that night. My stomach twisted, and I sat rigidly, fearful that someone would notice my sudden nausea. I breathed shallowly, fighting the urge to run to the bathroom. How could she survive this, night after night? Why wasn't someone helping her?

The suffering shared in the room was heart-rending at times, making my own seem trivial by comparison. I wondered at the tiny bird-like woman who kept pulling her sweatshirt sleeves down over the bandages on her wrists. She talked about her friend, sitting there with her, who had found her in time. She smiled, grateful, but tired, as if simply the effort of speaking her name was almost too much. But she was there. She was speaking, she was smiling, and she was trying hard to keep going. Maybe our faces, smiling and encouraging her, would get her through another week.

"I'm Audrey," said the woman next to me, with the heavy mascara. She had a ragged jacket, and a large leather purse that she hugged tightly against her chest. She talked in fits and starts, "I don't know if I belong here, but ..."

"You do," said the facilitator quietly.

"It's just that—" and she stopped, clearly struggling.

We waited quietly, looking down at the worn blue carpet in the center of the circle.

"It's just that he drinks so much and I don't really want to be around him anymore." She crossed her arms rigidly over her purse, then sighed deeply, gasped, and started to cry. Big tears rolled down her face as she fiddled in a pocket for a tissue and dabbed at the mascara on her cheeks. "I need to leave," she sobbed, "just leave. But where could I go?" She gasped again, "What am I gonna do?"

"There is a shelter on Brook Street near the elementary school," said the facilitator, "I can get you that information."

Audrey thanked her, shaking her head at the same time. "I don't know if I can go through with it. And my cat, how am I gonna keep her safe? He said he'd kill her!" She started crying again.

"Well, the family shelter can't take cats, but maybe you can board her somewhere until you find a place?"

The heavy woman from the other side of the circle smiled broadly. "Well, I, for one, am so glad that you are getting out! It's time. Way to go, Audrey! You've gotta protect yourself."

"Thanks, yeah. I'm not sure what I want, though," mumbled Audrey, slumping down further in her chair.

•　•　•

Later, I heard the group leader quietly talking to the bruised woman with the coiffed hair, handing her a slip of paper with some phone numbers. "They can help you," she said. "just ask. You can do it."

I wondered what it would take to stand firm and say *No more*. I knew I would come again. People here listened, and they cared.

•　•　•

My run that night was long and hard. I ran so fast that I gasped for breath, the trees whirring by, my eyes blurring from sweat or maybe tears, I wasn't sure which. I wanted the pounding to go from my feet up my legs into my stomach and chest, erasing the feelings which didn't belong there. I didn't want to care, I didn't want to feel, I just wanted to stay numb. But even as I ran, a part of me knew that my awakening was as inevitable as the season's changes. Where would it all end, I wondered? I feared that if I let it happen, if I let myself feel these emotions, then they might just tear me apart, leaving nothing behind but pieces.

CHAPTER 20

The tiny black-and-white barred bird, her head tucked under her wing and one foot pulled tightly into her belly feathers, looked like a child's handmade toy, a bit of fluff on a stick. I gazed into the cage, wondering what had left her crumpled in the grass on my front lawn. Drawn by Tom's avid focus, I had found her beneath the front window, after my morning run. I looked her over carefully for injuries, but finding none, had put her into a spare cage and brought her inside, safe from the sun and predators. Well, almost all predators ... It worried me that even Tom's steady gaze failed to rouse her. She needed a doctor. I changed clothes quickly and thrust an apple into my pocket, then picked up the cage, said goodbye to Tom, and headed for the closest veterinary hospital. Marlene would understand if I came in late.

"She's probably flown head-on into a window. Sometimes that happens when the light is just right and they can't see the glass." The veterinarian's hands were gentle, lifting the bird's feathers with one finger, peering into her eyes with a penlight. "I can't find any wounds, but I think she's probably got some head trauma. All we can do is treat her for shock and hope for the best."

The vet tapped a syringe he had prepared, then pushed away the feathers from the little creature's tiny abdomen, and slid the needle into her skin. She was motionless in his hand, not even blinking in the bright light of the examination room. He set her gently back in the cage. "Keep her in the boarding area, and check her vitals every fifteen minutes," he told his assistant. Turning to me, he said, "It's going to be touch and go for now.

We'll have to take one minute at a time." He looked at me briefly through his wire-rimmed glasses, then began making notes on some papers over at the counter.

"Can I see where you are going to keep her?" I hardly waited for his assent, following the scrub-suited girl who carried the cage down the hall and pushed through a door into a room filled with cages and dog runs. A few dogs clambered to their feet, barking desultorily, then settled down again, heads on their front paws. It smelled like dog and disinfectant.

The assistant opened a metal door and placed the entire cage inside, a cage within a cage. She hooked a lamp on the bars, "To keep it warm," she said, filling a cup with water and another with seeds.

I was reluctant to leave the bird behind. I had held her in my hands, sitting on the edge of my tub and ignoring Tom's inquiring noises from outside the door. She had been weightless in my curled fingers, a tiny warm bundle meant to be flitting quickly through the trees and the sunshine, racing from one shady spot to another, snatching up tiny insects or seeds as fast as she could find them to keep her wings strong and her eyes bright. But now, now, this little life was in critical danger, flightless, motionless, and caged. It was my fault. How long could she last in here?

I followed the veterinary assistant back towards the front lobby. She turned towards me, "Oh, I forgot to ask, can we keep the cage for now?"

"Yes, it belongs to Helping All Animals, where I work. I'm sure they wouldn't mind."

"Oh, I know that place. Don't you guys have a vet there?"

"Well, yes, but he isn't around this early, and I thought this was an emergency ..." I trailed off.

"Sure. Well, the bird's in good hands. We'll do the best we can for it."

Her, I said to myself. *She is a her. Or a him.* "Is there anything more I can do? Feed her, or something?"

"No, right now it just needs rest, and time for that medication to work. But we'll call you if there's a change. Thanks for bringing the little one in." She headed down the hall, opening a door and smiling at me over her shoulder, "Wish us luck!"

Luck, I thought, as the door shut behind her, dampening the noise of barking dogs. She'll need more than luck to survive not just the shock of her injury, but what must be the absolute terror of being handled by humans, cut off from the open air and the sun, injected with needles and caged behind two sets of metal bars in a room echoing with barking. If she was to survive, it would be despite all this.

·   ·   ·

Later that day I called the hospital, and was told that the little bird had died. "Thank you," I said, idiotically, hanging up the phone gently in its cradle. I stared numbly at the wall, imagining the little bit of fluff lying still on the cage floor, lifeless. It was almost more than I could bear.

·   ·   ·

There are risings within me. Pieces lifting up from deep places where they had sunk long ago, like snow swirling in a shaken glass globe. I feel anger at a woman leaning out of her car window, middle finger rigidly raised, yelling at the line of activists that cows were made for people to eat. I see her hate-filled face, and a wave rises from my toes, hot and burning, up through my stomach and chest. I want to scream back at her, but I don't. I want to keep feeling. I don't want to waste it on anyone who doesn't understand. It feels like power.

Then other mornings I wake with a sadness so deep that I can hardly lift my head from my pillow. I might have been dreaming of the calves who never knew their mothers, the mothers with aching swollen udders who will never know the touch of their babies as they suckle. Or maybe I'm thinking of feathers drifting, caught in the corners of the slaughterhouse, pulled from chickens who die at the tearing shock of electrified water. But my very real grief over this suffering is interwoven with something much more personal.

With these emotions bubbling to the surface, I am becoming more whole. It seems strange, but it's as if the parts of me I never knew were missing have been shaken loose and released by my work. And I have to take the bad with the good, because one pulls out the other, like the multicolored seemingly endless scarf of the magician. He pulls it out of his pocket, and it comes and comes and comes, turning red and green and blue, a never-ending circle.

I get angry at a cruel researcher, and there, lying in front of me, like a fish out of water, is my own brand-new anger at Mike. Red and blue the scarf changes, twisting and pulling and turning out of the hidden pockets. I cry over dying chicks in the classroom, and my hot tears bring with them a memory so intense it could be happening right now. A dark room, twisted sweaty sheets, and the terrible devastation of a small girl who doesn't know what love means anymore. Here the scarf comes, now yellow, now red again.

Sometimes, while I run, thoughts and images also rise unbidden, as if my physical exertion peels them away from a deep quiet place. Today, as my sneakers thudded on the asphalt and my breath heaved, I suddenly thought of the carefully coiffed woman at Al-Anon. I remembered her tear-stained face, and her continued love for her husband. And the terrible swelling bruises from his fists. I cried out and turned off the road into a field of corn, racing blindly down a row of tall green stalks, tassels waving gently high above my head. I twisted and turned into the field until I didn't remember the direction of the road. I stopped and stood bent over my knees, gasping, hearing only my ragged breath and the rustling surrounding me.

It hurt, deep inside. It hurt that I knew what it meant to love someone who treated me badly. Someone who knew just what to say, just what to do in order to cause pain in those intensely private tender inner places. I knew what it meant to feel shame simply for not speaking out, for letting him back in again and again, for letting it go on way beyond what was right, for letting something happen in the first place that had never been right at all.

I sat down in the middle of the cornfield and I cried, gentle tears that seemed to have no beginning and no end. I cried for the little girl I used to be. The girl with the pigtails who was too afraid to reach out for help and admit, down into her soul, that it would be better to say goodbye.

When I got home, my roommates must have thought my face was red from running. They didn't ask questions. But Tom knew. This linking of one emotion to another, of one story to another deep inside was a mystery.

But it kept happening. Like pulling a bucket out of a well, when I'm terribly thirsty. I haul on the rope, summoning the bucket filled with cold, clear water. But along with the sloshing water come other things stuck to the rope. I pick them off so that they don't fall into my life-giving water, but they get my hands slimy with unpleasant old encrusted sludge. Because from this particular well where I've been drinking, the water comes with a price.

Yet each time the connections are made, each time these unwanted memories or realizations emerge with that blessedly cold clear water, each time I look carefully at what I've found and peel it away, I feel cleaner, and the water tastes that much more sweet. And each time I curve my mind back to the past or find a link to a long-ago buried emotion, I feel just a bit lighter. I stand taller, and I am more whole. Seems like a good thing.

CHAPTER 21

One day in my cubicle, typing away, deep into an article, I heard a sound at my door. It was a small stuffed lion peeking at me. He had a big blue bow on top of his head. I stopped typing and grinned, looking at the little fingers holding tightly onto the lion, "Why, hello! Are you the lion who's going to help me get my work done?"

The lion disappeared, and I heard footsteps running down the aisle. I scraped my chair back and stood up to look, but no one was there.

Later I asked Marlene about the child. She explained, "When school lets out early for these teacher meetings, sometimes babysitters are hard to line up."

In the break room later that day, I saw the beribboned lion again, held by a freckle-faced girl of about five, sitting with a small group of HAA employees. The girl wore a bright pink jumper with matching tights. I waved, but she hid her face behind her lion, twisting closely in to her mother's body. While talking, the woman absently stroked her daughter's hair. I sat down at a nearby table with my paper bag lunch.

"Hi! You must be Mr. Big Blue Bow," I said. I couldn't see the little girl's face, but her mother turned to me and smiled.

"This is Miss Amber. Can you say hi?"

The little girl peeked at me from under her lion, and said, "Hi!" in a very tiny voice. Then she lifted the edge of her mother's jacket and hid again.

"Hi! What is the name of your lion? I like him."

Her mother patted the little girl's back. "Can you introduce your lion?"

No answer. She wiggled further under her mother's jacket, her dark hair falling over the lion. I reached into my lunch and brought out my sandwich. Her mother was pulled back into the conversation around her table.

"Lions don't like peanut butter sandwiches, do they?"

She lifted her mother's jacket and looked at me, shaking her head.

"That's good, because I wouldn't want him pouncing on my sandwich. Or is he a she?"

She rolled her eyes and tilted her head at me. "No, he's a he! Girls don't have manes."

"Got it!"

Her lips crinkled into a small smile.

"So is his name Mr. I-Don't-Like-Peanut-Butter?"

"No," she giggled and bounced up and down in her mother's lap, "it's Lanny!"

"Ah, Lanny the Lion. He's very handsome. I used to have a little tiger puppet. Actually, I still do. I'll bring him here someday to meet Lanny."

Now she was openly grinning at me, making Lanny jump up and down. "He's happy. He needs more friends."

"Me, too!"

She slid out of her mother's lap and began walking Lanny around the room, exploring the counters of the lunch room and sniffing the sugar canisters and salt shakers. She looked like she belonged there, comfortable in her pink jumper, comfortable in her skin. I ate my lunch and watched her explore the room, then walk Lanny back to perch on her mother's shoulders. I greeted two people who joined me at my table, but continued to watch Lanny.

I thought back to my first day of kindergarten. I remembered the fear, mostly. From the outside I looked shy and compliant, whereas inside I shrank down to a tiny spark of myself. I didn't know how to talk to the other kids, I didn't know how to talk to the teacher, I couldn't think when she asked me questions. Even lining up—something we did multiple times a day to go to the gym or the lunch room or the bus—was terrifying. Jostling all together, one in front, one behind, children turning their heads unpredictably, their bodies moving in sudden bursts, touching me. Touching me with their strange feels, smells, energies. Looking at me. I was invaded, overwhelmed.

Over time I survived, but I never fully relaxed. Every day, it would begin at the bus stop. Softly, invisible to anyone except me, I'd pull in my outward self and narrow my focus to a small space in front of me. If I blurred the edges enough, then I could get on the bus and share a seat with a classmate. My close cocoon protected me throughout the day, blunting smells, sights, and sounds, allowing only the focus of the book, the blackboard, the teacher's question. Stepping off the bus onto the street at the end of the day, I could finally breathe deeply, allowing the outside air in. Outside, alone, I could inflate, like bread rising, back into my skin. The whole process would begin again the next day.

Watching the little girl talking to her mother's friends, I felt inexplicably sad. There was something so carefree about her, something so natural and unselfconscious. Had I ever been like that? Even now, I was aware of the gaze of the person sitting at my table. Should I be talking to her instead of watching the girl? Or did I have some lettuce stuck in my teeth?

As a child, I remembered most clearly always wondering if everything was okay. Nights were the worst. When would he come to say goodnight? And if he didn't come, what had I done wrong?

CHAPTER 22

"Yeah, you and I know it, but the donors don't. That's where you come in."
Marlene handed my draft back over the cubicle wall, "Don't be so nice. Just
tell it like it is. Their money supports research that burns dogs. You want to
turn their stomachs."

I stared at the solicitation letter from the firefighter's charity with its
photo of a smiling bearded man, both arms bandaged, his yellow helmet
tucked under one elbow. Marlene waited, drumming her fingers on the top
of the partition.

"People want to help him," I murmured.

"What?"

"Donors think their money helps firefighters," I squirmed, rubbing my
forehead hard. "They feel good when they write that check."

"Yeah, and you're pulling the rug out," she said, grinning at me. She
looked at her watch. "You'll get it, kid," she said from behind the partition,
moving away.

I sat quietly, feeling my weight on the chair, my feet encased in my
sneakers, resting lightly on the floor. A tiny spot in my gut burned, a small
flame rising from a recent spark. Mentally I warmed my hands on that flame,
feeling heat and power rising into my chest, my throat, spreading outward
towards my fingers as they rested on the typewriter. That terrified schoolgirl
from those echoing long-ago hallways could not help me. I needed to move
her aside, perhaps reassure her, even throw her over my shoulder like a

firefighter carrying her to safety; something, anything to free my hands and heart, to lift my eyes beyond my own pain and fear and confusion so I could see my way clear. I needed to fight. It was time.

I took a deep, shaky breath. *Your local firefighter needs studies on human skin, such as tissue cultures and clinical studies of burn patients.* I wrote, *Dogs, whose skin has one third the layers of human skin, are poor models. Data obtained from burning dogs is much more useful for obtaining grant money than helping firefighters. Clinical studies on human subjects enhance our knowledge immediately, and are the quickest, least expensive and most effective path to better medical care. Our charities can do better. Your money can do better. Our heroes deserve better.*

I sighed and leaned back in my chair, my hands and arms tingling, as if I'd just had a hard run. Then I stood, suddenly needing to be outside, to stand in the breeze and watch the trees moving. The hall seemed longer than usual, but the fire door opened unexpectedly easily to my hard shove, spilling me out onto the pavement. I let the door clang shut and stood outside in the cool quiet air, leaning against the rough bricks. I watched the sun prickle through the thinning leaves of the nearby trees.

When I wrote a particularly compelling piece, I felt like a crusader. Other days, when my calls to scientists and witnesses weren't returned and the media wouldn't print my stories, I felt more like an idiot screaming at a blank wall. But today I felt like neither. I was remembering the woodchucks.

"You gotta grab them quick and lift, so they don't have time to turn around and bite you. And believe me, you don't want them sinking those big teeth into your hand."

One summer, while I was still in high school, I worked in a laboratory which studied woodchuck livers. I helped transfer the trapped wild ones into cages. I learned to grab their tails with a heavy leather glove, shaking their bodies if they tried to curl upwards, teeth flashing.

My trainer, barely older than me, reassured me, "Don't worry—they scream no matter what you are doing. But their tails are pretty tough. Doesn't hurt 'em."

How did he know, I wondered. Most were captured to study physiological changes during hibernation. These experiments seemed innocuous at worst, as the woodchucks slept their winters away in a cozy nest in a kennel, brought out only occasionally for blood tests. But the animals used for liver biopsies endured painful surgeries and frightening echoing empty steel cages. Instead of a straw-filled wooden den, they stood on wire-bottomed cage floors, their food falling into clanging bowls twice a day while they pressed themselves against the back wall, no way out.

The data gave us a lot of information on woodchuck livers. Was it worth it? I didn't know. But it brought in the grant money. And it paid my salary. The next time, I would remember to ask more questions.

The work at HAA left me feeling much cleaner, even though sad and discouraged at times. How long did I have to work here to finally make amends for hurting those woodchucks, if that was even possible? Wasn't I just as bad as the scientists? But at least now the sadness was farther away from my center, from my inner vulnerable parts. Now I could stand up and speak out for what I knew was right. I made a difference in animals' lives. I spoke for the ones who had no voice, and it felt good.

I argued with Marlene one day about people she was calling "horrible" and "stupid"—the ones sending money to a charity studying cystic fibrosis in pigs and ferrets.

"Don't they know that pigs' lungs differ totally from humans'?" she ranted, "How can they think they are helping kids? Really? Did they even go to school?" She reached over and picked at a staple sunk into the wall of my cubicle.

"Most people just don't think about it, Marlene. They just want to help. Those pictures of sick kids on ventilators really get to them."

"Yeah, well someone should get to them with the pictures of little dead piglets thrown onto a pile with intravenous tubing still sticking out of their legs," she growled.

"We all have to start somewhere. Maybe they didn't think about it—"

"Sure didn't. They just want to feel better inside. Throw their money around so they don't have to feel guilty. Help the world be a better place and all that."

I stood taller, breathing deeply. This felt important. "Maybe ... like me with those woodchucks."

"What woodchucks? What are you talking about?"

I sat down and returned her stare, holding my hands tightly together in my lap. I told her about the woodchucks I had helped capture, the way they would struggle to get free, frantic, whistling an alarm to their families as they were carted away. I believed what I was told, that the information from studying woodchuck livers would help people. But a thorough search of the medical literature on the subject was disappointing.

"Amber, what were you thinking?" Marlene said, staring at me, a frown crinkling her face.

"Well, I didn't know. I thought the scientists would be kind to the animals—"

"Hah!"

"And figured that the information gained was worth the price—"

"Amber! Woodchuck livers aren't the same as ours! For starters, they live in dens underground and sleep away the winter!" Marlene was horrified, "Were you in on the surgeries, too?"

I met her gaze, still seeing the terrified woodchucks in their metal cages, bellies shaved and long incisions puckered with sutures. Must have hurt, for sure. Marlene's relentless questions made me feel smaller by the minute, my insides twisting in shame. But something kept me talking, as if revealing everything I had done could ease my guilt. Right now I didn't feel so different from those donors supporting animal research. Eventually the questions stopped and I turned away, staring at the charity files on my desk. All was quiet, and when I glanced up again, Marlene was gone.

CHAPTER 23

Fall, along with its gorgeous leaves and rushing wind, brought HAA's anti-dissection campaign to a head. One of our investigators landed a job undercover preparing cat cadavers for biological supply houses. The bodies were bought by high school science teachers for their anatomy classes. The investigator documented the handling of the cats before they died. His findings shocked us all.

To our horror, the cats were not dead when the embalming began, because the company was cutting corners. Gassed a dozen to a chamber, they were barely unconscious before being strapped down, spread-eagled, to filthy wooden crosses, then injected intravenously with formaldehyde. Their jaws clamped and their paws curled over their bonds as the chemicals burned their way into the small stretched bodies. I felt sick as I watched the videotapes, not wanting to believe what I was seeing. I could almost smell the formaldehyde, imagined it burning my eyes and making them water. I collapsed inside, unwilling to allow the truth. But this was real. It had really happened, and it was still happening.

It was Friday, the end of a long day, the end of a long week. I sat late in the office, alone, working on an article about the torture. HAA was creating an information packet destined for teachers who most likely ordered from this company. We wanted the teachers to know that these cats were purchased from local animal shelters. Some of them could have been somebody's pet. And to die in such an unbelievably painful manner ... I thought of Tom and my mind veered away in horror.

I shook my head and tried to focus. I had to describe the torture so that our readers would accept that it was really happening. They needed to know. But putting the words to paper meant reliving the scenes over and over in my mind. It was almost too much for me to stand, but I did get a few pages written that I hoped would be useful in our campaign. I sighed shakily as I cranked the last page out of the typewriter and then carried the pages down the hall and slid them under the editor's door. Time to go home.

Sitting in my car, just breathing, I thought of Chris, and a warm soft feeling opened up in my belly. It calmed my inner trembling. Was he already finished with his dinner? Were his hands deep in the warm soapy water of his kitchen sink, dark hair plastered closely to his forearms? Did his hair smell like it did when I last buried my nose in it, yeasty bread and garlic and olive oil?

I started the car and maneuvered around the parking lot potholes, then turned onto the road. The trees lining the highway flashed past in my side-view mirror, and the air was hot, even with the windows wide open. The heat had returned, Indian summer-style. Tom and I might need the fan tonight.

I pictured Chris' face, his crinkly smile as he reached over to tuck my hair behind my ear. But his face faded and all I could see was row upon row of cats, dead and dying, paws curled over their restraints. I tried to remember the smell of the sage on the nearby hills, but for a moment my nose was filled only with the overpowering odor of formaldehyde and death.

Strong hands, dark hair curling up from raised blue veins and sinewy tendons. They gripped my arms, a heavy weight pressing me down into the mattress, holding me spread-eagled as he adjusted his position in the darkness. Panting breath, the soft drop of spittle onto my cheek, musty skin odor, the stink of desperation. Over it all, smothering me into silence, was my overwhelming fear.

I shook my head, pushing away the memory as I turned into my driveway. Meant nothing, anyway. I just had to keep putting one foot in front of the other, helping animals who deserved a better life. Once the science teachers found out the truth, they would make changes. It had to work.

That night, I sat on the couch alone, staring at the blank TV. This work was getting to me. The pain of the animals seemed harder to bear, closer to my heart than when I began this job over a year ago. Was my skin more sensitive, prickly and tender, or was it my insides that were more jumbled and confused? I worked hard, cataloging the gruesome evidence, but each night found me more twisted and unsettled inside. The suffering of these helpless, trusting creatures—how could I speak out loudly enough so that it would stop? I didn't know what to do, except work harder, watching the evidence tapes and carefully noting each agonized reaction; writing the reports, including facts and figures, so that we had something for the USDA veterinarians who enforce anti-cruelty laws. It was all we could do.

The Al-Anon meetings helped, because I could talk about my frustrations without being judged, and listen to other people struggling to work through their own difficulties. We were all in it together. Sometimes I even left those meetings feeling lucky. At least Mike didn't hit me. Once a woman talked about finally calling the police, then having them greeted pleasantly at the door by her drunken husband. Turns out they were his cronies from the pool hall, who saw only the scratch on his cheek from her desperate lashing out. It didn't matter that she was afraid for her life, her lip still bleeding from when she "ran into a door." The bruises on her face wouldn't show for another few hours. She could file a police report at the station, they said, shaking their heads as they strolled back to their patrol car.

She got more than a split lip that night.

The meetings often touched me deep inside in a way that I couldn't easily describe. Like a questing finger pointing down into my soul, calling out knowledge that I didn't know was there. One evening, sitting in the metal chair at my favorite spot, the far end of the circle, facing the door, I listened as the facilitator talked about honoring your child within. I thought how strange it was to first tell us to heal, then talk as if we had other unconnected pieces of ourselves that needed acknowledgment. Didn't the healing happen all together? All at once?

"Give your inner child love. Tell them you are here for them."

I squirmed, uncomfortable and wishing I was somewhere else, but I could not explain my unease. I thought instead about my upcoming work deadlines. Maybe I didn't need this group anymore if it was just going to stir up difficult feelings.

Meanwhile, my nights gave me less and less peace. I woke exhausted, unwilling to admit the sun's rising, knowing that another day of work would not bring me the calm I craved. Next Monday I would meet with the local district attorney to show him the evidence of torture occurring in his county. But as the meeting got closer, my mind, my insides, got farther and farther away, as if I was an automaton, soulless. I was trying to stand up for the animals, but just now I could only barely stand up for myself.

• • •

The weekend went by too fast, housemates busy with their friends. I tried to forget the cats on their crosses, but I kept seeing their agonized faces, bloody whiskers, and matted fur. Then Monday arrived right on schedule, not waiting for my readiness. I had painstakingly prepared the videos and my presentation, even practiced with Marlene, but it still didn't feel like enough.

"That'll work fine," Marlene had said, "you've got it, don't worry." When I was silent, she looked up from her desk, meeting my eyes. "Girl, you're just there to present the facts. Don't expect to move mountains."

• • •

I dressed carefully that morning, in dark slacks and a light blue blouse with buttons all the way up to my neck. The drive was too short, and the receptionist told me the district attorney was ready for me. She showed me into his office, a small room filled with metal file cabinets, piles of papers, and a videotape player and TV on a dusty counter, crammed in alongside a cluttered desk.

"Okay, let's see what you've got," he said, a heavy man with dark hair and a receding hairline, solid in his dark blue business suit and tie. He had a distant smile as he shook my hand, perhaps already thinking ahead to the next meeting on his agenda. His shirt buttons barely held closed against his belly when he leaned back in his chair after greeting me. He was relaxed and confident, whereas I felt like an impostor. But I had to tell the truth. He had to know. He was supposed to investigate Animal Welfare Act violations.

I wished we weren't alone in his office. I perched on the edge of the offered chair, pulling my blouse down away from my neck. I swallowed, bending over to grab the videotape in the stack of materials I had set on the stained linoleum near my chair. I handed it to him and tucked my legs in close, ignoring the drip of sweat that rolled down my spine. I watched his face during the few minutes of the video, expecting shock or dismay, but saw only a mild curiosity.

When the tape finished he said, "Yes, I see them moving, but how do we know that it's not just a reflex?"

I lifted my eyes to his, and saw only inner emptiness. I fought within myself, an invisible war against my fear, my complicity, and my overwhelming desire to be nice and pleasing. The clock ticked on the wall behind him, and suddenly I understood that his emptiness, his distance, his lack of compassion would hurt others a lot more than they could ever hurt me.

My voice was surprisingly strong and confident. "Dead cats do not have reflexes." I explained that killing cats by injecting formaldehyde into their veins is painful and cruel, causing immense suffering. I handed him the testimony from our veterinarian, which corroborated my observations and conclusions.

His smile returned, and he scratched his cheek while he leaned over to turn off the TV and video player. "Well, thank you, miss, I'll look into this. You have those numbers for me?"

"Yes, they are in the folder. And you can keep the videotape. Call me if—"

"Oh, sure, I'll be in touch. Thank you for informing me about this, young lady."

I shook his hand in the doorway, my eyes flicking over the hair curling obscenely from between the lower buttons of his shirt, and I was sickened, deep inside. Nothing was going to change. Why should he worry about a few stray cats, already destined for euthanasia?

But back in the car, tires humming on the highway, I smiled. I had done it. I had faced my fear. I had told the truth.

CHAPTER 24

The next morning I sat on the floor in my living room, cooling off from my morning run. "That DA," I told Tom, my appreciative audience, "he reminds me of Mike." Tom agreed, but didn't endorse his opinion in the usual way, by rubbing against me, because he didn't like sweat.

What was it about the DA? Perhaps the confident way he slung his arm across the back of his chair. Or the way he met my eyes, smiling and sure, so very sure, of his worth in the world. Nothing could challenge him, nothing could surprise him. Nothing could force him to change. But I had changed something. I took in a large lungful of air, my skin prickling, thinking of Mike's last visit. All I had done was stay out of the bedroom. Could it really be that easy?

I've got to talk to Mike. But how can I? What would I say? What evidence would be enough to make him close his eyes and say, "You are right. I am wrong"? I feared those words didn't exist, that my tongue wouldn't be able to speak them anyway, no matter how much I practiced them, that I had allowed his visits for so long that he would laugh at any attempt to put things right. Or at worst, that I would be thrown out into the darkness for speaking out. Hurt, abandoned, killed maybe. But as the sweat dried on my face, I knew I had to try something.

CHAPTER 25

The next day, we collected cages and gathered at the fairgrounds where the townspeople were gathering to shoot live birds instead of clay targets. Why? Pigeons are easier to hit. They are trapped from the surrounding areas, then released one by one from cages in front of the shooters. The entire town gathers in bleachers to watch the carnage, cheering on their friends and family members. Like a macabre baseball game, the stands are patrolled by hot dog and soda vendors, with beer available from trucks nearby. HAA brought a first aid truck to the site, so that we could collect and minister to any survivors.

I have always loved birds. These last remnants of the ancient dinosaurs remind me of their ancestors, with their scaly legs and beady eyes. But birds are so tiny and delicate that my heart almost breaks just watching them take to the air in a puff of wind. And their colors! Pigeons in particular have the most amazing plumage varieties, from coal black to all shades of gray to completely white, speckled with brown spots. If I had a choice, I'd wear feathers instead of clothes. They shed water, cuddle you close in the cold, shade your skin from the beating sun, and completely renew themselves every year.

Pigeons also have many voices, and they talk to each other a lot, bowing and quietly bubbling their songs, puffing up their feathers as they dance. Burble. That's the sound they make, like an underground stream rising from the cold wet rocks below, icy and clear.

"Why? Why?" she sobbed into her clenched fingers. I touched the girl's arm and looked into her eyes helplessly for a moment. Her long blonde hair fell over her face as she struggled to contain her misery. Part of me wanted to cry with her, let loose my own anguish, but it was buried too deep, tucked away. And people might notice. The shooters might hear us. Besides, the birds needed help, so I walked away, discovering another bleeding body behind the bandstand. This one, glowing white with speckles of brown across her back, had made it over the trees before tumbling down, red bubbles coalescing on her gaping beak.

As I gently collected her from the grass, folding her wings carefully in to her body and tucking her against my stomach, a small boy, about eight years old, stepped out from under the bandstand. His thumbs were hooked behind him into his waistband, and he wore a green baseball cap with a leaping deer, the visor turned backwards. "Nothing Runs Like a Deere," was printed across the back of the cap in bright yellow letters.

"What'cha doin'?"

"Trying to save her."

He was blocking my path. "Why?"

"Well, we don't believe in killing birds, so we're here to help the ones we can." My voice felt tight in my chest.

"But they're just pigeons, you know. There's lots more."

I edged by him as he craned his neck to see the bird. I had a sudden impulse to shove him, anything to get him out of my way. He was just a small boy, so it would have been easy. "Yes, I know that, but we care about all of them."

"Well, my Dad says you're all stupid. Buncha weirdos. Next year, he says, I'll be old enough to have my own gun." He turned to let me go by.

I stopped and looked back at him, feeling the bird's heart beating fast against my palm.

He ducked his head and looked away.

I hurried across the grass, my mouth dry. At the HAA first aid tent the vet tucked a gray barred pigeon into a cage, her wing bandaged to her body with blood-spattered gauze. She lifted her other wing, feathers brushing the cage walls, then folded it awkwardly down against the bandages.

"Here, I've found another one." But as the vet reached for the white bird in my hands, the bubbling stopped and the light died out of her eyes. I gasped as her small head dropped onto my fingers, surprising me with its weight. It was my fault. Maybe if I hadn't stopped to talk … The vet put his stethoscope into the feathers at her breastbone, then shook his head and gently added her to a growing pile of feathered bodies. I touched the place on my finger where her head had rested. So heavy, but only for a moment, as if her soul had paused just there before taking wing.

We stayed all day in spite of jeering hecklers, our trucks bringing wounded survivors to the veterinary hospital. Entire families cheered as the birds were systematically killed, dropping like spent leaves onto the bloody grass. Laughing boys swept the field in between rounds, grabbing any birds they found and ripping their heads off, ending their suffering even while sending shocks of horror into my heart. The loud voices of the crowd rolled over us in waves, lustful spectators cheering on modern-day gladiators. But this time, the enemies were only small feathered beings who simply wanted to live and fly again.

We tried to relieve their pain, collecting the fluttering bodies and bringing them to the first aid tent. Blood mixed into the bird droppings on my hands as I cradled another trembling survivor. He cheered me with his strength, desperately struggling to escape. His feet, clenched around my fingers, were hot and dry. I parted his feathers, knowing that any bird caught dazed on the grass had a good reason not to launch himself up, free, into the surrounding woods. There it was. A tiny hole, welling precious blood that his little body could not spare. Despite my tender handling, his broken wing bones grated terribly against each other. Applying antiseptic and bandages, the vet treated him for shock. "Maybe this one will live," he said, "though he might not fly again."

I turned away, nearly tripping over a small person, who had appeared behind me. I recognized the leaping deer on his green cap. He was holding a gray barred bird. "Here's another one," he said.

I rubbed my eyes on my sleeve and smiled at him, taking the bird gently. He backed up, wiping his hands on his jeans, looking around at the bandaged birds. Then he straightened, tucked his thumbs back into his belt, and sauntered away. "My mom likes hummingbirds and cardinals better," he said over his shoulder.

•　•　•

Chris called that night, as I sat exhausted in the darkened living room. "Amber," he said tentatively, "pretty awful today."

"Yeah," I said, not knowing what else to say. But the darkness lifted a tiny bit.

"Those people, what were they thinking?"

"They're just trash," I said.

"That's kind of prejudiced, Amber, don'tcha think?"

"No, no, that's what people are thinking about the birds. People call them trash."

"Oh," he said, "yeah, and they live in flocks."

"Yeah, and they poop on lawns and roofs," I added, "Why can't they use the Porta Potties?"

"Hear this?" he said, and a thumping sound came over the phone. "I'm beating my chest. I'm a warrior. I'm keeping my country safe from vermin."

I laughed, briefly, "Yeah, I know, a big macho illiterate moron showing off for your wife and kids."

"Well, I'm not macho, but I might be an illiterate moron," and he laughed, barely more than a sigh. He was tired, too.

A warm feeling came over me. I wanted him near me, I wanted to see his smile and feel his touch. "So, illiterate moron, whatcha doin' tonight, watching soap operas and eating bon-bons?"

He laughed, and I relaxed a bit more, "Yeah, I like the cherry-filled ones. They go with my eyes."

"Well, you should come over here some time and organize my sock drawer. Whenever you need something to do." We chuckled together, letting images of messy socks and cherry bon-bons push away the memories of the day. I think he cared for me, cared for how I was feeling. I wasn't used to that, but it felt good. Talking on the phone seemed safe, suddenly. It felt unexpectedly soothing, like gently rubbing an old itchy healing wound.

Tom came closer, responding to my laughter, his purr sending satisfied buzzes along my leg.

Tires hummed by outside, and a late bird called, the sound trembling in the darkness. The hard plastic of the phone against my cheek reassured me I was still there, still present in the world, still sitting on the old couch, deadbolt guarding the door and a friend holding my heart gently in his hands.

He breathed quietly into the phone, "So, you okay?"

"Yes," I sighed, "better now."

CHAPTER 26

My spirits rose as I stepped outside the next morning for my run. I gratefully filled my lungs with the cool air. The dust lifted with each footfall, marking my path as I turned the corner into the sunrise's light. My muscles, clenched and tired from wrestling nighttime ghosts, lengthened and stretched pleasantly out into the rhythm of my run. The trees skipped by as I sped up, breath rasping in my throat as I made that first hard mile, sweat suddenly breaking out on my back and dampening my shirt. The sweat felt clean, my own sweat from my own exertions. It felt right to be flying along the road, no cars in sight as the hills behind my house were touched by the morning sun's first rays. If I could just keep running, fly right out of my town and beyond, into the sky over the desert ... but I couldn't. I had to return for Tom. It was time. I turned around and pounded back home, feeling stronger and ready for the changes that were coming.

I thought of Chris as I arrived at my driveway, and the warmth in my chest expanded out to my whole body as my breathing calmed. I waved to my fuzzy friend in the window and leaned down to stretch out my hamstrings, thinking of the way Chris' eyes crinkled when he laughed, the wholehearted way he enjoyed my cooking, and the easy friendship he had with his housemates. Recently, he had invited me to his "bachelor's castle" and treated me with a delicious lasagna. He said it was his grandmother's recipe, somewhat modified from the original. "If she knew what I changed, she'd disown me," he laughed. I promised to keep his secret.

Chris' visits balanced out the difficult work at HAA. I was relaxing into our friendship, and Chris seemed content with our evenings spent eating, talking and laughing. I began to enjoy and even look forward to the kiss we would share before we said our goodbyes, and he never asked for more.

I turned towards my door, the dry fall leaves crunching underfoot. They smelled good, reminding me of deep Tennessee woods, and winter's approach.

• • •

That night after work I sought solitude to explore my new feelings. I had been distracted by thoughts of Chris all day. Who was this person who wanted to be close, who cared about how I was feeling, and who gave me things I didn't even know I needed?

I had watched other students pair up in high school, leaning on each other and mooning over each other's faces in front of their lockers. I wondered what it was like to have someone waiting for you when you got out of class, wanting to be with you, to walk you home, maybe ask you how your day went. I had admired some boys from afar, knowing that they were unattainable, surrounded by their solid ranks of friends. As far as they were concerned, I didn't exist. It was easier that way, slipping through the school day without anyone noticing. No ripples.

The bang on the door made me jump. Mike's lined face was at the window, probably wondering why the door was locked. I let him in and he brushed by me, heading immediately to the kitchen and opening the fridge. He was in a sour mood, like he often was lately, and there was no beer in the house. I stood in the living room, wondering what was going to happen. Did he notice a change, that I was more in my own skin? Separate from him?

He slouched back into the living room. "Where's the beer? What, you ran outta money or something? Need a loan?" His tone was nasty, mocking.

"Yep, sorry, ran out, my friends didn't get to the store this week, and then ..." I paused, reluctant to tell him that one of my housemates had taken the last beer, after I had specifically offered it to her.

"What, I wanna relax with you after a hard day's work and I have to bring my own stuff?"

I thought about how ludicrous that sounded, but I held back, keeping my tone light, "Sorry, Mike, I guess sometimes I don't live up to your expectations."

I was unprepared for the intensity of his outburst. Irate, arms whirling as if he was preparing to hit me, he stormed around the living room, yelling about a boss who didn't know what the fuck he was doing and the fucking customers who were always right and where the fuck does he fit in and he couldn't just have a peaceful time at the end of his work day because there wasn't any fucking beer left for him and does he just have to do it all himself ... I wanted to run, to fly out of the house, to leave his anger and hurt behind, but something stopped me. This was my place, this was where my heart lived. I would not run away any more.

Frozen, the door still held open in my hand, I stared at him as he slowed down and stopped, breathing hard, face red. I flinched as he looked right through me before heading out of the door, sweat moist on his cheeks. A bit of gray fur tumbled along the edge of the carpet in the wake of his heavy boots. As he lurched down the path to his truck, my fear intensified into a desperate clutching deep inside. What would he do out in the world without me, without smothering his feelings in my welcoming body? I had the power to contain his bitterness, or at least to ease it and send him out clean, his insides calm and quiet once again. Who was I to withhold that comfort? If I no longer soothed his terrible agony, what damage would he inflict, and who would he hurt? It would all be on my head.

The roar of the truck startled me. I rushed outside, tears wetting my face, forgetting even to wipe them in my urgency, oblivious of who might see my distress. His truck was already in motion, speeding too fast and wide out of the driveway and narrowly missing the trees on the other side of the road.

I stood in the dust, wondering what had just happened, the wetness drying on my cheeks as I felt the echoing silence within. The quiet and solitude of newly won freedom was frightening.

CHAPTER 27

It was a long time before Mike called again. I felt like a freshly paroled convict, learning to fit into life outside of solid concrete walls and barbed wire fencing. My life was becoming more my own.

One brisk evening I was chopping tomatoes when Tom ran to the door, looking up expectantly. Who needed a doorbell? The door opened with a creak of hinges and the whoosh of the weather stripping across the floor as Chris walked in, bringing with him the smell of leaves and fall wind. He handed me his traditional bread offering with one arm and leaned down to pat Tom, who was twining around his legs with little murmurs of greeting. Certain people just drew that cat out. He was like me in that way, I guess.

"He doesn't do that with me."

"Who doesn't do what?" asked Chris.

"Tom. I usually get a silent belly flop purr, no talking like that. He must love you better."

"Well, I am more lovable, you know." He tilted his head and sniffed appreciatively, "I smell that luscious sauce again!" He dropped his jacket on the couch and disappeared into the kitchen. "I'll give it a stir and check the spices. Got enough garlic for the bread?"

"Yup! In the fridge! Be right in," I said, hanging up his jacket and giving Tom another rub. I locked the door and stared out for a moment at the fall leaves swirling around the edge of the road. Then I joined the boys in the kitchen.

We talked as I finished the salad and he put the garlic in the bread, leaving every other slice garlic-free, the way I liked it.

"Maybe you can go garlic-free too so I don't have to smell it on you," I teased, tousling his hair.

He planted a quick kiss on my cheek, then started covering the bread in foil.

"I like your new shampoo, gives you a very masculine air. What do you call it? 'He Man Wash'?" I said.

"You nitwit, no, it's Zeppelin Rock Shampoo, haven't you heard of it?" He put the foil-wrapped bread into the oven, closed the door and began doing air guitar, bending and swaying in a convincing hard rock beat, his hair falling into his eyes. I laughed, feeling myself relax into the silliness, like falling into a nest of pillows.

I could let my guard down with Chris. After Mom died, I protected myself with blinders, keeping me from seeing what was happening during those lost nights. But now I was reaching out and pushing, moving away the partitions, opening the heavy curtains until the sun shone in. It was exhilarating and somewhat terrifying, but the more the sun came in, the more I wanted to knock those walls right down and rush outside, fully alive and living only for myself. What did I really want? I had never asked myself that before.

It didn't really matter. The fun was in the discovery, like opening a tightly wrapped present.

He put the imaginary guitar down and glanced at my face. "Amber, how's your part of the dissection stuff going?"

"Well, it's pretty horrible. Sure makes me glad I didn't take biology in high school."

"Yeah, so true. You gonna stay at HAA forever?"

"Oh, I dunno ..." I said, wiping tomato juice off the cutting board and picking off the seeds. Their slippery outer coating kept squishing out from between my fingers.

"Maybe someday we can start our own group. We wouldn't have to do protests anymore. We could just do rescues of needy animals, and adopt them out. And keep all the cute ones."

"Yeah, all the ones like you? Imagine a kennel full of Chris-puppies, all needing homes. What ever would I do?"

"We'd have to adopt them all out, because I won't allow any euthanasias, that's for sure."

"Yeah," I said, sobering, "that would be excellent. Do you think we could pull it off? Fundraising would be key."

"Well, this spaghetti would bring in some folks." We joked over our food, later relaxing in the living room, once the dishes were cleaned. My housemates came in later in the evening and finished the leftovers. I snuggled into his arms and told him I wanted to stay there forever.

"Okay, sounds good to me," he said, touching my hair. He pulled me closer, gently, as if afraid I might fly away. "You okay?"

I wondered why everybody asked me that so much lately. Something must be obvious on the outside. I didn't really know, but it felt good. Like a deep breath of cold autumn air in the early morning.

I told him about my nightmares, about the crushing weight that pressed all the air out of my lungs so that I couldn't even cry for help. Waking up gasping and sweating, afraid to move. There was a silence, then Chris simply tightened his arms around me, breathing softly onto the top of my head. At that moment, the nightmares seemed very far away. But my calm didn't last long.

"Okay," I jumped up, needing motion, anything to stop the sudden buzzing underneath my skin. "Let's play some music. How about Springsteen?" I knelt down in front of the dusty albums. Chris joined me. We flipped through the covers.

He nodded and murmured, "Here he is!"

We danced to our favorites, laughing, singing along with "Born to Run," almost yelling, and I imagined the wind in my hair, my arms wrapped tightly around Chris' slender frame, rushing down the highway on a motorcycle, no responsibilities, no entanglements ... We turned it down when my housemates came out and complained. But we were still smiling.

Later we talked quietly on the couch, Tom having joined us from the bedroom after things calmed down. Motorcycles were just too much for him, really. But he couldn't resist being between us once the excitement was over. We moved our hands over his soft fur, touching each others' fingers, feeling the connection and knowing it was good.

"Tonight, will you dream about motorcycle engine exhaust and dudes with beards and long hair?" he teased.

"I hope so. It'll help if this guy stops coming here." My words dropped like a stone down a long, long well, echoing inside me.

"What guy? You gotta lover I don't know about?" he smiled, still joking and relaxed.

"Nah. Just this guy who scares me. I don't really invite him, but he comes anyway."

Chris narrowed his eyes, surprised, "You aren't kidding? Who is this person? Why does he visit? What are you talking about?"

"I don't know ... he comes because ... I don't know." What had I done? Could I just curl up into a ball and disappear? Somewhere deep inside I thought that if I just told, just brought it out into the open, then things could change. Keeping a secret becomes the worst kind of suffering sometimes.

"But ... if you are scared by this guy, then call the police or something. Where did you meet him?"

"It's okay, I'll handle it, I'm thinking about changing the locks—"

"He has your key? Who is he again? Do I know him?"

I wanted to run and hide. How could I tell him the truth? He would be angry, horrified, disgusted, all the things I already felt about myself. I wanted to smooth it over and make Mike disappear again. Pretend it never happened. I was pretty good at that. "You don't know him. I think it's over, he's not coming back. It's okay, never mind."

Chris sat still for a moment, looking at me. "Well, okay, but you just call me if you need to, right?" He smiled, uncertainly, staring into my eyes, but the mood was broken. We both pretended that everything was still okay, but we were suddenly awkward, unsure of ourselves. Even Tom retreated to the windowsill, feigning the need to groom his perfect coat. His ears flickered at a passing car, and he raised his paw to a leaf which scraped briefly against the screen. The room was quiet as the last song ended, the click of the record player's arm echoing in our ears.

"Well, I gotta go, I have that early meeting with Marlene over the dissection stuff. But it was yummy, really, Amber, let's do another spaghetti night soon. Maybe I can bring dessert, too, do ya think?" He gave me a quick kiss.

"Sure, that would be good." I felt lost and abandoned. I couldn't move. Then suddenly he was gone, the air still moving from the swish of his jacket over his shoulders. After a while I noticed Tom, purring by my side. "Ah, Tom, what just happened? Guess he couldn't take me." My body felt old and hurt, and I didn't know how things had gotten so bad inside. Stirring it up sometimes felt like making it all bigger, more noticeable, instead of cleaning out the grime. Would things get better someday? It sure didn't feel that way just now.

CHAPTER 28

Tigee, the little hand puppet, covered in faded brown and yellow splotches, lay in my lap, button eyes glinting as if he was just about to speak. I smiled, settling him on the dashboard. "You wait for me, Tigee, I have a meeting. It's about beer, so you can't come. You're too young." The little girl at HAA had liked him, formally introducing Lanny the Lion to Tigee the Tiger as if they were going to be the best of friends. Now Tigee kept me company in the car. I told him goodbye and headed across the asphalt in the bright late afternoon sunshine.

I sighed, relieved, as I opened the heavy outer door of the church and heard the familiar murmurs of conversation inside the meeting room. Today, rather than simply a self-imposed duty, the Al-Anon meeting would be a safe place to celebrate. Mike hadn't been back since he found my fridge empty of beer. I smiled. This group would understand the importance of what had happened.

The sunlight streaming across the linoleum floor illuminated bits of crumbs fallen from a homemade coffee cake. I took a piece. Still warm, it was a crumbly sweet topping lusciously paired with moist lemony cake. The chairs scraped along the floor as we arranged ourselves into the familiar circle. I took a chair next to Audrey, smiling at her upturned face. She sniffed and rubbed her nose, looking through me.

I thought about my small act of unintended defiance. It was already fading in my mind, clouded over by worry and regret. Like caring for a fading plant clipping, I hoped that close attention would help it grow and become more real in my heart. Here, no one judged, no one labeled or put their own spin on my words.

I took a bite of cake to distract myself from the butterflies in my stomach. You'd think by now they would have settled down, but they were flying in profusion today.

"Hello, Amber, good to see you!" said our facilitator. Her face crinkled into a smile as she greeted me, and I wondered where she kept such a well of caring. To hear these stories every week, and still smile?

"Ah, yummy coffee cake, as usual."

"Yes, our baker is a master of his craft."

"I know. I'm getting another piece." I set another one next to the first.

"Well, hurry, we're about to start. And grab me one."

I handed another piece to her, settling back down and grinning my thanks at the baker, across the circle. We began, as usual, with introductions, because there was always a new face or two. The first speaker, a scruffy man in his fifties, still lived with his mother, paid her bills, balanced her checkbook, all while she was beating on him every night after she got drunk. We listened sympathetically, knowing how hard it was to make a change, and that simply talking could be the first step.

One woman had gotten her husband into a rehab facility, and we applauded, celebrating her accomplishment. Rehab isn't the final answer, but it's surely a great step towards more peace and harmony. And maybe now she could relax for a while.

There was a pause, and I knew it was my turn. I felt suffocated, my ribs rigid, but somehow I drew in enough air to speak. Audrey took a breath beside me, perhaps feeling my own desperation. I clasped my shaking hands tightly, as if the pressure could help me force out my story. I wanted to make it real, to bring it into the light of day. "Hello, my name is Amber, and something great happened this week with Mi—my—my dad."

Faces turned towards me, piercing beams of attention aimed right at my innermost self. Inwardly I shrank away, but my voice kept talking, because somewhere inside, my need to be heard had become larger than my wish to remain hidden. My stomach churned, fighting to stop the truth pouring out, even as a big part of me inaudibly yelled with triumph. I paused, feeling nauseous and wishing I hadn't had any coffee cake. The group looked at me expectantly, smiles on their faces, wanting, needing some more good news.

"I didn't have any beer in the house this time, so he left. Mike," I added for the new people.

Their faces were pleased, glad for me. But I had expected them to be happier, more effusive, so I continued, "He was mad and stormed around, and it was scary, but I realized that in the future if I keep beer out of the house, then maybe he'll stop coming by at all. The sex alone maybe isn't enough for him, because he likes to get drunk beforehand." The words wouldn't stop, and suddenly it was all coming out, the way he would wait until dark, drinking, then come into my bedroom after his cigarette outside. The bang of the door was the signal that my peace would be violated.

In my rush to explain my excitement, I didn't notice the fading smiles.

Many looked concerned, some even aghast, shocked. I finally stumbled to a halt, realizing that this was maybe more than they wanted to hear. They were here to talk about hitting, physical abuse, black eyes, or drunken rantings, not the sexual devastation of a small girl now grown.

"Well, that sucks," muttered Audrey. She patted my arm.

"Oh, God …" said a woman with a heavy red sweater, the one who had come before, her wrists freshly bandaged. "You mean, Mike is your dad?" She stood up shakily and headed for the door, avoiding my eyes as she groped for the tissue in her pocket, holding it against her nose. I watched her go, wanting to disappear with her, embarrassed and angry. Why couldn't they celebrate with me? I had heard so many sad and miserable stories before, but suddenly I was making them all uncomfortable when it was my turn?

"Amber, I am so happy for you," tried the facilitator. But her words felt empty, hollow, a recipe from some book on effective Al-Anon leadership phrases.

There was a silence while everyone shifted in their seats, and I could almost see my words sliding off their faces and onto the floor. One woman stared down into her lap, twisting the cords of her sweatshirt tightly around her fingers. Another avoided my gaze and starting urgently digging into her purse, and another rubbed her face, her previous sympathetic expression transformed into one of distress. Audrey stared blankly down at the carpet.

I sat in silence, keenly affected by the shocking loss of support. The scruffy man assiduously brushed crumbs off his trousers. My words, my revelations, would be swept up later with the coffee cake crumbs.

I kept myself from flying apart until the meeting ended, when I sprang out of my chair before the conversations began. Audrey reached for my arm, but I was moving too quickly. I left my coffee cake on the floor by my chair and put on my jacket as I walked, looking down at my sneakers. The lobby seemed huge as I strode quickly across it, gratefully stepping out into the fading late afternoon light. I breathed in deeply, feeling the cold rush down into my chest, and willing the heavy door shut behind me. My car, where was it? There, over at the edge, near the solitary young maple tree. It was warm inside with captured heat from the setting sun. As I drove away, I saw someone in the doorway, watching.

I drove in silence for a long while, radio off, not thinking. There were few cars on this quiet Sunday, and the sun drew long tree-shadows across the road. I finally flipped on the radio, turning it up loud when I heard a familiar refrain. Mick Jagger, singing about wild horses. The slow guitar chords pulled at me, as Mick sang of broken faith and tears that had to be cried. The music boomed, filling up the car and soothing my hurt places. Mick understood. His words crept right into my twisted emotions and smoothed them out. He knew about pain, heck, he even celebrated it and made it beautiful, without saying that all was going to be okay. Because just then, I wasn't so sure that it would.

Suddenly I was weeping, huge gasps shaking my chest and a flood of tears blurring my vision. I pulled off into a vacant lot, turned off the engine, and gave up, wailing until my throat hurt, until my ears rang, until I couldn't wail anymore. The hope was gone, the hope that some day he would explain, some day he would apologize, some day he would look at me and say, "Oh my gosh, honey, what have I done? I'm so sorry ..." It was never going to happen.

Eventually my racking sobs stopped and I felt myself aware again of where I was, who I was, how old I was. The car's windows had fogged up with the intensity of my outburst. I sat in silence, breathing, coming back into my own skin. The wind picked up, sliding around the car and whining at the windows. I stared out into the dimness, watching the light die as the sun finished disappearing behind the hills.

I opened the windows and waited while the fog cleared, then drove home. A hot shower. That's what I needed.

When I crept into the living room, Tom agreed. He settled on the couch, saving me a place next to his furry self.

•   •   •

The shower felt good, but only my skin was refreshed. After feeding Tom, I sank into the couch, reached for the afghan and pulled it over my feet, tucking them underneath me. I pretended to read my book as one of my housemates briefly joined me. I barely noticed when, after a few minutes, she said goodnight and padded down the hallway to bed.

I think Tom snuggled in by my side, but it felt like a dream. I was shrinking, getting smaller and smaller, while I stared at the book on my lap. As I shrank, the world around me faded, all hard edges lost, sounds deadened, sensations dulled. I wondered if this was what it felt like to die, simply letting loose all earthly connections, quietly floating away into nothingness. It wouldn't be that hard. A quick snip, the string severed, then I could lift up out of my sad aching body and leave everything behind, floating over the trees, lost to sight, a kite with a broken string. It would be better that way, just to be gone. Quietly gone, no fuss, erased from memories and places and events and time. Never to have been.

The world drew further away from me, losing its colors. Even Tom existed on a different plane, his soft gray fur a cloud, just faintly visible, as if across a great chasm. I stood up, feeling weightless, unmoored, and went into the kitchen, barely registering Tom's quiet complaint. I saw only my feet crossing the worn carpet, one toe showing out of a hole in my brown socks. The edges of my vision blurred as if I was following a dimly lit tunnel. I stood at the kitchen drawers. Something hard was in my right hand, and I wondered how it had gotten there. Who had placed the knife in my grasp?

The edge was shiny, unpleasantly glaring even in the dim light. I turned it curiously in my fingers, tilting the blade back and forth until my reflection stared back. My eyes looked dead inside, hopeless. The blade felt dull against my wrist, but the blood ran freely. Red. So red, dripping across the blade and down the handle, warm and slippery against my fingers. Suddenly the knife fell from my grasp, clattering onto the linoleum at my feet. I stared at my hand, wondering at the wet streaks left behind. I felt a sting, a small awakening, and saw the blood already beading along the wound.

Is this how it could work? Just bend over and retrieve the knife, then slowly draw it back along the wound, deepening it, gouging further and further until the physical pain matched my inner devastation? The string connecting me to life could finally be cut and my suffering released, rising up and away, out of this all-too-painful knowing. I was not good enough, I was terribly flawed, scarred unrecognizably, forever maimed, desecrated. It would be better to leave, and by leaving, finally gain the peace of oblivion. It would be better. I wiped my hand off on my jeans and leaned down towards the knife, eyes blurring with unfelt tears. Then my fingers touched an unexpected soft place, and I looked down, squinting, into Tom's concerned face. His good right eye was wide open, searching deep into mine, wondering. He made a small sound, a question it seemed, and the world came rushing back.

I collapsed onto the floor, boneless, the knife left forgotten by my side. Tom settled soundlessly beside me, curling his tail carefully around his front feet as he held my gaze. I touched his head gently, wondering at his sturdy frame, even though the rest of my world had withdrawn so far away. "I'm sorry. I'm sorry." Who was I apologizing to? Would I have left him forever? Would he have blamed me for my weakness, for running from the pain, the misery? My tears fell freely now, and this time, I could feel every single one.

It seemed hours went by until I heard footsteps cross the living room, and I sat up suddenly, holding my wounded arm close to my body and wiping the knife off on my jeans. Tom stood up, glanced at my face once more, and slipped out of the room. My housemate stepped into the kitchen and looked at me quizzically.

"Dropped it," I mumbled, scrambling to my feet and putting the knife in the sink. I rubbed my sleeve over the blood drops on the counter.

"Wow, this kitchen is a mess!" she said. "We got any milk left?" The question came from another lifetime ago.

"Sorry, I'll get to it now. Yes, I think—"

She opened the fridge and poured herself a glass, "G'night, Amber."

"Night."

I heard her footsteps receding down the hall, her door closing. I picked up the phone, hearing its tiny dial tone. I slowly dialed Lisa's number, watching the rotary click around, pausing so long between each number that I almost forgot what I was doing. Tom appeared in the doorway, then silently came to sit at my feet. I put my hand on his head, counting rings, one ... two ... Then her voice came on, her solid, dependable, friendly voice, and for a moment my breath caught in my throat.

"Hello? Hello? Who's there?"

"It's me, Amber." I picked at a stain on the tablecloth.

"Amber! How are you?"

"Fine, well, not so fine. I had a ... meeting ... Al-Anon." I got a glass of water, the phone cord coiling and quivering over my shoulder. I took a swallow, soothing the dryness in my throat. Then I sank down on the kitchen chair, the air whooshing out from under the vinyl. Tom hadn't moved.

"Great! But maybe ... not great? Sometimes the things people talk about are kind of overwhelming." I imagined her eyes crinkling in concern, her gaze intent.

"Yeah, well, they were fine. It was me they didn't like. I shared some stuff, and they were kind of, I don't know, disgusted?"

"No! Amber, how awful! I'm so sorry that they didn't support you."

I relaxed a tiny bit at her outrage. "Yeah, maybe I should find another group."

"Did you talk about your dad? His alcoholism?"

I opened my mouth to speak, my heart fluttering in my chest, my hands quivering. The blood had dried on my wrist, leaving a streak down onto my sleeve. I pulled it down over the wound, then slowly drew my feet up onto the edge of my chair. They fit, just barely. "No ... he's a ... friend ... who just comes by now and again, and sometimes things get a bit weird. If I could only deal with him, then I could make things better." I told her about my plan to keep beer out of the house.

"Well, I'm sad that this person is bothering you, and that your support group let you down," she was silent for a moment, then took a big breath, "You need me to come over? I will if you want me. I'll be there in a second."

I fought to hold back my tears, but they won, again. I was surprised I had any left. At least these were quiet ones. "Thanks, Lisa. I really appreciate it, but I feel better already."

I tried to smile at Tom, who was still watching my every move.

Lisa said, "Hey Am', let's get together sometime soon, okay? Maybe that bike ride you've been talking about?"

"That sounds good." I gently set the receiver back into its cradle, then turned on the tap, holding my arm underneath the stream. I rubbed soap over it and examined the wound. It was still oozing, but a couple of bandage strips would be enough. While the sink filled with hot, soapy water, I stared out at the moonlit tree limbs. The soap bubbles sent their perfume into the air, tickling my nose.

I washed and dried my dinner pots and dishes left from before the meeting, putting them away quietly in the cupboard. I pulled the drain and watched the water swirling down. "It's gonna be a cold night, Tom," I said. "We'll need our blanket." He agreed.

CHAPTER 29

The next morning my eyelids were swollen and tender. Sleeping after crying makes my eyes hurt, as if the suffering continues, amplified, during the night. I stared at my reflection in the bathroom mirror. I looked terrible. Maybe a run and then a hot shower would help erase some of the evidence. At least I didn't have any meetings scheduled at work. My wrist was stinging and uncomfortable. I peeled off the bandages, seeing that it had scabbed up, but the edges of the wound looked red and sore. I didn't know if there would be a scar.

I headed out for my run, and the exertion smoothed down some of the ache inside. Back home again, I turned the shower up extra hot, letting the water pour across my tender eyelids. I felt a stinging on my arm. It was the wound. I had forgotten about it during my run. Suddenly my vision narrowed to a pinpoint focus and I drew my hands up to my face. I was remembering other nights, long ago. Crying silently, afraid to make a sound, fearful of what might happen if he heard me. My whole body had ached to yell it out, to scream my pain and outrage and confusion as loud as my voice could get. But I never did.

There had been no one to turn to, no one to listen. By the time I knew that something was very wrong, that other fathers didn't visit their daughters' beds, my mother had been gone for a long time. I wonder what she would have done if she had found out? I imagined her strong arms taking me up, surrounding me with safety and a fierce protectiveness. Would she have chosen me over him?

I soaped up my hair and stood in the flow of water, watching the foam cascading down my arms. I imagined my cares sluicing away down the drain. Would be nice, I thought, if unhappy emotions could just be rinsed off like the dirt left over from a dusty run.

Breakfast was welcome. I ate quickly and then said goodbye to Tom before I headed out to the car. "Another day, another dollar, Tom." I turned to look before I got into the car, and he meowed soundlessly behind the window glass.

•   •   •

"Amber, you gotta see this. It's new footage from France. HAA has gone international." Marlene hurried me into the projection room. I don't think she noticed my red eyes, but I was grateful for the darkened room.

I sat transfixed, watching video footage from a *foie gras* farm in France. One by one, the geese were grabbed roughly by their necks, then squeezed tightly between dropping-encrusted denim-covered knees in a horrible parody of my gentle work with the young Canada goose last fall. Rather than careful gentle movements to minimize fear and pain, these men worked quickly and efficiently, with the total disinterest of those who torture.

The goose struggled to avoid the metal pipe shoved down her throat by the workers. After the pipe was in place, the man flipped the valve which pumped the bird full of food, much more than she would naturally eat, making her liver grow huge and fatty in a few short weeks. *Foie gras*. It sounds better in French. It's supposedly a delicacy, but fatty liver is not something I would ever eat, especially now after seeing the force-feeding which produces it. These birds were a pale wretched shadow of the geese I had cared for in the past.

They didn't even move away from the camera. They were depressed, dull-eyed, and silent, too exhausted to attempt any sound, let alone the outraged honks of a healthy bird. Their plumage was dirty and ragged, in such a state that would only be seen in severely ill birds. Almost like a ballet, healthy geese reach back and rub their cheeks against their preen gland at the base of their tail to collect bits of oil, which they studiously rub over their feathers. Then they carefully pull the feathers between their upper and lower bills to smooth out each one and keep it neat, oiling it against the ravaging effects of moisture and the normal wear and tear of flying. Feathers are an important buffer between their skin and the cold, the heat, or the wet from their beloved lakes. Without grooming or swimming, their feathers become ragged, dirty, and separated.

Glad I wasn't there. The smells alone would be overpowering in that place of horrors. I thought of a lady I met at a recent HAA *foie gras* protest. Dressed in a fur coat, she had come out of the restaurant and was staring at our posters of manure-stained geese crowded into the force-feeding sheds. "Ducks just poop all over the place, that's why their feathers are so dirty," she said, her red lipstick bright in the afternoon sun.

I wondered if she thought birds should be using a toilet. I imagined people crammed into a barn, with only enough room to sleep sitting up. How long would it take them to get smelly and dirty without bathrooms or showers? Geese aren't meant to be crowded into one place, no water for swimming or bathing, stuffed so full that they never again experience a normal healthy appetite for enticing foods. Strange how overabundance can be just as horrible as starvation.

The video ended and Marlene turned on the lights. "What's funny?" she said. She pushed her glasses up on her nose and peered at me before shrugging, then sat down and began studying her notes.

I stopped smiling. "No, no, it's not funny, I'm just thinking about the people who heckled us at the protest, and what their expensive clothes would look like after just three days in a place like that." I pulled some strands of hair off my face where they had come loose from my ponytail.

"Yeah, can you imagine, maybe then they'd understand that this isn't right. But I dunno—they like their fatty livers pretty well." She glanced down at my arm. "Did you hurt yourself?"

I pulled my sleeve down over the bandage. "Yeah, my arm got between my knife and my carrot last night." My face felt hot. "And they want everyone to know that they can afford it."

"Ouch. Yeah, that's the thing, you know, it's like a status symbol," Marlene said, "I wonder if that's the way to fight this? Instead of a status symbol, make it a mark of shame, of inhumanity? Like the fur coats covered in blood. But I really wish we could just storm the sheds and pull those poor geese out into the sun. Wonder how long it would take before they ever wanted to eat again?"

"Yeah, wouldn't it be great to bring a bunch of muscular men, rip down the fences and carry the poor birds out into the open air? Can you just imagine the geese having a swim in a clean pond after so many weeks jammed together in that horrible dark barn?" I held my arm still, trying to ignore the itching.

"Wow, that would be cool. I'd date a man who would do that for the geese," she said, "especially if he didn't mind getting feathers in his hair."

We laughed together. I imagined Marlene arm-in-arm with a hulking smiling football player, pulling bits of white fluff out of his eyebrows.

"Well, you know, that'll be the rage some day, probably," I mused.

"But I just don't know about getting any deeper into this issue. Where it would really count would be at the farm itself, rather than at the restaurant, when the geese have already been killed. Some food on a plate doesn't have the same impact as these poor birds do in person. People would get this. But we're not producing *foie* here in the States. Yet."

We talked more about plans for the film, and whether it could be useful in our campaigns. Marlene was not enthusiastic. She had to balance our limited time, employees, and funds with the likelihood of making a difference for the animals. "I wish we could save them all," she sighed, creaking up out of her chair and turning off the projector.

"Me, too." I wondered if some things were just lost causes.

CHAPTER 30

The sink sprayer head bucked powerfully in my hand as I sent soapy water cascading off a row of plastic cat litter trays. Loud rock music played from a transistor radio high on a shelf. It was our monthly service day at the local animal shelter. Some HAA employees complained about this required work, citing article deadlines, meetings, and other unfinished work that seemed more important, but to me, it was a vacation. No decisions to make, no suffering to witness, just cages to clean and floors to scrub. No hecklers, just happy families and adorable cats and dogs. Our work freed up the employees for more outreach into the community, thereby placing even more animals into new homes.

I toweled the boxes dry and carried a stack of them down the hall into storage. On my return, I passed the adoption ward and heard a high-pitched, excited voice. I turned into the ward, my wet sneakers squeaking on the linoleum.

"Ooh, look look look!" a little boy with a cowlick exclaimed to his mother, "Can we get that one? Please? Please?"

His mother laughed and asked me if she could take the golden retriever puppy out of her cage. The pup was wagging so hard her entire rear end moved from side to side, her tail making a drumming sound as it thumped against the stainless steel walls of her kennel.

"Of course, here. You sit down, and I'll get her out for you." I handed the gangly loose-limbed pup to the boy, settling her carefully into his lap.

"She's going to be pretty big, look at the size of her paws," I said, smiling and scratching her behind the ears.

She immediately flopped over in his lap, her big brown adoring eyes gazing upwards, begging for a belly rub. The boy obliged, grinning from ear to ear. He was mesmerized into silence, his small hands slowly moving through her soft fur. She licked his face, and he shrieked with laughter.

I looked over at the next cage in the row. I could empty it out and scrub it, making it ready for a new arrival. But then I noticed deep blue eyes peering over the edge of the cat box. A tiny white kitten was huddled in the space between the box and the rear wall. I reached back and stroked her gently between the ears, hoping to lessen her fear just a bit. Her body's tension eased slightly, and her eyes closed. I hung a towel over the bars of the cage door to help her feel safer, protected a bit from all the barking and the clanging dishes. Too young for life without her mother.

It was not all happiness here. Old and sick animals inevitably came in, but the shelter could not afford costly medical care or surgeries, so some were euthanized quietly in the back rooms. I thought about Tom. Would he have been adopted, or would that cute white kitten with the startling blue eyes have taken his place? I was lucky to have him home with me. I laid my hand briefly against the towel, wishing for goodness to come her way, and left to scrub the refrigerator with Lisa.

"Don't you just want to scoop them all up and take them home?" she asked.

"Yeah, but I think they'll get homes. This place does good work."

"Yeah," Lisa said, "but I still want the cute fuzzy ones on my couch. And someone else can clean the cat boxes."

I laughed, "Yeah, perhaps after they're done with that they can walk your dogs and then come clean my kitchen. Or scrub this fridge."

Lisa nodded vigorously and then left for more hot soapy water.

By the end of the day, the place sparkled. We drove away, smiling and content.

CHAPTER 31

"It's this way, Chris." I ran up the trail, following the narrow break in the desert scrub. The sun was heavy on my arms, but the breeze reminded me that colder weather wasn't far away. I avoided an inky black beetle on the path, warning Chris, "Watch out, stink bug!" I remembered my Mom's story of the mouse's stink bug dinner, and how he would first stuff the bug's rear end into the dirt, preventing the release of any smelly secretion.

"Dinner is eaten head first, because, you know, brains are the best part!" Then she'd pat me on the head and tuck me in. I would shiver dramatically, my hands wrapped tightly over my scalp, and she'd laugh and kiss my fingers. "Don't worry, your brains are much too big to confuse any mouse who lives around here." Then she'd tickle me until I screeched with laughter.

"Oh, yeah, so you're gonna make a race of this, huh? Can't take all day, right?" Chris joked, panting, coming up hard behind me.

We stopped suddenly as a fat brown lizard with little horns scurried across the path, disappearing under the wicked-looking spines of a cholla cactus. Wiping the sweat from our faces and sipping water from our canteens, we stood for a bit, inhaling the clean scent of sagebrush. Standing close, he lifted a strand of hair off my cheek. "To him, you must look like quite a monster." His bright red shirt was damp and smelled of laundry soap.

"Did you know those little guys eat ants? Don't you have an ant problem in your kitchen? Maybe you should bring him home. You could charge rent in ant carcasses."

Chris lightly punched my arm. We headed on at a more sedate pace, the cool air rapidly drying our skin, working up the side of a hill bordering a narrow canyon. We wanted more mileage under our boots before heading back, but the drive there had taken longer than we'd planned. The sun was past its high point and threatening to begin its descent.

"Hey, what do you think about Mexican takeout for dinner tonight?" Chris said.

"Really? Here we are on top of a mountain, nothing in sight but scrub brush as far as the eye can see, endless incredible poster-blue sky, and you're thinking about refried beans?" I laughed and touched his arm. "But you're covered. I got that spaghetti sauce already made, remember?"

I pointed to a pair of vultures soaring above us, floating just by the power of thought. I wondered if they had their eye on something, or whether they were just up there to get away. "What do vultures think about?"

"They're thinking about what a tasty meal you'd make if you would just stop moving." We laughed together.

Finally reaching the top of the rise, we gazed at the hills spreading out before us, a range of brown, gray, and yellow ridges curving away into the horizon. In the distance, something was moving, perhaps a pronghorn, picking his way along the top of the ridge, briefly silhouetted until he disappeared, stepping down the other side. I sighed, and Chris came closer. We watched the clouds move away, so slowly that their motion might just have been from the turning of the earth beneath. I leaned towards him and we kissed gently. His lips tasted salty, but underneath the salt there was just a hint of something sweet. Then, by mutual unspoken consent, we turned back down the trail.

• • •

It promised to be a good evening, finishing up a great day. I had the house to myself, as my housemates were all gone for the day. Chris had headed home for a shower, promising to bring something sweet for afterwards. I sniffed appreciatively, knowing that he would approve of my spaghetti sauce. And I had decided I liked chopped garlic on bread after all.

I was vacuuming around the couch when the screen door banged shut. I smiled and pulled the awkward machine around a few more times, covering the last bit of carpet. Then a meaty hand landed on my shoulder. I jumped, shocked, and saw my dad standing there, too close. The half-smile on his grizzled face wavered between anger and obsequiousness. The sound of the vacuum died, leaving us staring at each other. I wished I could pick it up and vacuum him out of the air, but instead, I pulled the plug and began wrapping the cord onto its holders. He stepped closer, touching my sleeve, and I flinched, unable to disguise my hatred and disgust. Whether it was disgust of me or of him, I wasn't sure, but he jerked his hand back, and his smile faded.

He pursed his lips and huffed, then headed into the kitchen, where I heard the fridge open and beer bottles clinking. Suddenly my insides exploded and I ran towards the kitchen, leaving the vacuum slumped on the floor with most of its cord in a pile. I shouted, "Those aren't yours! They're my housemates'! You can't come here anymore!" My socks slid on the linoleum as I came into the kitchen, panting, horrified at what had just poured out. Was that my voice? But I couldn't stop. "Go! I don't want to see you anymore! Leave!"

"Wha—" he began, and I moved towards him, the power of my anger pushing before me. He flinched, setting his beer on the table unopened, his eyes widening. "What's got into you? Got your period or something? You on the rag?"

"Just get out! Get out! And never come back!" I shouted, my throat feeling strange, but somewhere deep inside a small girl woke and took a huge breath, hoping against hope ...

He raised a hand and pointed at me as if about to speak, then dropped it and turned away. I followed him, vibrating with an immense energy that I had never allowed before; but not quite believing that he would go. Yet he did, walking jerkily to his truck. His movements were disorganized, as if he had forgotten what to do with his hands. He stared back at me from behind the wheel for a moment, then grimaced and leaned over to start the engine. I watched him from the doorway, still breathing hard, a fine trembling all throughout my body. As the truck moved down the driveway, I let out a huge breath. He glanced at me again, scowling, before accelerating onto the road, too fast.

Suddenly I was laughing. I slammed the door and yelled, scaring Tom, who had crept out from the bedroom. "It's okay, Tom, he's gone!" I was almost dizzy with a mixture of relief, fear, amazement, satisfaction, and remorse. "He's gone, he's gone," I chanted, feeling like the little pig in the brick house. I had chased the wolf away from the door.

I sat down on the couch, still shaking, wanting to cry and laugh, all at the same time. Tom came over quietly, and we sat watching the sun's rays glittering in the dust from the vacuum. A bird called outside, then I heard a car in the driveway. Tom's warm fur felt soft under my hand, but just underneath there was a muscular hard frame. I rubbed his back and thought about the space inside me. It was bigger now.

Chris came in quietly, a grocery bag dangling from his hand, asking about the truck that he had seen accelerating away from the house, "Who was that dude? He nearly clipped my bumper!"

"Dude? You are funny. He was just some salesman. Come on and taste the sauce. I think it needs a bit more garlic." I led him into the kitchen.

"I know you like chocolate, so here's some frozen dessert—a reward for all our effort today." He set the carton in the freezer.

I lifted the lid off the saucepan, holding out a spoon. Steam lifted from the deep red sauce, dotted with chunks of garlic.

Chris didn't notice my trembling hand. He took the spoon from me and delicately blew on it before tasting. "Mmm. Seems just right. I got the bread here, and I mixed up a new salad dressing I thought you might like." He turned and put his arm around my waist. "You're shaking! What's up?"

"It's nothing, I'm just glad to see you." When he wouldn't look away, I added, "Maybe I'm getting my period or something." I fought a crazy urge to laugh.

He gazed at me for a moment, then abruptly began collecting silverware. "That your beer?" he asked, smiling. "You gonna have one after all?"

"I think my housemate left it out." I returned it to the fridge, condensation wetting my fingers. I filled our plates with piles of noodles and large ladles of sauce, then turned to find him standing right behind me.

"I got you something. Do you have one of these?" He was holding out a Rubik's cube. "I dare you to solve it before tomorrow."

I shook my head, grinning, set down our plates, then took the brightly colored plastic cube and experimentally twisted one layer around. "I don't think that'll happen."

We settled at the table and I scooped up a large mouthful of pasta. Chris twirled his fork absently in his noodles. Usually he ate faster than me.

"Something bothering you?" I asked.

"Yeah, there was a news story on the way here. Made me so sad." He picked at his noodles.

"What was it?"

"A baby they found in a trash dump over near Santa Fe."

"Oh, Chris," I stopped eating and raised my fingers to my lips.

"Yeah, you know, we fight for rats and cats and other animals, but sometimes I just wonder, if people do stuff like that to each other, then how can we ever convince them to care for geese and cats and horses and dogs?"

I sighed and looked down at my plate, then up at him. "Well, all the people at our gala last night cared. They were paying pretty big bucks for their dinner," I reminded him. Our annual fundraiser had gone well, with over a hundred guests. Most of them stayed late, drinking and dancing.

"That's true. God bless those people and their money. They really help us out. And an appreciative crowd is nice for a change."

I agreed, "Besides, I think it's the same. The person who cares for other people usually also cares about animals."

"You really think so, Amber? Most people think that we are all a bunch of human-haters. Besides, who wouldn't be, after what we've seen? You've heard the things they yell when they drive by our picket lines."

"Yeah, well, maybe those kinds are the exception. The angry ones. The loud ones."

Chris jumped up from his chair, walked around the table, and wrapped me in a bear hug. "I don't know, man, but I'm glad you're here safe with me."

I hugged him back, then leaned away and wiped a bit of spaghetti sauce from his face. "You wasted it."

He took my finger and popped it in his mouth. I wriggled away, my stomach going tight inside.

"There, no waste," he grinned, relaxing back into his chair and examining his salad.

. . .

Later we lolled on the couch and watched *Magnum, P. I.* I sighed, sinking back into the cushions, my hand idly stroking Tom's fur. Tension I didn't even realize I had was slipping away in a delicious slow retreat. Chris shifted closer, lifting his arm onto the back of the couch behind me.

"That's a bottomless sigh. Do you really hate it that much when Magnum kisses somebody?"

"Well, he's kind of necessary to the story, you know? Somebody has to do it. Just like Captain Kirk in *Star Trek*."

"Yeah, I guess. I know you like Spock better. But not everything's about being smart."

I grinned at him. "In my book, it is. If you don't have brains, then how interesting could life really be?"

"You got a point there, my young Einstein," he stroked my hair away from my face. "But if you have no brains, then how do you know you're missing something?"

I smiled widely, then touched the small scar on his cheek. "How did this happen? Was it really during basketball?"

His body tensed as he drew a breath,"Okay, Spock, you can put down that eyebrow." He took my hand from his cheek and pulled it down to our laps, holding it gently. "It was my Dad. That's how he showed his love."

I held my breath.

"But now I'm bigger than he is." There was a pause while he looked closely at our hands, breathing quietly. Then he sighed and met my eyes. "What were we talking about? The importance of being smart? Well, I take the cake, right?" he laughed, his whole body relaxing closely in to me again.

I sighed, looking down at our entwined hands. "We were talking about not missing things. Like me, now. Can you see what I'm feeling?" I took a breath and smoothed a wrinkle in his shirt, feeling the warmth of his hand in mine.

Chris sobered, and gazed quietly into my eyes. "You seem happy. That's a good thing."

I was teetering on the edge of a vast chasm. I leaned out into space, kissing him softly on his parted lips, and he responded, pulling me closer. His mouth tasted like garlic, with another taste, dark and different. I pulled away, looking back at the screen. "See? There he goes again! He's always gotta have the women going nuts over him, doesn't he?"

"Yeah, I like that too," and he gently turned my face back towards his. We kissed again, this one different, with a subtle feeling of urgency behind it that reached way down deep into me, like a hook, tugging on something soft and very tender. I pulled away, fighting an urge to leap up and run. I turned towards the TV.

"Amber. Something wrong?" he said.

"Sure. You see? Now look, Magnum won't let her leave without a kiss. Does everybody have to be like Kirk?" I was babbling.

"No," Chris lifted his arm away and wiped his mouth slowly, turning back to the screen.

"What?"

"Not everybody's like Kirk," he repeated.

My thoughts were like birds, flying around inside my skull. I couldn't separate one from the other. "You want more spaghetti or anything? I'm getting a soda."

"No, that's okay, I'm full, Amber, thanks."

I paused in the kitchen, pressing the cold can to my lips. My hand was shaking again, a fine tremor deep under the skin, and I stretched out my fingers rigidly, trying to calm myself. *It's okay, you are safe here*, I thought. The Al-Anon greeting grounded me a tiny bit, and my shaking eased. I turned to go and then jumped to see Chris leaning in the doorway, smiling quizzically. His eyes widened.

"Amber. You look like you saw a ghost or something."

I put the soda down and shoved my suddenly sweaty hands hard into my pockets, looking at the floor. "I—"

"I don't have to stay if you don't want me to."

"No, it's not that, it's just that ... I get scared sometimes ... " I trailed off and there was a silence as Chris waited.

Then he straightened up from the door frame and came towards me, reaching out. I stepped backwards without thinking. He immediately stopped moving and raised his hands up before letting them fall back to his sides.

"See? Empty. No threat. You are safe. Amber, what's the matter? Did something happen to you?"

I couldn't speak. I stared at him, wishing I could be anywhere but here. I was full of an echoing silence, and he seemed far, far away from me.

"I'm not a bad person, you know, Amber. You can talk to me."

"I know, Chris, I just—I just—" I stumbled to a stop again, twisting my fingers together.

He stared for a bit, then turned and said he'd be on the couch. I heard it creaking and Tom's quizzical, "Mrp?"

I carried my soda with me, trying to smile at the sight of Tom presenting his belly to Chris. What was wrong with me?

"I'm sorry, Chris, I don't know what's the matter, I—"

"Never mind, it's okay, I get it." He sat rigidly, staring at the TV.

Magnum told his co-star, "Now I know what you're thinking."

I sat down and Chris got up, carrying his sweatshirt, and avoiding my gaze. Tom peered over his belly, then sat up and began grooming his mussed fur.

"Amber, I'm kinda tired. I'll see you at work tomorrow. Thanks for dinner." He reached the door and turned around, "It was good." Then he was gone.

I was stunned. My fingers, twisted tightly together, unclenched and lay still in my lap. After a few moments I picked up the remote and switched off the TV. Tom lay down again and stretched out, gazing up hopefully from between his front paws. I touched the soft fur of his stomach, rubbing in circles, almost as if that could soothe my sudden emptiness. His purr vibrated beneath my fingertips.

What could I say to Chris? How could I explain? I thought about the women in my support group with black eyes and bruises, tangible evidence of the harm caused by their ... abusers. There. I had said the word I heard often in the support meetings. Abuser. Was Mike an abuser? The only injuries I had were invisible painful wrinkles deep inside that got in the way of ... relating to people. Wrinkles that held dark, twisted, powerful fears that erupted at a touch, a word, a smile, a ... kiss. I remembered the professor at the slaughterhouse lecture, her motion picture flickering its grotesque images on the white screen. Had no one else felt the horror that had catapulted me out of my seat and sent me, desperate, clawing for the door?

Suddenly, violently, I wished Mike had hit me, that he'd given me a swelling bruise on my cheek, a black eye, even a broken arm. Instead of invisible injuries, I'd have proof of violence that everyone would understand. I'd have a hurt that could be fussed over, cared for, and best of all, some day, healed. I'd have a reason for pain, sadness, even anger. Who wouldn't be mad if they were trapped inside a plaster cast because of someone's bad behavior? Who wouldn't flinch if someone came too near, jostling the hurt places? The police would come, lawyers would get involved, the courts would tell everyone that the abuser was a bad person, and no one would question my need for special treatment. At least for a little while.

My housemates came home later that night, but by then I had cleaned up the kitchen and tucked myself away in my room with Tom. Their laughter and loud talking seemed alien, coming from another planet. I pulled out a book, staring at the words on the page, until finally they called it a night. Quiet at last.

CHAPTER 32

"Where to?" Lisa asked, tucking the ends of her pants inside her socks, "I know a great route out around the lake, and it's pretty flat." She looked down at her bike and picked a leaf out of the spokes.

"Oh, I don't know, that sounds nice. Bet I can beat you to that first curve down there." I leaned hard into my pedals and took off, spinning my wheels in the gravel at the side of the road. "Whoops!"

"Hey! I'm not an athlete like you, slow down! Do you even know where you're going?" Her voice got further away, snatched up by the breeze. I slowed and Lisa caught up with me, hair blowing into her eyes as she huffed around the corner. "Geez, what are you thinking, that this is a motocross race?" But she was smiling.

"Nah, I just felt like zooming for a bit," I smiled, taking a deep breath and feeling the air moving deep into my lungs. "Lisa, I'm glad you came over." I thought about Mike leaving, and it felt good. And Chris would be back, wouldn't he?

"Well, it's nice out here, now. Pretty soon it'll be too cold for this. Brrr!" she said as the wind rose and curled through the leaves in a nearby ditch. The clouds were moving fast, wisps of pure white heading towards the hills.

We cycled companionably down the road, heading toward the lake. I moved up beside her, feeling reckless. "I've made a good change in my life."

"Really? Tell!"

I looked into her eyes, and saw that her interest was genuine. Suddenly I felt especially wonderful, the sun warming my arms, the leaves skidding across the road, the horizon inviting us, the whole day to expand into, a friend with a good heart, and mine overflowing with excitement. My new internal space was spilling over.

"Well, there's this guy—"

"A guy! You mean Chris? Are you guys an item?"

I grimaced, "Well, I do like him, but no, there's this other guy ..." I slowed down, pulling onto the shoulder and watching a pickup approaching from far down the road. Suddenly I thought about Mike's truck and could almost smell his breath in my nose. But I kept talking, my eyes on the truck, not wanting this moment taken away. "He's kind of a jerk, and last night, I finally told him, 'Get lost!'"

"Wow, good for you, kiddo!" Lisa was really pleased, sharing my joy.

"Yeah, well ..." The pickup was closer, and suddenly I didn't want to be there when it passed us. I pushed off and pedaled down a side street, my heart pounding.

"Wait," she cried, "that's not the way, isn't it this way, over here?" I ignored her, pedaling madly to put some trees in between me and the truck barreling down the main road. What if it was him? What if he knew I was talking about him? Would he still be mad? Did he know it was me? What if he hurt Lisa? And then the truck was past, continuing down towards the highway, dust billowing behind its big tires, the stink of exhaust hanging over the road. I stopped, breathing hard, then turned back. Lisa had followed me down the road, and stopped to wait. She was staring at me. I hoped that my pounding heart wasn't visible through my T-shirt.

"I thought you were starting another race! You okay?" she asked, "You look like you saw a ghost!"

"Sure, I'm fine, just wanted to let off a bit more steam."

But Lisa knew. "Was it that pickup? Is he the guy?" She stared at me, then her face cleared. "Oh! He's the one you talked about at the Al-Anon meeting!"

I chuckled quietly, then sobered. "Probably that wasn't him, but for a second I thought it was. And yup, he's the one that the group didn't want to hear about." My hands were sweaty on the handlebars.

"Wow, he really spooked you. What did he do?"

I breathed in deeply, seeking calm, and we returned to the main road, slower this time. "He just stayed way past his welcome. I really haven't wanted him around anymore, but he kept coming back," I said, "without an invitation."

Lisa came closer, breathing hard, her bike chain rattling.

The wind blew my hair across my face, and I pulled a few strands away from my lips. "I'm going to insist that he should never come back."

Lisa wiped her hand across her forehead. "Well, be sure you have some good locks on your door and keep my number handy. I'll send that sucker packing if he tries anything." She grinned, but her eyes flickered over my face as if searching for something. "You okay?"

"Yeah, no, I'm good, just kind of deliriously happy right now. Wanna move on. Can we go faster?"

"Let's pretend I'm a sedate older lady. I am older than you, so I have the right."

We biked steadily for the next hour until we found a shady grassy spot at the lakefront. We lay our bikes down, took off our shoes and socks and waded into the water, the coolness blissful on our bare feet. The quiet lapping of the water on the sand was soothing after the dusty noisy ride along the road. Even our somewhat squashed sandwiches tasted good.

"You know, you're a great person, and things will work out just fine," she said. I believed her. Lisa knew stuff about people. Our ride back went quickly, both of us enjoying the breeze in our faces.

CHAPTER 33

I drove into the church's small parking lot, streaked with faded yellow lines. My hands were sticky on the wheel, and I wondered if this was a good idea. The late afternoon sun created long shadows on the parking lot, making a distorted outline of the cross perched high on its steeple. The bright pink sign in the window, "Al-Anon meeting tonight, four p.m.," reassured me I had remembered the time right. It had been a few weeks. But returning seemed important, after what had happened. I was tired of being afraid, tired of being the person someone else thought I should be. They needed to see me, hear me. I could do this. I didn't have to mention the sex again.

I walked in and was greeted by a smiling older woman wearing faded jeans and tennis shoes. A new facilitator. Her bright scarf cheered me more than her welcoming grin, but I smiled back, took the name tag, and looked around for a marker. I glanced around at the others. I didn't see the woman from before, with the bandages. There were lots of new people here I didn't recognize, except for Audrey, across the circle. She waved at me. I sat next to her, relieved to see a familiar face. We smiled at each other, both unsure, somehow already exposed, as usual, just from the fact of our very presence in this room. Yet even with so many strangers, I felt safe. Nobody would need me here.

"Hey," she said.

"Hey."

"Just so you know, I think Mike is a sicko. Glad you got rid of him."

"Thanks," I said, staring down at the purse at her feet. A plastic flower was tied to its handle. "He just doesn't know any better."

"Well, he's supposed to. He's your dad. What kind of dad …"

"Hello, everyone!" The facilitator's voice was loud, but I was grateful for the interruption. Audrey leaned back in her seat and crossed her arms, her silver bangles jingling.

We didn't come feeling powerful and in charge of our lives. We came for help, sometimes like slinking dogs, freshly beaten. But at least the beating would not happen in this room. That is, I hoped it wouldn't.

Invited by the facilitator, the first person began, talking about her alcoholic father who was out of a job and regularly yelled at her mother, blaming her for everything wrong in his life. As she spoke, and we listened, her body relaxed, and she stopped twisting her shirt in her fingers.

Audrey talked about her husband and his violence. She was gathering the courage to leave him, but she was worried about her cat. "Mittens is really my only friend, and he might hurt her if I left her behind."

My heart was already pounding. I was next. I took a big breath. "Hi, I'm Amber, and I finally kicked him out." Smiles around the circle. They knew it was a victory, a big one. They could tell. Some of them had been there. "He just wouldn't respect my space, and he wouldn't respect me, and it was time." I wished I could yell it out, but just getting the words spoken was enough. A great weight lifted off my chest, and I knew I would be okay.

Another woman began speaking, and I relaxed. I had done it. It was over. I had not only outlasted Mike in private, but here, in public, I had made it real. I celebrated quietly, deep inside.

As the meeting wound down, I followed Audrey out, saying her name quietly, "I was thinking about your cat, and I had an idea."

She turned towards me, stuffing a tissue back into her sleeve. She looked slightly surprised and somewhat guarded, like a person woken unexpectedly. "What's your idea? I am kind of desperate."

"I work for an animal welfare organization, and we could temporarily take … what's her name—"

"Mittens."

"Mittens. She would be well cared for until you got a safe place for yourself and for her."

Audrey's dark eyes widened, "Wow, that's sounds really cool. Do I call them? Will they charge me? How much?"

"I don't know, but I could find out for you. Want my number? I could also give you their number," I looked around for paper.

Audrey dug into her bag and brought out a chewed pencil and a notepad. As she wrote down the numbers, her face became more animated. She almost smiled, "Gosh, I don't know how to thank you. You know, he can get really nasty, and he's threatened Mittens before. Sounds dumb, I know, but that cat is the only one, some days, who cares about me. I just don't think she's safe from him if I'm not there."

"Your husband, right?"

She started talking fast, her voice low and breathy, as if confiding a big secret, "Yeah, we were high school sweethearts and then got married right away. Thank goodness I didn't get pregnant," she chuckled ruefully. "He's a real piece of work." She tucked my number into her bag. "I used to love him. I think I still do." A few tears dripped down her cheeks. She dug again into her purse and pulled out a dirty handkerchief.

"It's not our fault we're caught in these situations. And besides, he's not a stranger. He's family. It's confusing." I handed her a tissue from the box on the table. Her hands were small, the bitten nails showing specks of bright red paint.

Audrey sniffled and looked at me. "Yeah, I know what you mean. We can love the sons of bitches even as they are hurting us. Doesn't make sense, really, does it?"

"Not at all, but it's how it is, with us."

Her face was dry now, though her mascara was smeared. She smiled gratefully at me, "I'll call you. Or them. I'm gonna do this!" Her wave was cheerful as she pushed open the swinging door.

Tom had settled in for the evening by the time I came home. He looked up from his doughnut bed near the couch, hopeful that I had a tasty snack, which of course I did. I rubbed his ears as he gobbled the bit of canned food, laughing at how his purr continued even while chewing and swallowing. "Purrgurglepurrslurppurr ..." Licking his whiskers when he finished, he joined me while I warmed my dinner.

"I got some work to do, Tom, but you could keep my lap warm for me."

He didn't need to be asked twice, jumping up and settling in to lick his paws clean. While I ate, I did the final edits on an article about rats being deliberately addicted to cocaine. The research subjects suffered incredibly, and for what? I knew that if I was addicted, I sure wouldn't want anybody treating me based on rat data. I imagined small pink feet scrabbling uselessly in the wood shaving bedding, as the small white body is lifted out and pierced with a needle holding poison he would never have chosen on his own. Helpless in the face of someone so much stronger. Someone who should have known better, but only thought of the small furred being as serving his own goals and needs.

I shook my head and concentrated on my article, ignoring the ache in my lower belly. Maybe I had eaten too much. I was looking forward to a soak in a nice hot tub. That tub was one of the best things about this house.

• • •

The hot water soothed me, steam caressing my face and soap smells filling the bathroom. The door creaked open and Tom strolled in through the crack. He always thought I was peculiar. *Why do humans like getting so wet?* his expression asked.

I poked my toe out of the bubbles, and he smacked his whole paw down into the water, like catching a mouse, then ran away in a rush, as if my toe scared him. I could hear his paws scrabbling on the floor as he rounded the corner, running just for the fun of it.

"Excuse me, Tom, would ya close the door after yourself?"

The phone rang as I toweled off, Tom watching gravely from the counter as if judging my technique. "Hello?" It was Mike's boss. Mike had been admitted to the hospital with chest pains.

"What? When?"

"This afternoon. He's okay," he sounded frightened, "I made sure of that before I called."

"What happened?" I asked.

"I was discussing something with him, and he got angry, then just sort of turned all gray and sat down right on the garage floor. I knew something bad was happening."

I thanked him and put down the phone, dressed quickly, then stood for a minute in the middle of the living room, staring around. Had I fed Tom? Was the stove off? Should I leave any lights on? Bring any work with me? Did the car have enough gas?

Heading down the road, driving too fast, I paused at the first intersection, remembering the shorter route by the lake just in time. My hands fumbled with the buttons in my shirt. I had more button holes than buttons. Why had I picked this shirt? I pulled through the intersection and suddenly a deer was in the road. I swerved without thinking before she bounded away, impossibly light-footed in the darkness, disappearing beyond the reach of my headlights. I stopped at the side of the road, breathing hard, my hands shaking on the wheel as I stared out into the field. Could Mike maybe die? Deep inside myself, I felt a tiny spark of hope, before it was quickly buried.

• • •

The hospital lights glowed high above the parking lot, their brightness fading rapidly at the level of the scattered cars and pickups. I locked my car and trudged towards the front doors, twisting my hands together, finger by finger by finger. The skin had long since healed, with only a few reddened areas reminding me of that failed meeting with the science teacher. Seemed like years ago.

Just inside the entrance, I bought a bright bouquet. Red tulips. Seemed almost sacrilegious, bringing such beauty into a place of suffering, almost like celebrating illness; but the crinkly paper gave my hands something to do. I navigated the signs to intensive care, and asked the nurse at the desk for Mike's room.

"Cardiac patient, right? Dad's over there on your left. Nice flowers, but please leave them out here. None allowed in intensive care."

I felt strangely relieved as she took the flowers, while smiling brightly. "Don't you worry, hon'. We'll keep track of them. He'll get them soon enough." She turned away, with a flip of her ponytail.

I jammed my hands deep into my jeans pockets and headed slowly down the hall, staring into each glass-walled room as I passed. All the patients looked the same, gray-faced, drained of life and individuality. Would I even recognize Mike? And then I saw him, looking small inside a blue-specked hospital gown, white sheets pulled tightly over his legs. Wires and tubes crossed his chest, and his head was turned towards the window as if still hoping for a quick escape. A nurse bent over his bed, adjusting the wires and making notes on a clipboard.

"Hi, Mike, how ya doin'?" I said.

The nurse smiled at me and hurried out.

He turned slowly, his bleary eyes searching the room until he found my face. "Amber, hey ..."

"Dad, what happened?"

"Well, you know, the doc said I gotta cut down on fats and stuff. No more burgers for me, I guess."

"I've been tryin' to tell you that for a long time, you know. Heart disease, it's in the family. It's not like you're exempt or anything. Look at Uncle—"

"Just let me alone and be quiet for a bit," he snapped, letting out a big breath as if the anger had exhausted him. I watched his face redden slightly, which looked a lot better than the grayish color it was when I arrived. He closed his eyes briefly and sighed, "I'm glad you came."

"Is there anything you need? How long you gonna be in here?"

"Nah, I got everything," he looked up at me sadly, "they won't let me eat yet, until they're sure my heart's doing okay. They like to starve you in this place. I guess it's good for you or something."

I laughed, "Soon you'll be well enough for some green jello, I bet." I pulled over a wooden upholstered chair, then sat and lifted my legs over the armrest. I studied his expression. "I brought flowers, but they wouldn't allow them in your room."

"That's nice, Amber. You're a good kid." He stared out the window where a lone pigeon sat huddled on the brick sill, just outside the glass, feathers ruffled in sleep.

I sat in silence for a while, glancing at Mike's profile, confirming that it was really him lying there, helpless, and somehow smaller. I watched his hand lift and scratch at the stubble on his chin, remembering its sandpapery feel against my cheek, his wet mouth ... I dragged my eyes away from his face. "Mike, I'm gonna find a soda machine. Be right back." I escaped into the hall.

I walked aimlessly, sneakers squeaking on the linoleum, turning corners until I found the stairwell. The door was heavy, reinforced, and it slammed shut behind me, leaving me alone on the concrete stairs. I sat down on a step and sighed, listening to the far-off voices of the hospital staff. I felt strange, adrift, acutely released from an old fear. I was almost light-headed. Just like in the children's stories, the lion had lost all his teeth, and I was left with only the memory of his powerful muscular body forcing me down onto the bed in a desperate search for solace.

A desperate search for solace ... from what? Suddenly I remembered Mom telling me that Mike's Dad, my Grandpa, had done bad things to him. What things? I didn't know, but maybe the cause of his desperate need for solace lay far in the past. And I was the only one with him, after Mom died.

Now I felt only revulsion. Was that really how it was? Payback for his own hurts? I rubbed at my wrist, the tiny scar still itching. If it truly was a cycle, then it would end with me. I had seen his weakness, and right now, sitting alone on the cold concrete steps, I smiled. Behind me, the door rattled, and I jumped, looking down at the floor, my expression carefully neutral, wanting to protect my new insight from prying eyes. But the nurse, dressed in a starched white uniform, her hair pulled back severely into a tight bun, barely glanced at me as she hurried down to the next floor. I took a deep breath and retraced my steps.

The change was only on the inside. Hidden. But I knew that something was different now, and that other things were changing. Now, I was the stronger one.

I found the vending area and bought a cold soda, the can wetting my hand as I peeled off the pull tab. I sipped the cold fizzing sweetness, listening to the hum of the fluorescent ceiling lights. One was flickering, making shadows jump around my sneakers. I re-tied a lace that had come undone.

I took my time returning, wandering the halls and hearing voices murmuring from TVs in the patients' rooms. Mike was incapacitated and helpless, and yet he didn't need me. Since I was small, I had been the one to take care of him. I was the one he turned to when his grief almost overwhelmed him. Even as a child, I knew I helped him keep going. I kept our world together, so that he could keep getting up in the morning, looking in the mirror, making breakfast, walking me to the bus stop, and going to work. And without my father I would have been all alone in the world. It was a terrifying thought, even more terrifying than his nighttime visits. But now, I didn't know how to help. Maybe this time, it was someone else's turn.

I got back to the room and asked Dad what had happened. He said a customer had argued with him, and that he had gotten mad and thrown a wrench.

"Well, you know they say the customer is always right."

"Yeah, well, he called me stupid on his way outta the shop, and my boss didn't even hear him. But I heard. Then my boss yelled at me, said I coulda hurt someone, and then it was like I just couldn't breathe." He twisted the sheets across his stomach and stared at me, looking almost frightened.

"What is it, Mike?"

"I don't like it here. And I hate being sick. I just don't feel right."

"You in pain?"

"Not any more," he paused, "Aw, Amber it was like an elephant sitting on my chest. What if it comes back?"

"Well, I'm sure the doctors will take good care of you. I bet they told you to eat better and lose some weight, right?"

"Yeah, well, what do they know." He closed his eyes, clearly exhausted. The normal lines on his face were different, somehow, the deep frown creases softened, altered.

"Maybe you should get some rest. I'll hang out a bit in case you need anything."

· · ·

Back home that night, I sat on the couch with a cup of tea, hands steady again. Hospital smells lingered on my clothes, antiseptic and ammonia and another unidentifiable chemical. Mike's pains had not progressed, but the doctors were keeping him under observation. He was probably going to be okay. I had stayed until he drifted into sleep, his chest rising and falling under the starched white sheets. He looked small and shrunken, his hands splayed out on the thin blanket as if pleading for mercy.

I awoke late that night, body cringing from a dream. I reached out and felt Tom's soft fur. My touch pulled out his purr like the pull tab on a zipper. "Buzz, buzz, rumble ..." Wouldn't it be great if humans purred? Happiness communicated without the awkwardness of words. Tom was just happy. No complicated reasoning. Happy to be there, happy to feel my touch.

· · ·

The next day, I attended another Al-Anon meeting. I shared my confused feelings over Mike's hospitalization, and nobody seemed surprised.

"It's like we want them gone, but when they are gone we want them back," said one lady, fiddling with her soft, fluffy turtleneck and tucking her chin inside.

"Yes, we need to replace what's missing when they leave," said a young man with a blond crew cut. He rubbed his head and smiled at us, "But, I don't know how."

I felt almost normal that day, surrounded by other people who understood. The group leader said that these people we love, who hurt us, haven't learned to ask for help. When they hurt, they take it out on us, instead of taking their pain to a doctor, to a friend, or even to a punching bag at a gym. "And then, next thing you know, they'll confuse the heck out of us by bringing home a huge bouquet!" she said. There were murmurs of agreement around the circle.

I breathed a sigh of relief. At least, through this knowing, this inexorable tearing away of the veil that hid the wrongs he did me, I could finally see my own truth. I heard once that the strength allowing us to survive is the same strength that propels us into a better place. I hoped that was true.

My mother had loved flowers. "Oh, Mike, you didn't have to. But what a beautiful bouquet! You know how much I adore black-eyed Susans." Mom arranged the flowers in our best crystal vase.

Dad stood nearby, twisting the green tissue paper in his fingers. He looked pleased. "Well, I wasn't sure they'd have them, but then I saw them in the window. They had roses, too, but I knew you liked these. You deserve them after all you put up with from me."

"Oh, hon, they are perfect! Amber, come see the pretty flowers!"

I was already climbing up behind her onto the chair, my fingers caressing the sunny yellow petals. "Black-eyed nose-ans?"

"Yes! I like that even better than Susans!" Mom laughed, patting me on the head and doing a little dance step. "Shall we do the nose-an waltz?"

I giggled and reached up. She picked me up and we waltzed slowly around the room. I looked over her shoulder as we spiraled towards the door and saw my Dad's face. He sank down onto his recliner in the living room, patting his pockets and dragging the ash tray closer. "Where'd you learn all that fancy dancing stuff?" He sounded petulant, a small boy left out of the fun.

"It's easy. Anyone can do the waltz step. Da-dum-dum, da-dum-dum," she sang. I joined in quietly, under my breath. Sometimes being with my parents was like holding balloons in one hand and a mouse in the other. They didn't really go together, so much. Then my eyes caught Dad's as we twirled into the living room, and suddenly I wanted to get down.

"Where you going, baby?" She gently set me down, then saw Dad in the doorway. Her brow creased and her hands dropped to her sides.

"I found a frog in the back yard. Maybe he's still there." I ran out the back door, but stopped for a moment just outside, holding the door so it didn't slam. I knew how he hated slamming doors. I ran to my favorite tree, smoothing my hands down its furrowed bark. It was an old oak that had escaped the farmer's tractor a generation before the houses in our neighborhood were built. It had

known a lot of changes in its long lifetime. I wondered if it ever thought about its babies, carried off in the mouths of chipmunks and squirrels. Buried for a later snack. Did some get away from the sharp teeth, quietly hiding in the soft soil until green leaves uncurled and tiny bark bits appeared on the brand-new still-soft trunk? How long until it was safe?

CHAPTER 34

"It's the numbers. The numbers make the impact. They catch the reader's eye and make it all real," I told her.

The new girl reminded me of myself from a year and a half ago, barely out of high school and searching for her place in the world. Her brown hair was pulled back in a ponytail with a purple hair tie, and her earrings were tiny blue horses. She sat in my spare chair and stared at the papers in her lap.

I handed her another sheet covered in neat columns. "Take a look at these. You can see the breakdown by species, age, and sex. Remember your focus. We know these animals were harmed, and that they suffered, died even, but we need to get this information out to people who care, taxpayers who don't realize that they are supporting this torture. And our numbers must be accurate, verifiable, and compelling."

Manufacturers are legally required to test pesticides on various species of animals. After forcing the animals to inhale or ingest the poison, the test ends when fifty percent of the subjects die. It didn't matter that the metabolism of each species differed from humans, and that there were numerous alternatives available for these toxins. Rachel Carson's book *Silent Spring* had certainly alerted many people in the 1960s to the poisoning of our soil, but we still had far to go. When bald eagle's eggs began collapsing, because of the accumulation of DDT, killing the babies inside, that got more attention. I guess the eagle was more important, to some people, than the animals listed on this tally sheet. People cared about eagles.

She pulled some hair from behind her ear and began chewing on the ends. "But I don't understand ..." She sighed and rubbed her face.

"Not much to understand, really. It's pretty black and white, unfortunately," I grimaced.

"I know. I just ... well, maybe I can start with this one here." She straightened and squared her shoulders.

"That looks like a good starting place. You can build from there and make a case. Just be sure and include all the animals together, then individual species, then maybe count all the mammals separate from the amphibians." I glanced behind me.

"Got it. How do you do this all day?" She looked straight at me.

I smiled, "Sometimes I think that I'll go crazy and just run out and start shouting down the street, but then I realize maybe I can make a difference, you know?" I touched her sleeve. "Just being here, you are helping."

"But there's so many ..."

"Amber, got a minute?"

I jumped. Chris was leaning over the partition, his arms folded along the top. I looked at his face, and our eyes met for a moment. His gaze was guarded, but friendly enough.

"Sure!" I stood and smiled, "I'll be right back."

I followed Chris into the hall. "What's up?" I tried for a light tone.

"You wanna do a movie tonight? *Return of the Jedi* is playing. Do you like *Star Wars*?" He put his fists together and swept his arms through the air, making a whooshing sound. Then he shoved his hands into his pockets and looked at me with a half-smile on his face.

"Well, it's not as good as *Star Trek,* but Leia is kind of cool." I fiddled with my necklace.

He pulled his hands out of his pockets and examined his nails. There was a small bit of lint caught in his hair, and I thought about reaching over, but decided against it.

"It's worth a shot. What else were you going to do tonight?" he said.

"What time would be good?"

Marlene came out of the viewing room and started down the hall towards her office. "Amber, I need that fact sheet as soon as you can finish it," she said over her shoulder.

"Yup, after I finish helping our newbie." I grinned at Chris and turned away, "When's the movie? Seven?"

"Okay, good," Marlene disappeared into her office.

"I'll find out the times for tonight." Chris had his hands back in his pockets as he strolled away down the hall.

"Amber, could you please read over my article?" It was one of my research staff colleagues, with a scruffy beard and horn-rimmed glasses.

I faced him, "Sure, be right there. And would you talk to our new girl, kind of get her up to speed with what it's like here and give her any tips that might have helped you?"

"Sure, I guess," he adjusted his glasses and peered into my cubicle.

I looked for Chris, but he had already disappeared around the corner. "I'll send her over when I'm done with her. Thanks, I sure appreciate it."

• • •

Later that afternoon I was sweeping out the porch when the phone rang, jangling softly in the kitchen. I ran to grab it, briefly scaring Tom. He returned at the sound of my voice, looking sheepishly at me before relaxing again on the couch. Where was that warm spot again?

"Hello?" My stomach was tight, wary.

"Amber, girl, looks like a really nice night, huh?" Mike. I sat on the couch, the cord coiling behind me around the corner into the kitchen. I cradled the black receiver into my neck while I rubbed my hand down Tom's curved back. Mike was not happy, but at least he wasn't in the hospital anymore. He had been put on a strict diet, and cigarettes were strictly forbidden.

"Yes, Dad, what do you want? You doing okay? Eating right?" I had not seen him since the hospital, three weeks ago.

"Hah! Sure. I was just thinking about your Mom, how you look just like her."

My gut twisted. I was silent.

"I used to tell myself that I was working hard for your mother, that I was putting up with jerks at work so that I could bring home the bucks and buy her nice things. Sometimes I even had good days, when I took something into the shop that was broken, and then sent it back out fixed, even if I wasn't getting paid as much as those banker assholes with their fancy suits."

I listened to the silence over the wires, remembering ... "Dad, you are good at fixing things. Remember my old rocking horse from when I was little? Good as new."

He sighed. "I got Chinese takeout and thought you might like some. Unless you got plans, 'cuz, you know, I wouldn't want to mess up your social life or anything." I could almost see the sneer on his stubbled face. A doorbell rang in the background. "Hold on, Amber, somebody's here. Probably some stupid religious nut wanting to save my ass."

"Dad, no, I—" I heard their muffled conversation, and then something shifted in my mind, and I stood up and followed the phone cord back into the kitchen. I saw my hand quietly setting the phone back in its cradle. I stared at it. Then, moving slowly and deliberately, almost in a dream, I leaned down and unplugged the phone cord from the wall. I stared at the end of the cord in my hand, then gasped when the receiver cord coils moved across the kitchen table. Tom. He had pounced on the cord snaking across the floor, and was now flopped on his side, his rear toes scrabbling at the cord held between his big furry front paws. "You approve, do you?" I said shakily, dropping the cord and grabbing him up in a big bear hug. I danced around the room with him for a moment, then let him down. Tom wasn't a fan of dancing. He sat in the corner and tended to his mussed fur.

I filled a pot with water and set it on the counter, inhaling the aroma of peanut butter cookies that were packed into the horse-and-sleigh painted tin I had taken from Dad's house. Maybe Chris would come in for cookies after the movie. I knew he liked them. And here it was only Wednesday. Friday was our night, before. Before I'd pulled away from his kiss. Since then, it had seemed like he was avoiding me, until today.

"Friday is the best day of the week," he used to say. "The weekend is just around the corner. It's a day of wonderful possibilities. And Amber's spaghetti." We would always laugh together then. Maybe we'd laugh again tonight, and everything would be all right. I'd feed him cookies. "Quickest way to a man's heart, right, Tom?" My brown sugar was stale, which meant bits of sugar stayed hard and gave a special sweet burst to each bite of cookie. My Mom had always liked them better that way, too. I pulled out the cutting board and started chopping onions. Their familiar smell settled my nerves and relaxed me into the routine. If Chris didn't want dinner, I'd just have more leftovers for the weekend. In the background the TV news anchor talked about the weather. Sounded like tomorrow would be a good day, more sunshine, clear skies. Too bad, though, that we got little snow around here. No sleighs in Albuquerque.

Tom, having slayed the receiver cord, padded over and nibbled some food. He sniffed the air, almost squinting.

I laughed, "Not an onion guy, are you, Tom?"

He meowed and settled in at his plate.

"Well, more for me then." I bustled about the kitchen, setting out my best blue napkins and some special glasses—a graduation gift, rarely used. I buffed the outside of the fridge until it shone. Then I started on the cupboards. It felt like a time to celebrate, to start over, maybe. A clean slate.

Suddenly Tom rushed away from his food, disappearing around the corner. I laughed, running after him, in on the game of chase. But he was nowhere to be found. Then I heard tromping steps on the porch and knew, with a horrible certainty, that it was not Chris. I stood frozen, laughter gone. Had I locked the front door?

I hadn't. It was Mike, pitiful and sad, but determined, holding a large grocery bag. He tucked his keys away in his pocket, then grabbed a six-pack of Budweiser from just outside the door.

"Hey, Am', don't help me or nothin', it's okay, I got it."

I wanted to disappear under the couch with Tom, but I was simply too big. On the outside, at least.

"Here," he said, handing over the beer, condensation beading on the cans. "I called you back, but you didn't answer. Didn't you hear it ringing? You need to call the service guys, maybe?" He set the bag on the coffee table, the paper crackling as he pulled something out that was resting on top of the cartons.

"I—" Something inside me collapsed down to a familiar very small space. It happened so quickly I almost gasped. I started for the kitchen with the beer, thinking distractedly that his face looked much better, hospital pallor replaced with his usual ruddiness. I felt his eyes on my back as I turned the corner. Could I stay in here all night?

But he followed me in. "I brought a flower. You like it?" He pulled a tired rose from behind his back, brandishing it like a wilted promise.

I took it wordlessly, nodding thanks, opening the cupboard to look for a vase. Didn't we have one somewhere? Behind the cups I found a chipped glass that was tall enough. I pulled the paper off the rose and put it in the glass, adding water from the kitchen faucet. I set it carefully down on the windowsill. "Thanks, Dad," I stared at him, wanting to explain, wanting him to explain, wanting to apologize, all while a horrified inner voice was telling me to stay silent, bite my lip, do anything except tell him it's okay. Because it was not okay. It was never okay.

He met my eyes, slightly uncertain, but stolid and unmoving. "I hear *Knight Rider* is on tonight. I'll go turn it on. Bring me one of those cold ones."

I pulled a can off the six-pack and automatically turned the heat off under the pot of water. He doesn't usually like that show, saying that KITT is a car mechanic's dumb-ass wet dream. He used to come over on *M.A.S.H.* nights. I joined him on the couch, glancing at his face every few minutes. He had a small smile. Maybe he wanted to talk, maybe he wanted to apologize, say he's sorry, oh so very sorry for what he'd done.

No.

"Ah, 'Ber, what a day. I've got new routines I gotta learn, and here I'm not back from the hospital for what, just three weeks?" He leaned back and stretched his legs out in front of him, sighing. "These new cars've got warning lights on the dashboard, which means cars coming into the shop before the driver even knows something's wrong. I guess it's a good thing, but it's weird because I feel like I'm working with a computer instead of a car engine."

"Yeah, Dad, things keep changing, I guess, even cars." I felt far away. Something was wrong, I had forgotten to do something. What was it?

"I know, and here I am, like an old dog learning new tricks," he grimaced and scratched his ear, digging his finger deep inside. He rubbed his hand over his eyes, then left it there for a moment.

I watched him, feeling like a trapped animal. His presence sucked all the air out of my lungs, leaving me only leftovers.

His hand rasped down his chin, and I looked up, meeting his gaze. "Honey, Am', I'm sorry that I didn't do more."

I sat frozen, unable to think clearly, "Do more?"

"Yeah, to help your mother."

I breathed out, still and silent inside. A tiny flowering of hope crumpled. I heard a car outside, driving slower than usual. "I see," I shook myself subtly inside, like a dog with wet fur, trying to clear my head, and blinked rapidly. Then I straightened my legs out, feeling the carpet between my toes. "What could you have done, Dad?"

"Maybe made her see the doctor earlier, or did more stuff for her, I don't know," he sighed, smoothing his hands down his thighs, "When I was in the hospital, I thought about her a lot. I guess she put up with a bunch of crap from me."

I was afraid to move, to think, and yet a voice deep inside urged me to leap, to take a chance. "She did, Dad, and so do I." There. I had leaped off the cliff, and there was no going back.

"What do you mean? I'm good to you! I take care of you, Amber!" He leaned back away from me and the delicate new possibilities that I had sensed stretched away and fractured, just cobwebs in a sudden breeze. My chest was full of so many tumbling surging emotions; dark sorrow and fiery outrage impossibly interlacing with a fierce love.

Like a drowning man, he pulled my face close, staring almost furiously into my eyes. His glance flickered down to my lips. "You're one of those fucking pacifists. You think everything can be fixed with a 'sorry' and a 'please' and a 'thank you.'"

He let go of me, almost roughly, and grabbed his beer, taking a long swallow. We were silent for a bit, watching the lights moving across the talking car's front grill, its engine revving.

I was numb, my earlier elation completely inaccessible. It belonged to someone else's life.

"Listen," he tried, "I'm sorry. Okay, there, I said it. I shouldn't have gotten so mad the last time I was here. You're my little girl, my special ..." and his thick hairy hand rubbed my back, then laid heavily on my shoulders. I wanted to run, but maybe he was just apologizing, maybe things could get better ... then he pulled me closer, squashing into him, at first a hug and then more like a crushing demand, his breath wheezing out as his face came closer.

I raised my hand onto his fingers at my shoulder, trying to stop the flow of emotion that I no longer wanted. "Dad, it's not about last night. I mean when you—" I was interrupted by a loud knocking, then the screen banged open. I wrenched myself away from Mike's loosened grip, and there stood Chris.

His mouth was hanging open, shock in his eyes, mixed with terrible disappointment and horror. By sheer willpower, I shoved everything back inside, feeling desperately sick.

"Who the hell?" said Mike, pulling his arm back and struggling to release himself from the soft couch. He finally stood, wiped his hand across his lips, and held it out to Chris, "Hi, who are you?"

Chris just stared.

"Hi, Chris, this is Mike," I said, "he was just going. I was waiting for your call. Did you call? We can still—"

"Yeah. No. I called but ... No, I gotta go." He turned away when Mike approached, smiling, his large hand still held out. Chris looked at it over his shoulder as he practically ran through the door, glancing back at me in confusion and dawning anger. Then he was gone, leaving only the imagined echo of his car engine noise and his tires turning onto the road.

We stood there, frozen.

"Who is that kid?"

"A friend."

"Well, he sure had a bug up his jumper. Why'd he look so ticked off?"

"I don't know, maybe you surprised him."

"Well, I was taught to look a man in the eye and shake his hand. I don't know who it is you have for friends, but if they're all like that ... hippies ..." he sighed heavily and crossed his arms over his chest, a small smile flickering around his lips.

Suddenly I saw Mike through Chris' eyes, a graying slightly paunchy sad old man who had inexplicably wheedled his way into my arms. The walls crashed down around me, leaving the shambles of my newfound happiness broken at my feet. I walked dazedly into my bedroom and shut and locked my door. A sudden thought sent me to my knees to look under the bed, but there was Tom, tucked away into the far corner, a dust bunny hanging off of his whiskers. He looked back silently, wide-eyed.

"Hey, hon, whatcha doin'?" Mike turned the knob, then wiggled it, leaning his face close to the doorjamb, "Hey baby, let me in."

I was still crouched on the floor. I stared at the door. Trapped. No way to call for help. Then I remembered unplugging the phone jack in the kitchen. Chris had called. And I never answered.

"Hey, Amber, open the door!" Mike was getting more insistent.

Suddenly I had had enough. I unfolded from the floor, breathing deeply. I imagined gently taking the hand of the small frightened child inside me, hugging her fiercely, then setting her down on the bed, quietly. She would be safe. I would protect her. I stepped to the door, unlocked it, and wrenched it open. I stormed past my surprised father and strode to the front door, opening it and standing there, waiting, breathing hard. My heart was thudding in my chest so loudly that I couldn't speak.

Mike came slowly into the living room, staring into my face, considering, "What, he's someone you really like, huh? All that long hair, what is he, another protester?" His voice got louder with each derisive taunt.

"Dad, just leave. Now. Goodbye." I was trembling, angry enough to forget my fear. Something black and powerful was erupting out of my deepest insides, and it would not stop flowing. I remembered those lost long-ago nights, waiting in the dark for his visits, feeling again the desecration of a small girl who loved him oh so very much. I was no longer that small girl. I had a space inside of myself now, and that space was mine. I had no more room for his neediness, his terrible desperation that was soothed only in dark silent bedrooms.

"But, honey—"

"Dad. Go. Now. Goodbye." I would not bend, I would not accept his imploring gaze, I would not fold into his embraces anymore. I no longer fit.

He stared at me for a long moment, then grabbed his bag from the coffee table and stepped towards the door. He turned back at the doorstep, and said, "I just wanna say goodbye—"

I closed the door in his face, cutting him off, then locked it, firmly. I watched him walk heavily to his truck, climb in, glance back, then drive away.

"I already said goodbye," I whispered, furious at the tears suddenly streaming down my face. I plugged the phone back in before I went to bed.

CHAPTER 35

"Have you seen Chris?" I asked Marlene.

She shook her head, "Protest at McDonald's."

"Wow, it's early, isn't it?"

"They sell the most egg products at the morning rush hour."

"Yeah, that's right. Well, thanks," I set my lunch on my desk while I paced around my small cubicle, twisting my fingers together. Voices murmured, someone laughed, and I felt very small.

"You hungry?" A woman with a bright red knit cap stood against the partition, holding out some popcorn in its foil tray. "What could be better for breakfast?" She laughed.

"Sure, thanks!" I took a handful and sat down at my desk, pulling a napkin out of a drawer. I crunched one at a time, slowly, trying to think about nothing other than work.

The day went slowly, and everything was an effort. Calling charities to quiz them about their animal research, updating my records with the latest information, working on an article about studying human cancer cells instead of cells from mice with cancer. I worked like an automaton, without enjoyment. But at least the work got done.

When I walked into the break room for lunch, Lisa was there. She took one look at my face and wordlessly pointed to a chair at her elbow.

I sat.

She opened her lunch and pulled out a bag, "Fritos?"

I took one, avoiding her gaze, crunching the salty chip hungrily. Hunger. My body surprised me by still needing food, even when the rest of me was working in a vacuum, disconnected from the world. I opened my bag and pulled out my sandwich.

"They really that bad? Stale?" she teased.

I smiled weakly and took a deep breath. "Nah, just that ... Chris doesn't like me anymore, I guess."

"Why do you say that?"

"I've ruined everything." And suddenly the whole tale was spilling out. I didn't care who walked in. I told her about my "friend" Mike, about Chris walking in, the unplugged phone, our plans for a movie, everything. As if my distress formed an invisible barrier that repelled everyone else, we had the room to ourselves until I was done. By the time I finished, I was trembling, and Lisa had her arm around my shoulders. It felt good.

"That's a lot to take in. I can't imagine what you've been through."

In her eyes I saw only a deep concern. Through her touch, I felt only compassion and acceptance. No demands. The churning mass in my belly lightened and calmed.

"Amber. Mike is an abuser, he took advantage of you, and you kicked him out."

I sighed, not wanting the truth. That word again. Abuser. I knew it was true, but I felt complicit in the whole ugly business. My vision clouded as I remembered wondering, so often, why the battered women sharing their stories at the meetings didn't leave after that first black eye, that first split lip. Who was I to judge? I suddenly felt sick. I pulled away from Lisa's arm, rubbing my face distractedly. There was a vibration all throughout my body, a buzz of energy or emotion, with no place to go.

Just then Marlene came in, opened the fridge, and removed a bottle of juice. She looked at us curiously, then headed back out and down the hall.

"Who is this guy? He the one you told me about before? The one you talked about in Al-Anon? You know, we can call the police if he keeps bothering you."

I took a deep breath, "Yes. He's the one, and he's my dad. And he wants to get back in my bed."

"Oh, Amber," Lisa's hand flew to her mouth, then reached out for me.

I leaned away and snatched a tissue from a box on the table, rubbing it over my eyes. Someone might come in soon and I had to keep myself pulled together. I had to get a lid on my dismay so that I could function, get some work done, be around normal people. I sat, feeling Lisa's gaze on my face, waiting for the accusations, the horror, the disgust I knew must be rising to the surface. I waited to see her face change from care and concern to discomfort and disgust, but it never did. Had she heard me?

She reached out and gently touched my arm, her eyes welling up.

I jerked to my feet, thinking only of fleeing, of hibernating in a small dark place like a tiny furry animal.

But Lisa took my hand and pulled gently, insistently, directing me back down to my seat with a serious look. She dashed away her tears, almost in annoyance, then squeezed my hand, hard. Suddenly I felt grounded, pulled back to earth, like my wayward kites of so long ago. Yet I was dazed, and couldn't think straight. I was in danger of breaking wide open, all my rotten and diseased parts irretrievably revealed. This couldn't be—I couldn't handle telling anyone else about my shame. I shook my head, staring mutely at Lisa, imploring her to just let it go, just let me sink back into the woodwork.

She reached both her arms out, as if gathering in a frightened bird, and hugged me, almost fiercely.

I sat stiffly, feeling the warmth from her arms, and she let go, leaning back, looking again into my eyes.

Hers were dry now, and full of concern, along with something darker. "I'm on your side, always. Just know that." Her fierceness pushed away a bit of my own fear and self-disgust. We looked at each other mutely, and I felt the edges of my mouth rising, responding to her gaze.

Someone knocked and stuck their head in. "Lisa, I need you for a moment." She gently put her hand on mine before following him out.

I could hear them talking outside. I sat for several minutes, listening to their voices discussing normal everyday work matters. I concentrated on breathing, expecting my skin to tear, my insides to tumble wetly out onto my hands. I looked down at my fingers twisting, twisting in my lap. My trembling finally slowed down, then stopped. Like an exhausted swimmer gaining an unexpected sand bar halfway across a river, I had reached a bit of solid ground. I stood and opened the door.

They both looked at me, and I almost flinched. Then he thanked Lisa and set off down the hall.

"Okay, good, Lisa, I've got to finish my article." I studied her face, still seeing compassion.

She thought for a minute, "If you need a place to crash, we've got a spare bedroom. Betty would be pleased to have you. If you don't want to be alone tonight. Or whenever."

I straightened up, feeling my back lengthen, the tight muscles stretching out the tiniest bit, and thanked her. We turned in different directions and I walked quickly down the hall, squeezing around a group talking together about weekend plans, stumbling back to my desk, wishing I had a door I could close and lock. I tried to become invisible and lose myself in my writing, but churning thoughts kept me from making any sense. Did Lisa hate me now? Would she wash her hands in disgust, privately, revealing my shame to Tony? What would Tony think? How could I have let this go on for so long? Would Chris ever forgive me? Did I even want him to?

I finally stood, my fingers tired from the typewriter and my brain tired from writing in circles, and started reorganizing my filing cabinet. This was mindless—this I could do.

Sometime that afternoon Lisa quietly appeared with a burrito, placing it on my desk. "On the house," she said, touching me briefly on the top of my head before leaving.

• • •

That next morning at work I made a call. I took a deep breath as the ringing stopped and my landlord answered. "Can you change our lock? My housemates are okay with it, I checked."

"Maybe, why, you got a problem?"

"Well, I just worry about one of my friends."

"I tell you, don't be giving your keys to anyone else, Amber, I'm not gonna do this but the once."

Happily, the locksmith was available that evening. I watched him from the couch, his work belt hanging low and heavy around his waist. "Should be all set now, miss. Here's your key, and spares for the others."

"Thanks," I said, not quite believing that he would hand them over until they landed in my palm and clinked together. My small pot of gold.

CHAPTER 36

The weekend. Two days stretched in front of me, empty and meaningless. I had no desire to run, or hike, or watch TV. I had a library book, something about a war hero gone bad. I sat on the couch petting Tom and trying not to think. A flock of sparrows chirped outside, then flew away together in a rush, wings whirling. Had they made an agreement among themselves before they left?

Tom leaped off my lap and disappeared into the bedroom.

A moment later a bang on the door interrupted my reading, and it was my turn to jump. The doorknob rattled. "Hey, 'Ber, let me in." Mike.

I didn't move.

He tried to peer in, but he couldn't see past the bright new drapes Lisa and I had hung. They were deep blue, the color of a clear New Mexico summer sky. He banged again, more insistently. Could he actually break in if he wanted to? Was the old door strong enough?

I wanted someone else to keep him away, to insert themselves in between Mike's bottomless need and my unspoken, assumed acceptance. I wanted to exist undisturbed in my own skin, feeling the new outlines, like a tender spot on the gum, sore from a just-erupting tooth. Those last teeth we get as teenagers, weren't they called wisdom teeth? Funny.

"Ah, come on, let me in, I just wanna talk!" he whined. He knew I was there. My car gave me away. Keys jangled, and I tensed, but they rattled uselessly in the lock.

Maybe if I waited long enough he'd decide I was out on a run. Could happen.

"I brought your favorite. Chinese food. Ah, come on, babe. Open the door!"

My anxiety deepened as I pictured his big hands crashing through the door. Would he get angry and lose control? I remembered those hands flying around, raging at me and my mom, long ago. His emotions were so tangible they nearly boxed us on the ears, as if they were the most important things in the universe. "Pay attention!" he would yell. And we did.

"What's the matter? Got that new boyfriend in there? I wanna meet him, Amber, come on!" My heart pounded in my ears as I sat frozen on the couch, willing him to leave.

He slammed on the door again, and the book slipped out from my nerveless fingers. He wanted to meet Chris. I smiled grimly, my shaking easing somewhat. Wouldn't that just be so easy? Have Mike come in and shake Chris' hand, just like old buddies? They could laugh together and slap each other on the back and everything would be all right. Or even better, they could fight over me. Chris would beat him up and push Mike out the door.

Right. In my dreams. In reality, Chris had simply left, blind to my need and horrified by what he had seen. Besides, Mike was twice his size. So, I was alone. But I wasn't helpless. I had myself, complete with a new sense of my own unique boundaries. And, stubbornly, I wanted to be the only one within them. The space inside my skin was reserved now, a special exclusive club just for me. Now that I knew I was in there, now that I could feel my own outlines and follow the curves and bends of my own muscles and bones, I wanted to stay, to keep my newfound awareness, and luxuriate in my oneness. To feel that when I moved, my muscles and nerves and blood and bones came along, propelling my body as my mind wished, moving through the world with its sunshine and rain and wind, feeling dust and heat and sweat on my skin, feeling blood pumping and lungs inhaling and senses tingling, all mine.

I shook my head as Tom crept to my side, surprised that he would return despite the continued pounding. But finally I realized that the pounding I heard was only in my ears, together with a churning burgeoning excitement. All was quiet. All I could hear was the quiet hum of the refrigerator, and Tom's purr. Mike had gone. I had done it! I had actually kept the badness outside, resisting the urge to give in to the begging and pleading. I had a new key, and I was keeping it for myself.

I sat quietly, staring sightlessly at the pages of my book while stroking Tom's sides. His warm body lay heavy on my leg, vibrating. The house was so much quieter than I'd ever remembered it being, even when I was the first one home after a long day. I got up slowly, opened the front door, and stood on the shabby porch, looking into the haze over the mountains. I thought about what it would be like without my father in my bed at night.

I had avoided this subject with a vengeance, for years, ever since his first visit just before I started kindergarten. As the years went by, unwilling to admit to the details, I had convinced myself he was an older boyfriend. That's what my housemates thought, and he never set them straight. He thought it was funny. Besides, I always felt that I owed him. I grew up thinking that a daughter is supposed to care for her father, wasn't that what they always say? How had I survived?

I returned to the living room and rejoined Tom on the couch. "Trees, Tom, it was the trees. They helped me." Growing up, I had spent a lot of time out on my own, climbing trees, trying to feel the outline of my skin apart from his. In each new place we lived, I introduced myself to every climbable tree within bicycling distance, just to be ready for that next summer storm. I remembered the muscle-tightening scramble from one branch to another, the reach to the next one smaller as I climbed higher. How far was too high? Moving my feet closer to the trunk as the branches got thinner and the ground disappeared into the leaves beneath my bare toes. The wind rising, tearing loose the leaves, whirling them around my arms and face. Finally alone. Branches too thin for him up here. Wind gusting stronger, whipping through the branches, and the slow groaning sway of the main trunk, like an unbelievably large prehistoric creature waking. Then a quick scramble down—much faster than going up—as the first large drops spattered down, bursting as they hit leaves and bark and face. Skin tingling with the electricity in the air, sluicing away the man smell.

He's gone now, it seems, and things will not be the same. I've kicked the monster out of the closet, and I don't think he'll fit back in there. But I can't worry about it all now. Tomorrow we'll be working all day, loading neglected horses onto trailers and removing them from a farm. Over fifty horses had been left to starve there by the landowner, and many had already died. They couldn't survive on the sparse scrub growing in their tiny fenced lots. So I needed my rest. "Right, Tom?"

He blinked and rubbed his whiskers against my fingers.

CHAPTER 37

That next evening, after a long cold day spent coaxing desperately skinny horses onto trailers, I screwed up my courage and called Chris. We were so busy at the farm that we hadn't had a chance to talk, let alone even smile at each other. I wanted to explain.

"Hello?" His voice made me catch my breath.

"Hi, it's me," I said, cautiously.

Silence, breathing. "Hi." Flat, no rounded edges.

"I'm sorry about what happened the other day."

"Yeah, me too. So, what're you calling about, Amber?"

"Ah, I ... wanted to know if you ..." A long pause.

"Amber, listen, I got some things to do, so ..."

"Yeah, well, never mind. It's just that Dad has been going through a lot lately, and he gets weird when he's been drinking. You see—"

"That guy, that was the creep you told me about before?" His voice receded further and further away, reaching me across another country, another planet even. "He's your dad? Jesus Christ." There was a moment of dead silence, and then the line clicked.

I listened to the dial tone for a while before replacing the receiver gently on its hook. I sat on the couch for a long time, hearing and seeing nothing, until a gentle nudge on my knuckle alerted me to Tom's presence.

He was obviously concerned. I smiled at him. Why did he keep going on as if nothing had changed? How could he act so normal, so ... Tom-ish? Wasn't the world collapsing?

I cleaned out his litter box. He watched appreciatively from the toilet seat cover, as he always did. Then I collected my dinner dishes, slipping Tom's little white bowl into the warm soapy water. The small tasks of a normal day calmed me, averting the incipient internal storm. Really, maybe nothing had changed, except myself, deep inside. Maybe I was the changed one, and only those who deeply cared for me, rather than for what I did for them, only those people would come with me into my new life. Tom, Lisa, they were the beings who loved me in spite of what I could do for them. The others, well, they tugged hard on my heart, but really, the tugs were for them, not for me. They were never for me.

CHAPTER 38

The winter was a long one, tiresome in its details of Freedom of Information Act requests, gruesome cataloging of animal deaths, and researching the terrible suffering of experimental laboratory subjects. It was important to get it right, to note each life lost. No exaggeration, no sensationalizing, just the facts and figures. When taken all together, hopefully the numbers decided whether the campaign would attract enough public attention and encourage action. Regardless, each hash mark represented an individual soul who had suffered and died. What made any one more important than another? Who was anyone to say that having eye liner that was tested safe on a rabbit was more important than that rabbit's eyesight? Not me. Rabbit eyes react differently than human eyes, making them a poor model, in any case. Their corneas are thinner, allowing more substances into the eye. I'm not the one to judge, really, not wearing makeup myself, but I did not want those animals blinded and killed for me, and certainly not for eyeliner.

Today, however, I was looking forward to work, because I had another article nearing completion. It was a good mixture of dry facts and personal connections that spoke to the hearts and minds of our readers. I had developed a style that was meant to draw our caring compassionate subscribers into the discussion. Their letters supporting our work and commenting on my words cheered me and rewarded my efforts. Together, we could get more done.

I discarded my sweatshirt in front of the house before my run, setting it on the side of the crumbling driveway. I'd rather start cold than end my run too hot. As I stepped out onto the road, I was greeted by the liquid loveliness of a hidden bird's song. A few days ago I had spent time listening to recordings at the library, determined to find out who was singing so beautifully. I thought the singer would be someone exotic, like a red-eyed vireo, or a hermit thrush, but no, I found that this song was from none other than the humble American robin. Kind of like the ugly duckling, maybe. Unexpected beauty from the plain Jane of birds.

I headed down the road, hearing the mourning doves with their soft melancholic murmurs. The sun was just rising over the hills in the distance, lengthening my shadow and gilding the new leaf buds on the aspens lining the road. It was going to be a good run, I could just feel it. Some ducks passed overhead, calling to each other as they headed over the trees, looking for water. My legs felt strong, striding down the road, able to go forever, the early morning breeze drying my sweat as it appeared on my face and neck. My lungs filled with the moist smells of a New Mexico spring, sagebrush scents invigorating my body and welcoming me to the new day.

My life was opening up since Mike was gone, and everything was stirring, not just in the outside springtime world, but deep inside of me. He hadn't been back for weeks and the world seemed a bigger place, more exciting. There were possibilities I had never thought about before.

Leaving the robin and the doves behind, all I could hear was the quiet thud of my sneakers on the edge of the road. Not a car in sight this early. The silence was welcome, mirroring my new inner calm, and my insides expanded out towards the horizon. I was running into myself for the first time, instead of away.

I turned down a different road this time, my legs humming from the road and the miles. I passed a community center, and a new notice on the outdoor bulletin board caught my eye. I slowed down and stopped, breathing hard, reading about rowing classes. I ripped off a copy of the information number from the bottom of the notice, and tucked it into the pocket of my sweatpants. A new skill, involving physical exercise and water and boats—sounded like a good combination. But why would anyone need training to row? Something I was misunderstanding?

The mourning doves were still murmuring as I returned home, my muscles pleasantly tired and my skin glowing from the inside. I took deep breaths of the still-cool air, marveling at how the taste and smell of it changed so from day to day, even hour to hour. A dog barked in the distance as I stretched down, touching the driveway with its broken bits of sun-warmed asphalt.

Once inside, I hung my sweatshirt near the door and greeted Tom. I rubbed his ears while I pulled out the bit of paper with its typed phone number. Too early to call yet, so I started the shower. If I still felt like it, I'd call tonight after work.

CHAPTER 39

The week was very satisfying. We successfully redirected a brand-new charity away from supporting the use of animals and towards research based on human tissues and genetics, instead. Our no-fur campaign placed lovely fake fur coats in more stores, and our shelter had a huge run of new adoptions. At times like these, I was proud to do the work. But it was still good to get away and relax. Today I was going rowing.

When I had called about classes, the teacher's voice was bright and friendly. There was a smile in her voice when I said I'd never rowed before and was interested in learning.

"Yes, we offer rowing classes at the lake dock off Governor Street. You interested?"

"Sounds fun! I've taken out canoes before, and had a good time."

"Oh, you'll have much more fun in a shell. Canoes are so much slower. It's like the difference between Fred and Barney's stone car and a Porsche."

The lake was like glass, reflecting perfect images of the trees along the shoreline. I found the boathouse road, following it to a large parking lot ending in an asphalt ramp leading down into the water. A middle-aged woman with a faded yellow T-shirt, jeans cut-offs, and flip-flops came out of a metal-sided warehouse with a weathered sign on it that read, "Governor Street Boathouse."

"Hi there," she said, "you must be Amber?" She shook my hand. Hers was hard and calloused. "I'm Jane. Come on in, I'll show you our boats. I'm so glad you could make it."

We walked into the shed together, our footsteps amplified by the concrete and the cavernous space. The boats rested on metal racks, massive and sleek, shining in the overhead lights. There was a metal contraption splayed out on the concrete floor, looking like a very large insect. It was a practice machine.

Jane showed me where to sit, how to strap my feet into the man-sized shoes, and how to move the oars, scraping them lightly against the ground. We worked for the next half hour, practicing the basics of a rowing stroke. Much more complicated than running!

"It's easier once you get on the water, because then you can feel it pulling against the blades and feel the boat moving in response."

I couldn't wait. Today's lesson was only on dry ground. Next week I'd join the class of beginning rowers. I let out a deep sigh, and realized that I hadn't thought about Mike or Chris for at least twenty minutes. It felt wonderful.

CHAPTER 40

The phone rang, jolting me out of a sound sleep. I fumbled for the lamp, knocking it and my book onto the floor with a crash that sent Tom flying from the room. I followed his indignant meow out to the living room. The receiver was cold against my cheek. "Hello?"

It was Audrey, and her voice sounded strange. "Amber, I don't know what to do—I think he's going to kill me or something," she wept.

I came wide awake, my stomach clenching into a hard knot. I heard a crash over the phone, and she gasped.

"Audrey, you've got to get out of there. Do you have a car?"

"Yeah, but Mittens ..." She was whispering now.

"Get Mittens, get in your car, and get out of there."

"But where am I gonna go?"

I thought for a second, looking at the clock. 2:30 a.m. Then I took a deep breath. "Come here. You can flop on my couch until you find something."

Audrey sighed deeply, a low moan, "I don't know how to thank you." I heard a male voice yelling, then she screamed, "Shut up, you bastard!" and dissolved into more gasping sobbing.

I quickly got her number and gave her directions, then hung up gently, hoping I hadn't woken my housemates. My hands were shaking as I fumbled in my closet for a robe, pulling out my extra sheets and a blanket. I carried them into the living room and spread them on the couch.

Tom was sitting near the kitchen door watching everything.

"It's okay, Tom, I'll keep Mittens in the bathroom for now."

He looked unconvinced.

I sat on the couch to wait, and awoke with a start when Tom pushed his head against my hand. "What, Tom, it's not morning yet ..." then I jerked fully awake, and for a moment could not remember why I was lying on the couch in the middle of the night. Actually, it was near dawn. I stood and stretched, gazing out the window onto the deserted street. The street lights were still on, but the sun's light warmed everything with its morning glow. I stroked Tom, then hugged myself. "She didn't come, buddy."

I left for a morning run after putting out some food for the very pleased Tom. My thoughts were jumbled and confused. Had she been hurt? Had she changed her mind? Were they both in jail? Should I call?

• • •

Later that morning Lisa was sharing her thoughts on my new dissection alternatives fact sheet, and I asked her what I should do. I could not stop thinking about Audrey.

"She called at two in the morning? And then didn't show up? How do you know this girl?"

"She's from Al-Anon. Her husband drinks too much and then gets violent, but she has a cat and is afraid to leave without her."

"Amber, you can't get involved with her. You don't know her, and he could be dangerous, making you a target. They say that the most dangerous time for a battered woman is just after she leaves her abuser."

"You should have heard her husband yelling. It was scary! Should I call the police?"

"I suppose, but probably whatever was going to happen already happened last night."

I curled into myself and put my head in my hands.

Lisa explained that as an adult, Audrey had little chance of receiving help unless she would leave him, or at least call the police if he was hurting her. Even then, the police might believe his word over hers.

"It's hard, Amber, because as soon as the cops arrive, he'll become Mr. Charming, and she's a total angry mess. She'll be the one who looks guilty," said Lisa, shaking her head. "She's just gotta get out of there."

• • •

At lunch I took a deep breath and dialed Audrey's number. My hands felt sweaty on the receiver.

She answered after the first ring, sounding distant and wary, "Yeah, I couldn't find the cat carrier and then when he realized what I was doing he got all sweet and told me I didn't have to go. He got me flowers, Amber. Daisies."

"Well, that's nice, but you gotta get out of there. Go find the cat carrier and come now."

"What? I can't! I promised him I'd make a nice dinner for when he gets home tonight."

I was silent for a moment. "Audrey—"

"I know, it's just that I promised, and the flowers," she trailed off. "Amber I gotta ... go. Thanks for calling." The connection went dead.

I stared at the receiver, listening to the dial tone, picturing wilted daisies set in a little vase. The plastic of the phone felt heavy in my hand. I imagined throwing it down as hard as I could, pieces shattering, scattering across the linoleum. What was wrong with her?

Then I remembered all the times I'd unlocked the door and let Mike into my house. Again, again, and again. I let out a shuddering breath and carefully placed the receiver back on its hook.

• • •

That night, sitting with Tom on the couch, I didn't want to think about Audrey, so I thought about the exercises my rowing coach had taught me. She had been so patient, tucking her hair behind an ear as she bent forward countless times, adjusting my grip or changing the angle of the oar. I felt like a newborn foal just learning to stand, with legs way too long to control. Would it feel better on the water?

· · ·

Saturday I spent curled up with *Lord of the Rings*, sharing hobbit facts with Tom, who always listened seriously, as if he was considering a change. I read myself to sleep that night. But my peace was all too brief. I awoke with a start to pounding on the door. Tom was gone, probably hidden under the bed even before my eyelids fluttered open. "Wha'?" I mumbled, my hands still numb with sleep as I shoved off my covers and pulled a sweatshirt over my pajamas. My stomach was hard, hurting, as I arrived at the door. What would I say to him? Should I call the police?

But it was Audrey, tear-stained, peering between cupped hands through the window at the edge of the curtain.

I opened the door, and it creaked loudly in the silence. "Oh, Audrey, what's happened?"

Her face was bruised, the blood already pooling beneath her left eye. Her hair was hanging in long dark curls all around her face as she picked up a cat carrier at her feet. She came inside, silently, wiping her nose on her sleeve and catching her breath when her sleeve brushed against her cheek.

I pointed to the couch and sat down next to her, glancing inside the carrier at a frightened calico cat. She cowered against the back of the carrier, her wide eyes peering out at me. "This must be Mittens."

"Yes, I got her … I got her safe."

I handed her a tissue from the end table. "And you safe, too. Oh, Audrey, I'm so sorry. He's hurt you."

"Yeah, well …" She tucked some hair behind her ear and wiped at her eyes with the tissue. Then the words began pouring out. "I burned the dinner and then tried to make it right by mixing up his favorite drink, but I messed that up too, and then he started throwing things. I don't think he meant to hit me. He was just kind of going all lunaticky and swinging his hands around, and I got in the way."

"You got in the way."

"Yes, you know, I was getting Mittens out of the room because I thought he might kick her or something ..." Her voice trailed off and she sniffled into the tissue.

"Well, you're here now. In the morning you can call the police."

"What? I can't do that! He's my husband!"

"That doesn't give him the right to hit you! What do you see in him?" Then I wished I hadn't spoken.

"He's really a good guy at heart. He does love me. Ever since high school, when nobody else did."

I brought her my spare sheets and blanket. "Let me get a cat box set up in the bathroom for Mittens."

Audrey already looked half asleep, her breath coming slower as I gently lifted the carrier and brought Mittens into the bathroom. Tom was nowhere to be found. I closed the door and opened Mittens' carrier. She hissed defiantly, and I suddenly remembered Tom's belligerent face, staring out of the carrier's grate as I took him away from his first home. "It's okay, Mittens, you just stay in there if you want to. Come out when things feel right. You're safe now." I poured some litter into a box and set down some food and water. She would be fine in here. I hung a sign on the door handle for my roommates. Hopefully, they would understand.

Audrey was already asleep, curled up under the blanket. I looked at the welling bruise on her cheek. Probably would be better if she applied some ice, but I was not going to wake her. I checked the lock on the front door and headed back down the hallway to my room. It was a long time before I slept.

• • •

"Ya got any cereal?" Audrey was standing in my doorway picking at her fingernails.

I glanced at the clock. Seven a.m. At least it was Sunday.

Tom, pretending to be invisible, glared at Audrey over my hip.

"Yeah, I've got some cereal in the kitchen. Help yourself—"

She was already gone, rummaging through the kitchen cupboards.

"Audrey, look for stuff with my name on it ... it's the cupboard on the far right," I yelled, then put my hand over my mouth. We'd wake everybody, and then I'd have to explain.

"Where's the bowls?" I heard from the kitchen, silverware clattering.

I looked down at Tom, who was staring at me as if I'd lost my mind. "Well, Tom, it will be an interesting few days." He blinked at me, silent.

I joined Audrey. "Drawer to the right of the sink. And keep your voice down, it's pretty early for my housemates."

"Oops, sorry, I didn't realize."

"You are going to have quite a shiner, there."

"Yeah, well, what's new?" She chuckled and touched her eye. "Mittens seems fine. She wants to come out, though."

"I'd rather keep her in there until we can get her settled in at HAA. I don't know if Tom would get along with her."

"It would probably be okay. She's not mean or anything."

"I don't want to upset him, and we can keep her comfortable. I'll find her a spot at work tomorrow."

"What do you do there?"

I took a breath, "I collect information about people doing illegal things to animals and collate evidence so we can help bring attention to it and get it stopped."

"Wow. They got any openings? I can type, I think. I gotta make some money." Audrey poured cereal into her bowl and got up, searching in the fridge. She brought over a carton of milk.

"I don't know, you could call them—sorry, you can't use that, it's not mine. I use orange juice on my cereal. I don't drink cow's milk." I found the juice in the fridge and joined her at the table, moving my chair into the remaining space. Felt a lot different than when Chris sat there.

"Ew! Why the hell don't you drink milk? It's good for you!"

"I don't really like how they treat the cows, and besides it's really meant for their calves, you know?"

Audrey stared at me, her mouth open. "You serious?" She picked up the carton and looked at it. "Orange juice on cereal? What a concept. Is it good?"

I laughed, "I know, weird, huh? Hope you like it."

"Can we get some real milk? Maybe we can go shopping together."

"Audrey, we can get what you need, but have you tried the shelter?" I was twisting my hands in my lap again.

She scooped up a mouthful of cereal and chewed thoughtfully, absently touching her cheek where the bruise was turning darker. "Yeah, I got that phone number, but Amber, I gotta call him first, to be sure he's all right. He's probably really mad right about now."

"Audrey! He's probably still sleeping it off. You gotta stay away. You are here, and that's the first step, right? First, keep yourself safe. He's no good for you, and he's no good for Mittens."

She sighed, leaning back in her chair and fiddling with her spoon. "I know, but I don't really want to go to a shelter. I like my house better. I can handle him."

"Have you looked at yourself? Half your face is black and blue." I jerked out of my chair and walked into the living room, barely able to speak. Mittens called from the bathroom. "You need to give her some breakfast." I heard a chair scrape and the fridge open.

"I found a can. Can I feed her this? I'll pay you back."

"Sure, that's okay." I hugged myself fiercely as I stared out the window. Pretty quiet this time of morning. I dropped my arms, grabbed my sneakers and headed into the bedroom, where Tom was still curled up in the covers. "You got the right idea, sir." I changed into shorts and a T-shirt and brushed by Audrey on her way to the bathroom. The T-shirt said, "E.T. phone home." I liked how the bicycles floated up towards the stars. Free at last.

"Where you goin'?"

"Headed out for a run. See you in a bit."

"Can I hang out for a while? Or is your Dad coming over?" She thought for a moment. "He doesn't hit you, does he?"

"Yes, you can stay, and no, he doesn't hit me," I muttered as I pulled the door closed behind me.

• • •

My breath heaved in and out to a comforting rhythm, and as the trees steadily passed by, my emotions settled. I spit out the saliva building up in my mouth, as if ridding my body of a bad taste. But it was still there, the certainty that I knew exactly why Audrey found it so difficult to leave, to get herself safe.

I couldn't run forever. I had to get back, to be sure Tom was okay and figure out what we were going to do with Mittens and Audrey. I had to be an adult, someone who could make decisions and help get my friend onto the right path. I looked around, thinking that the light seemed different. Had more time passed than I thought, or had something in me changed? I didn't know, and I didn't want to examine myself any more closely. Time to go home.

•   •   •

When I returned, Audrey's car was gone. I walked into the house, calling Tom, who came running out of the bathroom as if he had not seen me for decades.

He was licking his whiskers.

"Wouldn't want it to go to waste, huh, Tom?" I rubbed his head as he settled down for a good wash in the middle of the sofa. "She went back, Tom. I'm sure of it." I found the phone number for the Al-Anon facilitator, and told her what had happened. "I don't know where she's gone, she just packed up her cat and disappeared in the time it took me to have a run. I had to blow off some steam."

"Did something happen?" She sounded concerned, "Does she have any children?"

"No kids. But yes, she had a pretty good black eye. And when she called last week he was beating her up. There was lots of yelling and screaming in the background. I told her to grab her cat and get out of there." My heart began beating faster, remembering.

Tom came close and gazed up at me seriously, unblinking.

"Now that she's gone, I don't know what to do."

"Sadly, there really isn't anything we can do. She's an adult and makes her own choices. We can't force her to leave him."

"Audrey's afraid that he'll get even madder if she stays away too long." I heaved a huge sigh. I thought about Mike, peeling out of the driveway. I could almost taste the dust churned up from his tires.

She told me to call again if I needed to.

I hung up and absently stroked Tom, staring out at the sunlight on the tree out front. A tiny bird was hopping from branch to branch, twisting and turning as if searching for something. He flitted away so fast that it was almost as if he blinked out of existence. I searched for him, but he was gone. My stomach rumbled, and Tom turned over to present his belly. I chuckled, "Well, you, I guess I can help you out, there."

CHAPTER 41

"Marlene, here's my summary of the Draize test alternatives. Let me know if you need any more facts checked," I said, putting my papers on the stack at the corner of her desk. I had had to do some digging, but I had found scientific articles describing the testing of dilute substances on human volunteers, studies of changes in cultured human corneal cells, and also experiments studying the action of the toxin on proteins embedded in gels, instead of spraying the chemicals into the eyes of living rabbits. Satisfying work. I waved away a few fruit flies that hovered, hungry for leftover juice from the bottles in her trash can.

Marlene grunted and bent lower over her typewriter, mumbling something about deadlines.

"You okay?" I asked.

"Sure, but why does everybody keep asking me that?" She jerked her fingers off the keys and glared at me, pushing her glasses up on her nose.

"Just ... nothing. Sorry to bother you." I turned away quickly, and nearly collided with Lisa in the hall. I followed her into the lunch room. "Lisa, what's with Marlene? She's even more grumpy than usual."

"I guess it's no secret. She and David are getting a divorce," Lisa said, pulling a bottle out of the fridge.

I stood in the doorway, my fists clenched in my pockets. "Is there anything we can do?"

"You know Marlene, she'll carry on. Who knows, maybe she'll find somebody more suitable. You never know!" Lisa smiled a bit sadly, offering me a sip of her juice.

I shook my head, sighed and leaned back against the counter. Then I told Lisa about Audrey.

"Good for her! And lucky she had you!"

"Yeah, well, she left this morning while I was on my run. I think she probably went back to him."

Lisa grimaced, then nodded, "Audrey has to really want to get out of there. She has to be ready to be on her own. If there was a child involved, that would be different. Then you'd have to get the law involved."

"What about an animal?"

Lisa explained that if the cat was being harmed, then we could report animal cruelty. "Same as with Audrey, I guess. If she's hurt, then we could call the police."

"Well, she was, there was a huge bruise on her face."

"Even so, first she'd have to stand up and say what he did."

"Yeah, and she's not gonna do that." I turned and left the break room with a shrug, walked back to my cubicle, and slowly sank into my chair.

What would have happened if I had called for help so many years ago? I imagined dialing the number, trying to be quiet, then explaining ... what? That my dad came into my bedroom almost every night and touched me in places that didn't feel right? How could I have explained what he was doing? How did I know it was wrong except for the terrible emptiness I would feel after he left?

Lying rigid on the bed, staring at the doorway, waiting, waiting, waiting for the footsteps in the hall, for the loud breathing, for the blankets to be pulled away, the cool air to hit my legs, waiting to go away and leave my body. The leave-taking—it always happened just in time.

My office chair felt hard, as if I'd been sitting there for hours.

"Here's those reports you needed, Amber."

I jumped a mile, almost gasping, as Marlene laid some pages on my desk. "Sorry. Daydreaming?" she smirked.

I mumbled an unintelligible response and took the pages, staring down at them without seeing anything. Typewriters clacked around me. Voices were briefly raised in an argument, then someone laughed. I sighed and refocused my eyes on my work. I was writing an article about a little dog who was discovered chained in a back yard without food, water, or shade, in one hundred degree weather. The responding officers went to their car for bolt cutters, returning to see the property owner standing next to the pup. Arguments ensued, but during it all the dog stared up at the face of her abuser, wagging her tail madly and asking only to be petted and loved.

It was difficult writing about that day. I wanted the dog to savagely bite the leg of the person who had chained and starved her. Instead, her eyes never left his face, craning her neck towards him even as she was carried away by the humane officers. That hope is something that both Audrey and I understand all too well.

CHAPTER 42

Early Saturday morning, and it was time to row. Today, all the beginners would row for the first time on the water. I had had trouble sleeping the night before, imagining being strapped into a boat, dependent upon other people, all moving together. I was used to the autonomy of running, just myself and my sneakers on the asphalt. The thought of moving in time with a boat full of people made me anxious. But I was determined.

The sun was just rising as I drove around the lake, glowing in the trees at the edge of the water. The air was still brisk. I turned into the boathouse parking lot and drove into a spot facing the lake. Some ducks were gathered at the edge of the water, heads still tucked under their wings in sleep.

I got out of the car and saw a group of people who looked as clueless as I felt. They milled around, chatting about how early it was and how pretty the sunrise was. I stood by myself, looking over the boats waiting in their metal racks. I touched one and felt the smooth curve, imagining water sliding over the hull.

"Okay, everyone, grab yourself a pair of oars," Jane was energetic, signing every new arrival into the log book. "We've got a great day, calm water. It's a perfect time to be out on the lake."

We all selected oars and brought them down to the ramp, the clattering of the wood louder than the birds in the nearby brush. They were long and unwieldy, and several of us almost smacked the oars into the next person in line, stooge-esque, as we turned from the oar rack after making our selections. At nine feet long, and carrying two together, it was hard not to scrape the ground or knock over the person walking behind me. I smiled at a woman close to my age. She was also struggling, obviously as inexperienced as me. One oar would go down and the other would go up, almost like the balance point was different in each one. But we successfully deposited our oars in a raggedy line at the water's edge, and joined the group back at the boathouse.

"Today we'll take out the quads, because they are very stable and we can get used to stroking on water. I'll be nearby in the launch."

I saw the motorboat waiting in the water. Coach Jane would be there, ready to rescue us if needed. Still, I was glad I could swim. I could take care of myself if I needed to, just like I always did. I looked around and saw a few nervous expressions, which calmed me. I wasn't alone.

The next step was getting the shell into the water. Our quads were already out of the boathouse—sleek fiberglass hulls resting in slings in the yard. Coach lined us up, four to a shell, and explained the process. "First, I call 'hands on' and you place your left hand across the boat to grab the other side. Your right hand stays on this side. Then when I call 'roll up to heads, ready, up' everyone lifts the boat, turning it upside down over your heads." Then we would "split," she said, meaning half would have our heads on one side and half on the other side of the boat as we lowered it to the tops of our shoulders.

Awkwardly, we got the boat up and settled on our shoulders. It was heavy and cumbersome, but the commands coordinated our actions and we made our careful way down to the water. I was lucky, not being the tallest one, who carried the most weight.

The ducks commented loudly while they paddled away. We looked like a giant centipede heading down for a swim. It was strange carrying something with other people. Every time they moved, I had to move, and every time I moved, the boat affected the other people as well. We all had to work together, and we weren't even in the water yet! As we grew accustomed to the weight of the boat and fell into step, I began breathing easier and focusing more on my teammates instead of the churning in my stomach. We stepped into the soft sand of the shore, and waited for our next command.

"Up to heads, ready, up; roll to waist, set it in."

We plopped the boat down into the water and there was a collective "whoop" of excitement. Our first hurdle. It bumped gently against my shins as I wriggled my toes in the swirling sand. The water was cool on my skin. The breeze lifted the water into tiny wavelets that tap-tapped against the side of the shell, like invisible fingers.

Jane demonstrated how to attach the oars into their oar locks. She showed us where it was safe to put our feet so that we didn't damage the shell, and we all began moving. I stepped carefully into the shell, sitting down and settling my feet lightly on its bottom. I pulled my socks out of my waistband and awkwardly worked them over my wet feet, then held my oars and waited for further instructions. Barely above the water line, I sat and looked doubtfully at the shoes screwed into a plate at my feet. Did I really want to be strapped in? How well did I know these people? I turned around to the rower behind me and realized that my expression probably matched hers. We smiled together.

"Okay, everybody, get your feet into the foot stretchers," said Jane.

"Foot stretchers? Is that what they're called? Sounds like a torture device!" The voice came from behind me.

Coach Jane leaned back from the shell and gave a great big belly laugh. "Now, I've heard a lot about the suffering of a crew team, but I've never heard foot stretchers called torture devices before. Hah!"

Her laughter, and those of my teammates, flowed over me like soothing music. I breathed in the rich smells of the lake and felt myself relax. The rower in front of me pushed her feet into her shoes, so I followed suit. If she could do it ... Easier to row without your feet sliding around, I guess.

Coach waded out into the water, pushing our shell out away from shore. "Hold your oars flat on the water. They work like a stabilizer, keeping the boat set."

It was true—they were like large outriggers. When I experimentally pushed down on one oar, I could feel the shell tilt away just a bit. I imagined what it would be like in a single shell. Tippy!

Coach got into the launch and began organizing our movements, guiding us through strokes, at first one at a time, then by pairs. We discovered we could make our shell pick up speed, and we found ourselves out in the middle of the lake, the landing area a small bare patch of asphalt in the distance.

The hour went by quickly, as I focused on coordinating my body parts. We learned to start our motion from our arms and back, then bending our legs so when we unwound back the other way, we had the longest stroke possible. When we were moving all together, without clashing oars, it was exhilarating. We did not move very fast, but I could feel the power of everybody else added to my own. The compounded strength made me catch my breath and want to whoop with surprise. By the time we returned, we had changed from a group of strangers to a team with a shared purpose.

The woman behind me grinned, "Wow, I didn't expect to be so tired!" No longer looking anxious, her eyes shone with excitement and perhaps pride. I knew how she felt.

Coach docked her launch and instructed us to step out, one at a time. I welcomed the lapping of the cool lake water on my legs.

Somebody fell into the water as his foot caught the lip of the boat. We all laughed with him while Coach held his arm and helped him up. "Jeez, we make it all this way without a problem, then I gotta go and fall in!" he groused. He pulled a red bandanna from his pocket and squeezed it out, his lined face grimacing as the water dripped into the lake. The wind tousled his straight gray hair, scattering it around on his head in wispy clumps. He stuffed the bandanna back into his pocket with a wry smile.

The middle-aged woman who had rowed behind him clapped him on the back. "If it hadn't been you, it woulda been me, believe me, I came this close!" She held her fingers out, nearly touching. My breath caught in my throat as I felt the support of these strangers, all learning together, taking risks and laughing at themselves, without fear.

We lined up our oars on the shore and then gathered back at the boat. This time, we knew what "hands on" and "roll up to heads" meant, so it went much more smoothly. We settled the shell on our shoulders and carried it back up the ramp. Handing it down into the slings was easier than putting it in the water, even though we were all tired.

"Good job everybody! Nobody flipped!" said Coach, her tanned face crinkling into a smile. "Now go put your oars back in the rack." She rubbed some lake weed off the hull.

We collected our oars, settled them into the rack, then helped wipe off the shell.

"That's it, thanks, see you all in two days. Good class!"

I started towards my car, waving goodbye.

"You did great!" Coach called out, and I nodded, pleased, "You looked like you enjoyed yourself."

"Yes, definitely. I am hooked already!" I turned away, and saw Lisa in the parking lot, leaning against her old Chrysler, squinting against the sun.

She waved, "I watched you out there, and you all looked very powerful."

I smiled, feeling a rush of warmth, "It was awesome! We all work together and the thing slips through the water like a fish! I'm definitely going to learn this stuff. And did you notice the sunrise? It was beautiful! " I stopped when I noticed Lisa looking at me and grinning, wordlessly. "What?" I asked.

"Nothing, it's just that you are kind of ... I don't know ... glowing?"

I sobered, thinking.

Then she added, "And, I like seeing that."

CHAPTER 43

"It's just not right. We are supposedly standing up for the calves, but all we do is pat the abusers on the head and nod, smiling, saying what a good job they are doing. It's not right. It's not what I signed up for," Carter said.

I resisted flinching from his angry gaze, feeling the cold wetness of my soda bottle drip over my fingers. We were sitting at a tiny table in Pete's Tacos, where my former coworker had agreed to meet after work. Country music played from a nearby jukebox, and the air smelled like a combination of cigarettes and fried hamburgers.

Carter's heavy shoulders slumped as he looked at the menu. I had not seen him since that long-ago lunch with HAA as a new employee. He was still upset about the veal calf campaign.

"So that's why you left HAA?" I crinkled a napkin in my hand, soaking up some of the wetness. The late afternoon sun slanted in through the round windows high on the wall, outlining the curls touching his flushed cheeks. He was too tall for the table, his legs coming out the other side, his stomach pushing against the edge.

"Yes. I'm sorry, but I can't celebrate these so-called victories anymore. The calves might be more comfortable for a few months, and that's good, that's great ..." he pressed his palms onto the tabletop, pausing and looking down at his bitten fingernails, "but we've essentially given the farmer who kills them and sells their starved meat a license to continue doing what he's doing! We say, 'Good boy!' and we promise to leave him alone. It's just not right, and it's not why I had come to HAA!"

"So what do we do? Tell the farmer that everyone should be vegetarian? Go open the pens and free all the calves?"

"No!" he practically shouted.

I sat up straighter and eased my chair back from the table, putting my drink down carefully.

The waitress appeared and asked if everything was okay, and we reassured her and ordered some tacos. Carter, calmer, put his menu down, resting his hands in his lap. He looked steadily into my eyes. "Of course not. They'd just starve to death somewhere out in the mesa. But we can shift the conversation away from cruel farming practices and focus instead on why it's wrong to use and kill animals at all. Talk loudly about what we really think about these things. Publicly support a lifestyle that respects other living beings. Don't you get it?" He stared at me, looking for a reaction.

I looked away across the smoky room, thinking, wondering now why I had wanted to meet. But I had to understand. I met his eyes, wondering if he was really as angry as he sounded. "I do get it. But it seems like if we make the farmer mad, then we wouldn't get anywhere." I hoped that my voice wasn't shaking.

"Make him mad? What are you, Mahatma Gandhi or something?" I flinched when Carter suddenly reached out to grab my arm, dropping the soggy napkin I had been twisting. His large fingers were moist and hot, but strangely comforting. "Amber, Amber, we can't just give up halfway because somebody does something a little less horrible. It's like releasing a convicted pedophile because he promises to tuck his little girl in at night afterwards."

"Oh, yes, I get it, that's crazy," I mumbled, pulling my arm away as the waitress arrived with our food.

Carter ate quickly, his fingers tapping softly to the jukebox's music. "I'm sorry. I just get so mad." He chewed and swallowed, looking at my plate. "Aren't you going to eat?"

"Nah, I just realized that I forgot to feed my cat." I signaled the waitress. Carter laughed, "We gotta take care of our own first, right?"

I had the food boxed up and stood quickly, smiling and thanking him for meeting with me.

"Call me again sometime," he smiled, "you remember what I said, okay?"

I would remember. I remembered the smell of crisp clean cotton sheets tucked around my legs. And cigarette-laden breath on my cheek. And the smell of desperation.

CHAPTER 44

Her voice was an anguished whisper. "Amber! Is it you? Amber, I need help! Can you take Mittens?"

"Audrey! What's happening?" I heard a crash in the background and a deep voice, yelling. I held the phone tightly to my ear and sat down on the couch, twining the phone cord around my fingers. It was late Thursday, and I had just finished brushing my teeth before bed.

"Audrey?" All I could hear was heavy, panting breathing. "Audrey?"

"You shit! You leave her alone! Let go!" Then came a scream that shocked me right down into my deepest being, cut off with the click of the line going dead. I sat alone on the couch, listening to the dial tone. Eventually I rose and replaced the handset on the cradle, relieved when the dial tone ended. I stood in the kitchen staring at the phone, hearing the chirp of a cricket. He seemed out of place, hidden in some dark corner, singing his cheery song to no one. My heartbeats were loud, the pulses rising up my neck until I thought they might choke me.

Tom wandered in and I crouched down, wondering at his calm. But of course, the phone call, it was for me, not him. "Tom. I'm calling her back." I rubbed his head and felt his purr, coming from deep inside his sturdy body. Then I picked up the phone.

No answer. I found her address in the phone book and mechanically dialed 911, my fingers trembling on the dial. The operator, cold and efficient, told me to stay by the phone in case they needed more information.

She emphasized that I should stay home, and that I must not go to the residence for any reason.

I collected Tom from the doorway, where he was watching me. We tucked ourselves into our warm bed, but the only one who slept much that night was Tom.

· · ·

"Amber, can you come here?" my housemate called out, seven a.m. the next morning. She sounded frightened. "The police are here, and they're asking for you."

I put down my cereal and joined her at the front door. Unsure of what to do, I awkwardly invited the officer in, a tall dark-haired man, mid-thirties. He looked tired. He sat down on the couch and took his hat off, turning it in his fingers before setting it down and taking out a pad of paper.

"Did you get a phone call last night from a woman name of Audrey Jones?" he began.

"Yes, about ten," I said. "She was screaming. They were having a big fight. Is she okay?"

He shifted and put the pad of paper down on his lap, then breathed in deeply and looked at my face. His eyes were unexpectedly kind. "Well, no, ma'am. I'm sorry. Mrs. Jones is deceased."

My housemate, standing in the kitchen doorway, gasped.

I saw the officer's lips moving, but heard no sound over the roaring in my ears. I sank into the couch, closed my eyes, and put my hands to my face, wanting only to disappear, to float up and out, to be anywhere but here. I saw again Audrey's bruised face, the blood pooling around her eye, her smirk as she poured orange juice on her cereal. Flowers. He had bought her flowers.

"I ... I tried to get her to stay with me," I began, "But she wouldn't ..." I took my hands away and looked down at them, my fingers twisting together in my lap. My roommate sank to the carpet at my feet, her eyes wide and shocked.

The officer reached out and placed his hand lightly on my shoulder. I felt a brief weight, a warmth, and a tiny bit of peace, before he returned his hand to his lap. "You did all you could. She made the choice to stay with him." He picked up his pencil.

I looked up. His eyes were a deep brown, with tiny creases around them, which could have been laugh lines or frown lines, I couldn't tell. He was still, his gaze quiet as he waited, pencil poised, "Did she say anything about her attacker?"

"Her husband?" I stood, looking out the window at the distant hills, avoiding his gaze. I watched the rays of sun flicker through the leaves in the yard as I recounted our conversation, "Just that she had to get away. She wanted to get her cat and leave." I gasped and looked at the detective. "Mittens. Do you have the cat? Is she okay?"

"Some lady came to get it."

"Her."

"What?" he said.

"Her. Mittens is a her." I shoved my hands deep into my pockets.

"Ah. Her. Somebody came. I think it was the sister of the deceased," he looked closely at my face.

I let out my breath, "I didn't know she had a sister. That's good, that's good. Thanks for telling me." I was absurdly grateful.

My housemate gave me a hug, saying, "I gotta get to work, Amber. I'm so sorry about your friend." The door shut quietly behind her.

I talked with the officer some more, mostly about Tom, who liked him. My heart was calming by the time he left, but our polite handshakes seemed a small thing against the enormity of what had happened. Audrey was gone, taken. Irrevocably. And there was nothing I could do to bring her back. I put my hand on my shoulder, still feeling his touch.

CHAPTER 45

The wind was fierce, spending energy saved from the heat of the day. It flung leaves against the window and made tossing tree shadows on the wall of my bedroom. Three a.m. I had woken to a branch hitting the side of the house. The sheets were secure around my legs, and Tom was quiet at the foot of the bed, but I couldn't get back to sleep. My mind raced with worries about tomorrow, when I would give Marlene notice. Would she be angry? Resentful? Whatever happened, it was time to leave the animal protection business. I was not cut out for convincing people to be kinder, more loving. I just wanted it all to stop. No more sad stories.

Lately, most days, I was angry. Angry at researchers who withheld medical care, angry at hoarders who allowed their animals to breed and breed and breed, even though they had no money to feed and care for them properly. Angry at biological specimen companies who gassed cats to death en masse to save money. Angry at myself for not successfully convincing people to do the right thing. Just ... angry. I came home most nights tense and anxious, taking sometimes two hours to fully relax. On bad days, I relived the most horrible stories all night long in my dreams, waking still tired, jaw muscles aching from grinding my teeth.

I smelled the cookies I had baked yesterday afternoon, and my stomach rumbled. Tom's head lifted from the blankets and I scratched his neck. "Tom, I'm tired of being mad."

He purred and stretched up against my fingers. Cats. They always know how to feel right at home.

I lay back on my pillow, followed by Tom, who decided that more rubs were a good thing, even at three a.m. His fur tickled my nose and I sneezed twice, making him jump. His eye glowed in the light from the streetlamp as he stared at me. I reassured him I was done sneezing, and he settled back down. I twined my fingers into his fur and imagined celebrating a new job with Lisa and Tony. Maybe I'd get a better paying job, and could take them out to dinner as thanks for all the meals they had shared with me. I sighed and turned my face to Tom's belly. Before I knew it, the sun was shining and the wind had gone, and it was time to get up and face the day.

$$\bullet \quad \bullet \quad \bullet$$

"So, kid, we're sorry to see you go. You accomplished a lot in two years. You helped a lot of animals." Marlene smiled and pushed her glasses up onto her forehead. She rubbed her eyes and squinted at me.

I felt a small swell of pride.

"You started out in the kennels, and ended up in the press, giving abusive research scientists hell for what they're doing," she smiled, and crossed her arms over her chest.

I met her eyes, "They deserved it. I just called it what it was."

She chuckled, "Well, don't be a stranger." She looked back down at the work on her desk.

I waited, twisting my fingers together in my lap, clutching Marlene's praise against my sense of abandoning something important. "Thanks, Marlene, I'll get my things." I stood.

She pulled her glasses back down onto her nose and picked up her pen. "I'll probably see you at Lisa's sometime. And there's the wedding. It'll just be me, of course. I'm fancy-free now!" She wiggled her empty ring finger at me and grinned.

It didn't take long to bundle my personal effects into a cardboard box that I found in the mailroom. I was in a daze, feeling adrift and aimless. I stopped by one cubicle to hand over my cruelty-free charity files, and slipped my dissection alternatives article into the editor's inbox. I hoped I wouldn't bump into Chris. On my way out I walked by Lisa's cubicle. She was bent over a report, scribbling in the margins, muttering to herself. I set my box down and imitated her muttering.

She looked up, frowning, then grinned, a sudden sunny smile that made everything easier. She grasped my hand.

I remembered her touching the arm of Gloria, the hoarder at my very first rescue with HAA. "How do you do it, Lisa?"

"Do what?"

"You keep loving people, no matter what they've done."

"Oh, Amber," she looked at a picture of Tony on her desk. "I just have the right people around me." She looked back up at me, "Like you."

I sighed, aware of footsteps passing by, a murmur of voices from the other cubicles, the clack of typewriters. "I may come back, but for now, I'm done."

She leaned forward, suddenly serious. "Amber, it's okay to take a break. Fighting bad people does not mean relinquishing your own peace. You'll always be a good influence in the world, just because of who you are." Her voice was vehement.

I rubbed at the back of my neck, feeling some tense muscles easing. Her parting hug was warm, lasting just long enough.

At the front door, I nearly collided with Chris, barreling in from the parking lot, his hair wild.

"Need any help?" he paused in his headlong rush.

"I got it, thanks," I wanted to say something smart, something to make him smile at me the way he used to, but my throat was dry, and by the time I took a breath, he was already gone.

I put my box in the trunk and then sat in my car for a bit, the solitude easing my tension. I looked around, then carefully wrapped my arms around myself for a moment. A hug from the person who knew me best. It worked. I felt more secure inside, lifted. I started the car and turned towards home.

CHAPTER 46

It didn't take me long to find a job at the local grocery store. They had lost a stock clerk, and I walked in at just the right time. Monday was my start day, and that was a whole two days away. I stretched out as far as I could in my rumpled bed, reveling in the late hour, carefully avoiding Tom on the pillow. My housemates were away for the weekend. I had briefly roused when I heard them leave early, before first light, then I had reached for Tom and snuggled back to sleep.

He was being patient for breakfast. Perhaps he understood things had changed. I crawled out of bed and sleepily spooned some food into his dish, watching while he curled his tail around his front toes and settled down to eat.

I sat down at the table with my cereal, brushing a few crumbs away, and thought about a recent Al-Anon meeting. The facilitator had said that if we were treated badly growing up, then we might similarly neglect our own needs. She told us that writing often accesses child-like parts of our selves that had been left behind, shut down or silenced—just writing with no goal, no deadline. "Just a letter to that lost part of yourself can work wonders." Her words reached down deep into me and gave me pause. I didn't really know how to care for any child, let alone an inner one, and really it seemed a bit silly, but I knew that sleeping late and enjoying homemade biscuits for breakfast felt good, so that was what I was going to do. I finished my cereal, pulled out my cookie sheet, and began measuring out the flour.

The biscuits were delicious. After finishing my last bite, I sat back and licked my lips. Tom licked his, too, and I laughed. "You liked your breakfast, too, did you, big guy?" I gave him my plate, which needed polishing. I rubbed my stomach and realized that I felt good. My insides were less crinkled up, more accessible. Inside, somewhere, was a new part of me that no one else had shaped. No one was there now, but me. I felt a certain relaxation that was both scary and interesting at the same time. I absently pulled over the pencil and blank pad of paper that I had near the phone, and began writing.

I didn't mean to hurt you so badly. I didn't mean to push you into a dark closet, clothes falling over your shoulders, your skinny legs stumbling over jumbled dusty shoes. A careless shove, a rough turning away was all it took. I, being stronger in worldly power, growing every year into the privileges awarded to maturity, found it easier and easier to rest my eyes in places you were never allowed.

I didn't mean to silence you. But each time you lifted your head, you met my tense stare, a stiff denial of the truth your words may have held for me, if only I had listened. Over the years your attempts to speak became weaker. You came to expect the rebuke that was made all the more cold by its softness, its firm unrelenting gentleness.

I feared your words, those truths of a child unjustly accused. They threatened to drown me in their shadow. It seemed too much to bear, for to listen meant looking directly into the light. But every year the shadow grew and grew, no matter how I opened my curtains to encourage the light's presence, no matter how I painted bright colors over my walls. Every attempt to lighten these rooms only made the shadows stand out in sharper relief.

Until now. I finally acknowledged your timid presence beside me, seeing you for the first time as just a kid. The monster locked inside the closet has become a little girl with pigtails, eager to show me the pictures she made at school. She teaches me that even monsters smile now and again, even terrible scary beasts sometimes need to simply weep, and the wonder of wonders is that I can let them all cry on my shoulders. How could I keep my secrets locked away once I looked into the face of this innocent child? How did such tender beauty survive so many years locked in with the savage memories I sought to forget? She beguiles away my fear with her forgiveness.

I face the world differently now. I have a precious new friend whom I want to hug. We walk hand in hand, marveling at the beauty in the world, watching the leaves drift down in autumn and the grass grow in spring. The first time she cried, I was only a little bit afraid. She and I have become stronger every day, until finally, one day, she honored me with her anger. The monster had finally spoken, and I heard only the terrible lost wailing of a child ignored for so many years.

I have come to love this monster, this angry child, and my love has finally let her grow into a woman who no longer seeks pain as proof of her existence. We are done with hurting, done with helplessness. I am riding on a wave of growing intimacy between my child and myself. The paralyzing fear is lifting, and my power lies beneath, waiting for me to finally claim it.

I caught my breath, surprised by these words, as if they had come from someone else. I felt cleaner, as if someone had lifted the bad hurt places up and away. And it felt good. My pencil dropped onto the table and I got up to scrub the biscuit pan. The day was going to be good. In a few hours I had another sculling lesson. I opened the kitchen window and breathed in the cool, soft air flowing in from the back lawn. The air responded to the new lift in my heart with its own uprising, mingling perfectly with the lingering smells from the warm oven.

I wandered into the living room and found Bruce still on the turntable. Just the man for the morning, I thought, carefully lifting the needle arm into position over the spinning record. Born to run. Springsteen's words spoke directly to me. I sighed, turning the sound up, the guitar chords sinking down into my skin and soothing something deep inside, like a hug from a lover. I sank down upon the couch, leaned back, and closed my eyes.

Suddenly the door banged open and my father stood there, large hands loose by his sides, frowning. I jumped up and stood there, shaking, watching his lips move, he was saying something, why couldn't I hear what he was saying, it was the music, it was too loud, I didn't hear his car drive up, the door had been left unlocked, where was Tom, what is he saying, the whirl in my mind finally settling on Bruce singing about wanting to be my friend and guard my dreams. I lifted the needle from the record, concentrating fiercely on my shaking hand. Before I could turn around, Mike's hands curled around my waist, his skin warm and moist through my shirt. I twisted away but he held tightly, breathing into my neck, "I've missed you, 'Ber, I ..." and he kissed me, lips wet and squishing flatly on my jaw.

I leaned away. "Dad, yeah," I said, my voice trembling. I tried to control my breathing, fighting against rising panic, and pushed weakly at his arms. "Let's just sit a minute. What's going on with you?" My question sounded far away, coming from someone older and more in control, wiser. I waited, taking another slow breath, my vision flickering as my focus lifted from the still-spinning record to the picture on the wall. Daisies in a bright blue pitcher.

Finally, Mike released me and I turned abruptly down the hall, saying over my shoulder, "I gotta find Tom, Dad, he's disappeared, I think he might want more breakfast ..."

"Tom? Who's Tom? Some boyfriend I don't know about?"

"No, Dad, he's my cat, I think he might be—" I knelt in my bedroom, lifting the sheets away from where they brushed the floor. I wanted the touch of someone who loved me.

Heavy footsteps behind me. He knelt next to me on the floor, and a voice in my head urgently whispered, *Stop, back away, just leave,* but I couldn't stop my hand from lifting the sheet. It was light blue with tiny yellow flowers, which rippled as something shot out from underneath the bed. My father grabbed and held on. Tom became a whirling growling hissing ball of fur in his hands, and Mike yelled and threw him across the room.

I screamed, scrambling to my feet. But Tom was quicker, shaking his head briefly while he tucked his legs underneath him, ran to the door, and slipped around the corner. Mike and I stared at the doorway. There was blood dripping from a long scratch on the back of his hand. "That's Tom? That motherfucker nearly ripped my hand in half. What, is he wild? What's the matter with him?"

I ran into the living room, my scream still ringing in my ears, and knelt down to peer under the couch. Tom was trembling, but he looked unhurt, his one eye glaring balefully back at me. I reached out, but he backed away. "I'm sorry. I was stupid. It's okay, boy, I'm getting rid of him. You wait there."

In the bathroom I grabbed some bandages from under the sink. I met Mike as he left the bedroom, thrusting them into his hands. "Here. Now go." My body was solid against the floor, my stomach settled into a hard place. I stood quietly and watched him.

"What? Amber, you gotta get rid of that thing. Where is he? He's dangerous."

"Dad, you are not welcome here. Go now, or I'll call the police."

He started laughing, but stopped when I walked into the kitchen and dialed the phone, "Yes, hello, my name is Amber, and I have an emergency. I have an intruder in the house."

"Wha—? Amber, for Chrissake, calling the police on your old man? What will you tell them?"

"Yes, he's already hurt my cat and I'm worried that I'm next. My address is—"

"Jesus! Amber, hurt you? Okay, okay, I'm leaving." He turned towards the door and I put the phone down on the table. A voice came out of it, tiny, asking a question. I stared at my father, standing with his hand grasping the doorknob.

"Dad, if you've hurt Tom I'll never forgive you. And you'll never hurt me again."

"What do you mean?"

"It's not right, Dad. We can't do this anymore."

"What, eating Chinese food and watching movies?"

I felt sick. "No, Dad, what you do to me in the bedroom afterwards." My voice felt far away again, but sure, so sure. My words were the kites, flying somewhere above my body, but I held firmly to the strings and watched them curve in the air between us.

Mike was staring at me, white bits of bandages sticking out from his fingers. The voice came out of the phone again, and I set it gently back on its cradle. Then I stood and walked towards Mike. He recoiled as I reached towards him, just a slight intake of breath and a tiny movement backwards, but it was enough. I took a bandage and opened the wrapper, flipping the safety strips away and smoothing it over his scratch.

"There. Now you won't get blood in your truck."

Mike's eyes widened, then he turned and left, letting the door slam. I stood still and listened to his motor start, the tires on the driveway, then the engine noise fading down the road. Then I shook myself and called Tom. I rubbed his body all over, gently feeling his muscles, his ribs beneath the long gray fur. He seemed unhurt, staring calmly at me as if he, too, knew that it was finally over. He sighed deeply, then placed his head on my hand, laying it across my palm like a benediction.

I called Lisa. "It's me. Something just happened," I said. "Mike tried to hurt Tom, so I called the police."

"Oh my gosh, Amber, is Tom okay? Are you okay?"

"Yup, we're just fine. Excellent, in fact. You are the best, really, you made this possible," I paused, realizing that my hand was resting on my opposite shoulder, as if seeking that small place of warmth. "And also a detective I talked to ..." I trailed off.

"Well, then, I'm relieved. You really threw me for a loop!"

I reached down to Tom, and smiled at his purr. For the rest of the day, layers kept settling inside me, filling in lost lonely places with recovered parts of me that had never had a chance to speak. Now they were speaking volumes.

CHAPTER 47

I looked forward wholeheartedly to my time on the lake, perfecting my technique, celebrating my successes and those of my teammates. I even conquered my fear of flipping. It happened when I was in a single and moving too close to a newly submerged tree, fallen from the eroding embankment. My oar caught on the leafy branches sliding under the shell. As it was pulled from my fingers, I instinctively grabbed harder, and immediately realized my mistake when the shell leaned hard to the side. I was in the water before I could think. My concern about being strapped in evaporated as I hit the water, floating freely beside the shell. The dreaded flip was really just a slide and a splash. Swimming, I could do. I yelled out my triumph, startling a pair of Mallard ducks who paddled quickly away, one iridescent green head turning back to eyeball me.

Turns out that getting wet was the easy part. Getting back in was much harder. Embarrassing, too. I floundered around for a while like a beached whale, finally pulling the shell to shallow water so I could step in. The experience only made me ready for more.

Even off the water, I often relived the delicious pull of my arms against the oars, the push from my legs that made the shell leap through the water. So different than running. Team practice was even better—I moved in time with the other rowers, trusting them to respond with me, all working together to race the wind. Exhilarating.

CHAPTER 48

"Almost as good as Tony's cooking!" I teased Lisa as we munched our bean tacos in the tiny park outside the takeout place. A tree, almost larger than the park, moistened the hot desert air just enough and we settled ourselves in the bit of grass beneath its spreading branches.

A breeze ruffled the hair around Lisa's face, and she smoothed it back behind her ear. "So you're sure that you're okay being a bridesmaid?"

"Only if I don't have to wear a dress," I bit off another piece of taco and elbowed her, then pretended to scrape refried beans off her sleeve. "Oops."

"Sure, don't worry, I can use your dress for washing my car. I picked out pink-and-purple striped overalls especially for you. They'll go with your eyes."

"Anything for you, dahling, but with pink and purple I might be prettier than you."

She chuckled softly, "I can't believe it's finally happening." She stared down at her plate. The breeze picked up a few dried leaves and swirled them around our sneakers. She sighed, "I wish I could share some of this ... this happiness ... with you."

I felt a soothing warmth spread down my stomach. "I'm doing just fine, buddy. No worries. It's funny, now that I have more space around me, I feel so much better, more ... I don't know ... real. But Lisa," I shrugged, "You *are* sharing your good stuff with me. I have a big smile inside, kind of matching this one." I pointed to what must have been a loopy grin, with a bit of taco sauce attached.

Lisa's happiness, the coolness of the tree shade, even the taste of the taco, all melted warmly into me and filled in more of the empty places. I licked sauce off my fingers and leaned back against the rough bark. It was warm from the sun, as if the tree had its own heart beating within, sending body heat out in response to my touch. I put down my plate and curled my fingers into the hard ridges of bark, imagining the strength of the tree flowing into my hand and up my arm, dancing around my heart.

Lisa was looking at me. "What do you mean, more space around you?"

"It's hard to describe." I scooped up some dusty soil from near my feet and held it, tipping my palm, letting the dry grains trickle back down to the ground. "It's like having enough room inside, enough awareness, or presence, to feel every bit of soil falling out of my palm. That little rock moves across the base of my pinkie and tumbles down onto the bit of bark there, and I feel them both falling. I feel the impact on the ground, and I feel the lightness left behind." I looked up at her, knowing she would understand.

She was silent, a small smile on her face. She tilted her head. "I think I know. It's space that was taken from you, and now, you are taking it back."

"You know, your fiance is a lucky guy."

She beamed and leaned back, gazing up into the leafy branches. "We're traveling around Europe for a bit. We've got some money saved." She looked at me. "You gonna be okay without me?"

I laughed, "Things are great with me, you know that. And, Lisa ..."

"Yes?" she was looking at me with her mouth slightly open. Such a dear friend.

"I have forgiven him." *And maybe myself, too,* I thought.

My words hung in the air. Lisa looked at me and closed her mouth, no longer smiling. "Why bother?"

I rubbed my palm along the tree bark ridges. "It's about holding something almost ... tainted ... inside me, that he left behind. Like a placeholder to somewhere I never want to revisit. I'm pulling the bookmark out of that page."

Lisa sat quietly, smiling at me. Then she reached out, awkwardly, and we hugged. An old man coming out of the restaurant stopped briefly to stare at us. A paper bag crinkled in his fist, and time stopped for a moment. His long gray hair shifted in the breeze, and I thought I smelled the heavy odor of cigarettes. Then he smiled and shuffled away.

Lisa's hand was on my knee. I put my hand over hers, watching the old man settle his bag into a rusted grocery cart tucked behind the dumpster. The wheels of the cart shrieked and clanked as he pushed it down the sidewalk.

"He remind you of somebody?" she said.

"I guess so, in a way." I straightened away from the tree trunk and brushed dried bits of bark out of my ponytail, grinning at her. "But it's true. I called him and told him. All is forgiven."

"How did he react?"

"He didn't care. He doesn't think there's anything to forgive. But that didn't really matter."

"But—"

"No, really, it felt like the right thing to do. It was like a big bubble inside my guts. I needed it out to have more room for me. It's a good thing!"

"You're so weird. But I believe you. Sometimes forgiveness is more about the forgiver than the ... forgivee?" She laughed again, a dry chuckle that came up from deep within. She understood. "But just so you know, *I* will never forgive him." She picked up a leaf from where it had fallen into the grass and examined it carefully, rolling the curled edges between her fingers.

I watched two gulls fight over a piece of bread, their high-pitched cries merging with the creak of the tree limbs above us. Then I took her hands. "Thank you." I wasn't sure if she heard me over the traffic going by, but then she met my eyes and her expression cleared.

"You are welcome, my dear, you are welcome. You really don't know what a good person you are. You amaze me."

We walked to our cars and smiled goodbye across the hot parking lot.

CHAPTER 49

The halls of Central New Mexico Community College were lined with bulletin boards covered in brightly colored notices. Orientation classes, book groups, support groups, Ultimate teams, there was something for everyone. My sneakers squeaked on the linoleum as I searched for Room 103, "Writing from Experience." Here it was, a corner room just past the water fountain. I walked in, adjusting my backpack on my shoulders.

"You must be Amber." A middle-aged woman with gold-rimmed glasses sat at the desk by the chalkboards lining the front of the room. She held out a manicured hand and with the other one delicately pushed her glasses up her nose and tucked a stray bit of brown hair behind her ear. Her red blouse matched her earrings.

"Yes, that's me." I shook her hand, liking its firmness. I had wanted to slip in unnoticed, but no other students were here. I was early.

"Welcome! You can sit anywhere you like." Then, answering my unspoken question, "I could tell it was you, because you are the only woman in the class."

I relaxed into a seat near the back and looked around. The room was bright with sunlight. The blackboard sported neat lines of chalk and the teacher's desk had a bright green vase overflowing with black-eyed Susans. The chairs with their attached desks sat in rows facing the front of the room.

A long-haired student took the seat next to mine, smiling shyly. He pulled a notebook out of a battered canvas satchel and settled into his desk.

The room filled quickly, the door making a whooshing noise every time somebody arrived. A frizzy blond sat down on my other side, with a button-up shirt and a tie. He greeted me soberly, looking down at my jeans, and then the class began.

The material was less interesting than I had hoped, but my confidence was boosted because I knew a lot of it already. My two years at HAA had taught me more than I had realized. I felt like a construction worker laying a foundation for something bigger, something full of new possibilities.

For ninety minutes we busily took notes as the teacher discussed the difference between exposition and narrative, and why one is more useful than the other. "If you know your goals, then you can make good decisions based on that knowledge."

I wondered if she had been reading my thoughts.

After class, the sound of rustling papers being tucked back into notebooks reminded me of high school, though the students were older, and wanted to learn. I headed down the aisle of desks towards the door, but a touch on my back made me jump and turn around. It was the long-haired fellow. "Sorry I startled you!" He did look sorry, with a small hovering smile. "I'm Alex. You taken classes here before?" He had a faint mustache and a solid handshake.

"I'm Amber. No, this is something new for me." I edged backward towards the door.

"Cool. I figured it would be helpful for my kite-making business." He slipped between the desks and followed me. "You parked out here? I'll walk with you."

I slowed down and glanced at his face, watching his lips spread into a slow smile. "Yeah, my bike is here. You said you make kites? That's neat ... what kind?"

He laughed, clearly pleased by my curiosity. "I'll try my hand at any interesting idea. Often it's a lot of animals. Lions and tigers and bears, oh my ..."

"So you make unusual shapes? Not just, you know, regular kite shapes?"

"Well, I have a couple people who do that for me. My part is the fabric itself. You see, there's a special material called ripstop nylon that is super lightweight and yet really strong, which of course is really important for—"

"Flying things! Of course, makes sense. Your own invention?"

His whole face lit up when he talked about the kites. "Yeah, it was my idea to make kites out of it, and that was what got this whole thing going. Then I decided that a good press release could only help. So, that's why I'm here." He fingered some stray papers sticking out of his satchel. "What do you do?"

"I stock shelves over at Safeway," I paused, "But I'm hoping for a job at a paper or something." We stopped in the parking lot near the bike stand and looked at each other awkwardly. I fumbled with my bike lock.

"Hey! That's what I did after school, too, until my kites started selling. Stocker. You the kind who lines everything up perfectly, or do you just throw things on the shelf and worry about it later?" He was smiling.

"Hey, my aim is pretty good, especially with the non-breakables."

His whole body moved when he laughed, slapping his knees with one hand. "And your boss wants neatness, without sacrificing efficiency?"

I thought that with Alex in the class I could relax and feel like I belonged. He spoke my language. I coiled the lock chain around my seat post.

"That bike's been well loved. You live nearby?" Alex squinted in the warm air while I settled my backpack on my shoulders and maneuvered the bike out from the rack.

"Yeah, not too far. And it's mostly flat."

"Well, see you next week, Amber, and don't forget to examine your goals, whether expositively or narratively," and he laughed again.

I felt a tug as he walked away, but damped it down quickly. I held my breath and gripped my bike handlebars so tightly my fingers turned white. I called out, "Alex, bring some of that ... what was it ... ripstopper fabric you are talking about. I'd like to see it."

His smile was huge. "Sure thing!" He waved and turned back towards the line of cars, rattling a group of keys in his hand.

I went the long way home. I wanted hills. I stayed hard on the pedals going downhill, steadily working my way up to the highest gear. When another hill approached, I flew up it, over the top and down before I could lose much speed. The wind in my hair and the humming of the tires pushed all worries out of my mind for a brief blissful time. But the next hill was higher, and my momentum wound down, the bike slowing dramatically. By the top, my breath was spent, and my heart pounding, just like after a fast run. On a bike, however, I was faster. Best of all, I could sit down the whole time, if I really wanted to. But for the next hill, I stood up as I pedaled, to get the last bit of speed and make the crest. I was invincible.

I got home before the sun started to set, and greeted Tom. My mind was far away, remembering the kites I had loved as a girl. They were cheap and plastic, but if they could fly high and stay there, then they were beautiful to me. Some part of me would fly up the line, riding high in the wind, tugging and pulling on the string. From the ground, it felt as if a racehorse was begging me to loosen the reins. *Faster, higher,* the kite would say. *Just let me go and I promise to come back. I'll see sights you've never dreamed of if you just. Let. Go.*

I never did it on purpose, but at times the string would break, and I would spend hours looking for my lost steed. One time, I found him in a tree, and recaptured him so he could fly again. A rarity. They usually simply disappeared, escaping to some imagined invisible other world.

I rubbed Tom's head and dialed the phone. I had promised to call Lisa. "My class is going great, and there's this guy," I told her.

"Do tell!"

"Well, he's got a kite business. Isn't that cool?"

Lisa laughed merrily, "Oh, Amber, just like you to hook up with a hippie."

"Yeah, well, maybe I find them more interesting." I hugged the phone to my ear with my shoulder and began filling a pot with water for tea.

"Whatever rocks your boat! By the way, my rehearsal dinner is next Friday. Five p.m. good for you, at Pete's? They've got some good vegetarian fare ideas for us."

"I'll see if I've got anything nice in the closet."

"I just hope that people are happy with where I've seated them. Family!" I could almost see her throw her hand in the air and roll her eyes.

I joined Tom on the couch, and he gazed up at me as I rubbed his head. Cats really can smile, I thought.

"I miss you, Am'." We agreed to meet after work the next day, and shop for dresses together.

After I hung up, I opened my closet and gazed at the clothes on the rack. Tom looked with me. Nothing really fancy. Most of my nice clothes hadn't been worn in years, and none seemed suitable for a rehearsal dinner for my best friend. I pulled out a black dress and sat on the bed with it in my lap. I fingered the silky material, remembering other hands.

"What about this one, honey?" my mother said, holding out a card of buttons shaped like cat faces. Each one had tiny stripes and green eyes.

I laughed, "A little kitty! These are the best, Mommy!"

"These will look great on the sleeves." Every year she made me a new dress for Easter. We would go on a special shopping trip together to pick out the finishing touches. The newest one was even better than last year's, dark blue with long buttoned sleeves. "Amber, you have such great taste." She touched my face and smiled, looking deep into my eyes.

I put the dress back in the closet, carefully smoothing out its creases. Mom would understand my forgiving Mike. She didn't hold grudges, and she knew how hard his life had been. It seemed like she had been gone forever, yet my memories of her were as clear as yesterday. I could still smell her shampoo and hear her laugh, saying, "Why buy perfume when you can have flowers in your hair for a fraction of the cost?" Her laughter was like bells, sweet and chiming.

Her sickness came on suddenly, a mysterious illness that wasted her away to almost nothing in mere weeks. Nothing the doctors did helped. That was when Mike had gotten so strange and needy.

CHAPTER 50

"Well, I think that one's the one, but if you don't feel good in it, then let's keep looking," Lisa squinted at me critically in the dressing room's mirror.

"Yeah, it's just too form-fitting. I can't breathe."

Lisa laughed, "Well, you've got a form that is worth fitting."

Heat rose into my face. "Lisa, cut it out!"

"Well, it's true! Must be all the running. Or rowing. Still doing that?"

"Yeah, and it's great fun! I saw a crane fly overhead yesterday. He was amazing!" I pulled on the dark blue dress with the lace at the front. I paused at the mirror, looking at curves that I rarely acknowledged. Could I really wear this, in public? Suddenly I took it off and said, "This is the one. I'm done." It felt like taking a deep breath and jumping off a cliff into a bottomless lake, terrifying and exhilarating all at the same time. All over a dress.

"I like it, too. You'll be the belle of the ball. You know, why don't you bring your new hippie friend?"

"I can't simply ask Alex outright, just like that! I'll come alone. Can I sit with your family or something?"

"Of course. We'll find you the perfect spot. No stress."

We linked our arms together as we headed for the cashier. I paid for the dress.

Lisa was fingering the lace on a frilly blouse. She sniffed and dug into her purse for her handkerchief.

"Lisa, something wrong?"

"I'm worried about my Mom. She's still in the hospital, and not doing well. I don't know if it's just being away from home, or if she is getting sicker. She kind of sinks into herself whenever I get ready to leave, after a visit. I think being there makes her sad."

"She's in good hands. Do you want to visit her together, you and I, before we meet for dinner?"

"She's really uncomfortable lately with anyone but me. She gets all stern and twitchy, and makes me worry even more. But thanks. I'll give her your love when I stop in tonight." We walked to our cars, waving goodbye across the rows of metal roofs. I rolled down my window and sat for a moment before I started the car, listening to the gulls calling out to each other.

CHAPTER 51

The door blew open as if Lisa had been waiting for me. "Hi Amber, come in, I was just telling Tony about the class you're taking."

I groaned, "You just reminded me I have a take-home test to finish. How's Betty?"

"Oh, that reminds me," she handed me a pink envelope with my name scrawled on it in spidery handwriting, "she left this for you."

I tucked the letter into my back pocket and thanked her.

"She's hanging in there. They're trying a new drug that's supposed to help her breathe. At least I got her laughing tonight when I visited, telling her about your hippie boyfriend."

I thought of Alex, and the way his whole body moved when he laughed. "I don't think you could call him a boyfriend yet, but he's interesting." Mentioning a male friend out loud felt like bringing two magnets close together. The world liked instant pairings. I preferred the long road, savoring sights, smells and sounds along the way. Then there was touch. Like wading into the cold ocean, I needed time to acclimatize, time to accommodate to the new temperature before I was ready for the deep, where I might lose contact with the comforting familiar sand. Was there an in-between, where I could linger, somewhere after meeting a new friend and before being named a couple?

We talked lightheartedly as we enjoyed our meal, a salad with my homemade cashew cream dressing, bread, and Tony's delicious and wonderfully nourishing lasagna. I watched Tony and Lisa talking, so relaxed and spontaneous.

"The rehearsal dinner went well, didn't it?" I asked, looking between the two. I had enjoyed meeting their relatives. There were many stories from the past, and amusing updates about those who were missing the gathering. All sent their regards to the happy couple. The evening still swirled in my mind, hugs from strangers and merry irreverent toasts.

They agreed, but both were glad it was over. "We're trying to keep a low profile for the wedding, because the invoices keep rolling in. Maybe balloons on the tables instead of roses," Lisa said. It was a relaxed and peaceful evening, topped off with a new ice cream called Tofutti that Tony had found, made from tofu. Who knew? Something else to celebrate.

• • •

Later that night, after having finished my test, I pulled Betty's letter out. The bedside lamp glowed softly, Tom purred on my pillow, and the rain tapped lightly on the window. The yeasty odor of bread I had left rising scented the air. The rain ... I always felt safer with rain coming down. It kept more people indoors. I picked up the small square envelope and sniffed. Baby powder.

My dearest Amber, it began, *I am so grateful that you are my sweet Lisa's friend. I would wish that all her friends were such deep-to-the-bone good people as you are. I know that wherever you end up going in the world, whomever you meet, you will always be a pure soul who cares for her friends, including the animal ones. That's it really—sometimes my brain gets flustered when I'm with everybody at dinner, so I'm setting down my thoughts for you in a straight line that I know you'll understand. And welcome to the family!* She signed it, *Affectionately, Betty (Mom).*

I held the letter in my lap and stared at the rain slipping down the window outside. Each drop, on arrival, flattened itself on the glass before it bulged outwards again, holding tightly for a tiny moment before breaking loose and sliding down. I sighed contentedly, fingering Tom's soft fur as he slept, oblivious, bonelessly sprawled across my pillow.

CHAPTER 52

"She looks really peaceful, doesn't she?" Lisa had her arm tucked into mine. She lifted a handkerchief to her nose and sniffled. "What a dear soul she was. She helped me through a lot of ... things that happened after Dad died." She tightened her arm in mine, then reached for a rose from a nearby bouquet, rubbing the petals between her fingers. "She always scowled at flowers, saying that they were prettier left to grow instead of being killed. Maybe these are more for me than her."

We stood in the viewing area, among scattered wingback chairs and a painting of a rural country scene with a heavy gilded frame. There was a peculiar smell in the air, something in between musty old perfume and cleaning solvents. Lisa gazed into Betty's coffin, murmuring quietly, then took my arm again. "I'm ready to greet more people now. I've got to do this. I owe her a lot."

I was relieved. I had so far avoided looking at Betty, feigning sleep in this strange room, all silent and still the way she had never been in life. We walked back to the receiving line. "Lisa, Marlene's here, and she's brought more roses," I said, "I'll take care of them."

"Hey kid, how's that terror of a cat doing?"

"He's turned into quite the gentleman. His favorite thing in the world now is a belly rub." I took the roses and looked around for an open spot near the photo display.

She chuckled, "Maybe he just needed a good lesson from your rabies pole."

"Nope, never needed that again, even at the vet's," I said. "Here, they'll look beautiful here," I inhaled deeply as I settled the roses on a table. Flowers for the things we hadn't said.

There was a steady stream of friends and family, murmuring together over the photo display, speaking softly to Lisa and Tony. Handshakes, comforting shoulder pats, warm or perfunctory hugs.

More pictures were set on metal easels. The wedding, Lisa beautiful in her veil with her mom beaming up at her. "God must have spoken a word to get Betty home for the wedding," said Marlene. The ceremony had been brief and lovely, Lisa glowing with happiness.

I turned back to the photos. Here was the wedding party; me with an awkward smile. Then here, a young Betty with an armful of puppies, her smile huge. A teenaged Betty holding a trophy from her debate contest.

I stepped back from the pictures and watched Lisa hugging an older lady with a velvety black cap pinned to her hair. I breathed in slowly, then approached the large wooden coffin. I blinked, then looked down at Betty's face. I let go of my breath and held myself there, supported by the murmurs of conversation behind me. She did indeed look peaceful, lying so still, a small red rose surrounded by delicate baby's breath pinned to her jacket. Her hands were primly clasped together and resting on her skirt. I imagined them flying up, exaggerating a phrase, lending strength to an argument. She was pale, but that was better than the heavy rouge I remembered on my mother's face from so many years ago.

I heard footsteps behind me, so I turned away, unwilling to be caught up in anyone else's grief. I sank into a wingback chair, leaning back into its cushions and smoothing my hands over my dress. I picked a bit of lint off my lap.

This leaving, this loss, was hard to accept. It was much easier being the one who left, I thought. As a girl I would carefully write down addresses for my friends before it was time to get back into the station wagon with Dad. If I was lucky, I'd have time for one last goodbye with the one or two girls I had gotten to know, but often we packed up and left almost before the sun had come and gone. Letters would be exchanged for a while, decorated with hearts and stars in colored ink, but eventually the friendships faded and we each grew into our separate lives once again. A seamless transition, most of the time.

As the one who did the leaving, there were exciting changes ahead—a new house, a new neighborhood, new places to bike, new forests to explore, trees to climb, and farms to discover. But now, I was the one left behind. The only change was that my life was made smaller, more empty.

"Amber."

I jumped and shook my head, rubbing at my eyes and looking up to see Lisa.

"You were far, far away! How you doing?"

"I'm the one who should be asking you that." I lifted my hand towards the coffin. "She always did like that outfit."

"Yeah, I picked it out. I wanted her to come before her Maker, or whatever happens, looking her best." Lisa smiled and touched my hair, almost whispering, "Amber, you are the sister I never had."

"My life would have been different then, I think," I said, "a lot better."

"But I wouldn't have you any different than you are now, not for the world." Lisa's gaze softened, "At least Mom was able to come to the wedding. I've finally grown up, and she got to see it happen." She paused, "I'm doing okay. Actually, Tony is having a harder time than me. He's really broken up."

I hugged her, then settled back in my chair, watching groups of people come and go. They talked softly near the coffin, as if they might disturb Betty's rest. I imagined her sitting up and demanding to know what all the whispering was about. I remembered the dark suit and tie my father had worn at my Mom's service, buttoned tightly across his stomach. He had kept awkwardly pulling at his collar with a finger, grimacing. That was the last time I had seen him in a suit.

Finally I said my goodbyes, hugging Lisa and Tony. I could feel Tony trembling, but he smiled into my eyes as I left. He was going to be okay, I thought. I imagined he and Lisa holding each other after everyone was gone, quiet in the night, talking and remembering, touching each other's faces gently. Maybe they would smile a little, maybe they would cry, but they would be okay.

I drove home slowly, wondering if the friends I had moved away from had missed me. Did their lives change after I was gone? Did they eat different foods, play different games, talk about new things? Or maybe my passing left no mark, as if I had never existed in that town, slowly fading from their memories, until the last letter was read and then forgotten?

CHAPTER 53

The sun was gentle on my shoulders as I pedaled back home from class. The midterm test had been difficult, but I finished in time. As we had filed out of the classroom, Alex handed me a bit of paper with a phone number. I grinned at him and tucked it away.

As I coiled the lock around my bicycle seat post I replayed his laughing, "Now, don't lose it," in my mind. He had an interesting way of tilting his head when listening, as if capturing every stray bit of spoken word that might have gone unnoticed by anyone else. I wondered what it would be like to have him in my kitchen, making a salad or frying up his special stir-fry with mustard that he was always talking about.

Despite the still-warm sun, it was a cold ride home. Crisp brown leaves had collected along the shoulders, obscuring bike tire dangers like rocks and roots. It would be time for the car soon.

I turned into my driveway and saw Tom's face peering out from under the curtain, like an old lady in a lacy bonnet. He disappeared and the curtain fell. I wheeled the bike onto the porch and pulled out my still-shiny key, pushing it into the deadbolt.

Tom was ready for dinner, as always. I pulled off my shoes, fed my one-eyed friend, and stretched out on the couch. Tom ate quickly, then came running to me. I laughed as his belly swung, "You'll bruise your knees if you run any faster."

I worked at the kitchen table while eating my salad and waiting for my soup to boil. Tom was on the windowsill studying a bird stepping jerkily through the grass.

"What can he possibly find for food, Tom? No bugs in this weather, I would think."

The fur suddenly lifted on Tom's back and he thumped to the floor and sped off down the hall, inviting a chase. When I got there, feeling a little silly, he was nowhere to be found, so I scrabbled under the bed making cat-eating-monster noises. A blur of gray fur whisked by my ear, paws thumping on the wood, as my hand touched a small square foil packet. I reached in and pulled it out. My father's brand. The tears came easily, sliding down my cheeks and pooling on the packet, but they didn't last long. I sighed and wiped them away, feeling empty and yet changed, ready for a different life.

It had been almost six months since I last saw Mike. He called often at first, after the day I drove him out of the house and locked the door. Once he even came over and tried his key in the lock again, as if he couldn't help himself, twisting it around and clawing at the door. I was frightened but determined, fiercely reminding myself of my wish for solitude. Hard-won knowledge that gave me little solace at first, but as each week passed it felt more and more right, more true to myself. My inner sacred places had to remain free of his need.

I rose, leaving the packet where it lay. I put my hand into my pocket and felt the tiny scrap of paper. I pulled it out and stared at the neatly penned numbers, then tucked it away into my pocket again and stood at my bedroom window. My chest rose with a deep breath, and I felt the expansion still happening deep inside, secure within my innermost self. The wind kicked up outside, tossing leaves against the screen, each one clinging briefly, wanting in out of the cold. I sat down and put my hand gently on Tom's head as he curled around my leg, my fingers feeling inner rumbling. He pressed back, pushing hard and arching his back, guiding my hand down his spine. I rubbed the solid muscles underneath his plush coat. Outside, a sudden gust reached the aspen tree and detached a single leaf from its upper branches. Brown, dry, and curled, it dipped and swayed on its way down to the dry earth.

CHAPTER 54

Winter flew by and spring was ushered in by robins. I was finally free of the sadness that had surrounded my days at HAA. Good things were happening, as if the outside world mirrored the inner. I had an interview with the local paper, and I had also joined a rowing team training for recreational races. Practice was today.

Arriving at the boathouse, I saw the sleek shells resting in their slings, reminding me of greyhounds waiting for the starting signal. Thankfully, I thought, shells don't share the same sad fate as living, breathing, racetrack dogs. My team had eight people, two groups of four, and they were an enthusiastic crowd, ranging in age from a sixteen-year-old and his father, to a middle-aged housewife, to a slightly older lady college professor, a white-haired retired policeman, and a few others in between. But when we lined ourselves up in the shells, ready to row, our differences dissolved and our breathing quickened together. We all shared a common interest—speed. Nothing more complicated than that.

I joined the father and son duo, carrying oars to the waterside. We chatted about the regatta coming up next month.

"Do you think we'll be ready?" I asked.

"Sure! We'll do our best and that will be good enough, right?" the father said.

"Absolutely!" I replied, and shared a grin with his son. He was smiling from ear to ear. I watched him set down his oars, then splash his father, who yelled in mock outrage. The boy ran, shrieking and laughing, when his dad threatened to toss him in the water. The laughter made his freckles almost glow where they spread across his cheeks.

Jane was adjusting something in a shell, muttering quietly. I came closer and watched her move one of the racks that holds the foot stretchers. She stood back and examined her placement. "That should be about right for two seat. You were having some trouble getting your full stroke in, and that should make a difference." She caught the older gentleman's eyes.

He was absently tucking his socks into his waist band, and then his eyes cleared. "Excellent!" he said. "Maybe that'll help me match my power better to Amber, here."

I smiled, "You're only gonna make me work even harder to keep up with you!"

The rest of the team chatted together, planning our post-regatta party. We laughed while we stretched, commenting on the weather and the water conditions. We felt like old pros, hoisting our shells and getting them smoothly down into the water. No more stooge-like moves, though I almost missed that part of it.

We warmed up at a slower pace, then increased our speed, and I was breathing hard as we began our first sprint. Cool water splashed on my leg from the next seat's oars, and it felt good, a benediction directly from the lake itself. As I pulled hard on my own oars, thoughts of Mike floated up. Kicking him out was like conquering my fear of flipping. It had happened in stages. Once done, I could do it again, as many times as necessary, each time with less fear. Unbidden, exultation rose in me, flowing from my feet to the straining muscles in my legs, up my back and out my arms, streaming seamlessly into the water rushing by our shell. I felt the pull of the foot stretchers, anchoring me and sending me into the next powerful wave of motion, one with the team.

I didn't think my life was changing because of foot stretchers, but they had been an immediate catalyst for change and a challenge to my insecurities, once I felt those straps tighten. Now I welcomed this new feeling, I liked the closer connection to life, almost as if I was part of a single, larger, organism. And I had great company. With my team, I could be myself, and I belonged. Who needed makeup?

We surprised the egret fishing along the bank and raced the heron as she glided. The other boat, slightly ahead, disappeared into the mist hanging above the water in the early morning, the sun briefly shining beneath it, lighting up the opposite bank.

• • •

I was about to dial when the phone rang in my hands.

"Amber, I have big news," Lisa's smile traveled down the phone line.

"What, you've discovered how to make calorie-free candy? We're going to be rich!"

"No, you nut! Tony and I, we're having a baby!"

I took a breath, "Lisa, that's wonderful! The world has just changed forever, and for the better! Congratulations!"

Lisa was quiet, and I waited, hearing her breathing slow down.

"Amber?"

"Yes?"

"My dad, he would have been proud of me. Even though he hated my work, he hated my boyfriends, he hated ..." She took a shuddering breath, "This is one thing he would have celebrated. Somehow that makes everything better. I can almost feel him nearby now, smiling. I'm finally letting that old bad stuff go. And I wish I could share some of this peace with you."

"Oh, Lisa, you are. You are."

"Good. And you're doing okay?"

"I am. I've even started volunteering with the shelter on weekends. It's good being with the animals again, helping out, settling them into good homes, finding foster families for the orphaned kittens. I'm even working with the vet there sometimes, during spay and neuter surgeries. She's amazing and I'm learning so much from her."

• • •

I found Tom in my room, picking him up from his nap and simply cuddling his soft self, nuzzling his fur and feeling his quiet purr beginning and spreading. "What a pair we make, Tom. You and me, the invisible and the unseen." I thought about Lisa and her happiness, and suddenly realized that I was happy too. I kissed Tom between the ears, gently returned him to my pillow, and told him I had to make a call.

"Remember me?"

"Good to hear your voice!" Alex and I talked for quite a while, and it was effortless. We saw a lot of things the same way. We set a plan for dinner on Saturday. I put down the phone, smiling. "Tom, I'm only slightly amazed at myself."

CHAPTER 55

The dinner went well, our conversation flowing easily. I could get used to this. But I wanted to be sure. No surprises, I thought. I'd had enough for one lifetime.

"There's something I want to share with you, Alex," I said. If it was possible, I was holding my breath and talking at the same time.

"What'cha got?" he grinned at me, wiping some guacamole off his hands with a napkin and taking a sip of soda.

I took a deep breath, preparing for a dive into deep water. "I had trouble with a man."

Alex got very still and looked into my eyes. His body was relaxed, but his focus on me felt intense and suddenly very personal.

I wanted to escape, take a bathroom break, make a phone call, anything to move out of that intense focused gaze, but I steadied myself and said, "Well, it was kind of messy, and what made it worse was that it was my father."

He was silent, concentrating hard. Was he curious? Did he care? Did he hate me?

I kept talking, wanting this moment over, wanting him to do something, say something, yet I wasn't sure that I would be ready to hear it. "It's okay now. It's over."

He reached out slowly and took my hand, shocking me.

I hesitated, then tightened my fingers around his warm solid palm, larger than mine. I mumbled, desperate to get it out, "I wanted to celebrate. With you."

Suddenly Alex let go of my hand and grabbed a passing waiter. My heart thumped in my chest, and I felt nauseous. I needed to leave, or at least simply disappear.

"Do you have any champagne?" Alex asked the waiter, who looked sternly at him. "Okay, some sparkling cider, something festive?"

The waiter smiled and nodded.

"Then we want some."

The waiter glanced at me, then grinned and headed for the kitchen.

Alex turned back towards me, his face suddenly serious, then said, "Is cider suitable? Is it okay with you?"

For a moment I couldn't speak, thoughts whirling in my mind like fall leaves caught in a wind storm. "Sure, but for what? Why?"

"Celebrating!" he said, sitting back in his chair and crossing his arms, gazing at me.

"Celebrating?" I smiled and nodded, grinning and feeling my eyes fill. I wiped at them and laughed, "Of course!"

We waited for the cider, fiddling with the bits of chips left in the bowl, smiling at each other, looking out at the tree branches moving across the window. Nearby conversations flowed over me and my skin prickled.

"Good kite-flying weather," he remarked. The waiter finally arrived with a flourish, two clear glasses of sparkling cider held on a silver tray.

We toasted each other, the bubbles fluttering in my stomach. "My dad, it was ... he was ..."

"An abuser?"

I leaned back, mouth open. I stared at him, but saw only caring and curiosity. "Yes. How did you ... ?"

"My big sister. She had the same thing happen."

"Oh my God, Alex," I was silent. His hand on mine was warm, steady.

I wiped at my eyes again. "Your sister, how is she? How does she cope? Did you help her?" I was almost babbling, my words released from some intense internal pressure.

He lowered his eyes, picked at a stain on the tablecloth, then put his napkin over it. He glanced up at me, his face solemn, and said quietly, "She didn't make it."

"What do you mean?"

"She took a bottle of pills."

I put down my glass and leaned towards him, the enormity of his loss flowing over me. "Oh, Alex, oh ... " I put my hand on his knee and felt a fine trembling in the muscle there, just beneath the skin.

"It happened two years ago. She told our mom, but Mom didn't believe her. I had no idea about any of it until my sister was gone. Some days I wonder, if there had been something I could have done, something I could have said, I don't know ..."

"Alex," my words stumbled in my throat, but I pushed forward, wanting, needing to step into that place with him, "I know about wanting to die. And it wasn't about what you did or didn't do. I'm sure you loved her."

"I—yes, I did. I loved and admired her."

"Then you made her life better than it would have been otherwise. Know that."

We talked until the restaurant closed, finishing our cider, the bubbles floating up and bursting on our cheeks. Our conversation pulled feelings from deep within us, sharing colors and nuances and memories and regrets and also, sometimes, blessings. Hidden agonies, tended for so long deep within our private suffering places, blended together in their release. Through this deep communion, our shared distress began to ease. By the end of the evening, when we said goodbye under the lone street light, the velvety warming air of spring touching our faces, the delicate wings of a lone moth floating past, I knew I had found a friend. And along the way, I had found myself.

ABOUT THE AUTHOR

Wendy Jensen grew up in three different countries, landing finally in New Hampshire to practice homeopathic veterinary medicine and play violin. She received her veterinary degree from Cornell in 1987. In 1990, she left to spend four years working for People for the Ethical Treatment of Animals and then the Physicians Committee for Responsible Medicine, where she discovered homeopathy. She has written frequently for holistic animal health magazines, and lectures widely. She published *The New World Veterinary Repertory* (Narayana Verlag) with co-author Dr. Richard Pitcairn, and her own textbook *The Practical Handbook of Veterinary Homeopathy: Healing Our Companion Animals from the Inside Out* (Black Rose Writing). She has served as an advocate at her local crisis center since 2017.

NOTE FROM THE AUTHOR

Word-of-mouth is crucial for any author to succeed. If you enjoyed *But I Already Said Goodbye*, please leave a review online—anywhere you are able. Even if it's just a sentence or two. It would make all the difference and would be very much appreciated.

Thanks!
Wendy Thacher Jensen

We hope you enjoyed reading this title from:

BLACK✿ROSE
writing™

www.blackrosewriting.com

Subscribe to our mailing list – *The Rosevine* – and receive **FREE** books, daily
deals, and stay current with news about upcoming
releases and our hottest authors.
Scan the QR code below to sign up.

Already a subscriber? Please accept a sincere thank you for being a fan of
Black Rose Writing authors.

View other Black Rose Writing titles at
www.blackrosewriting.com/books and use promo code
PRINT to receive a **20% discount** when purchasing.

www.ingramcontent.com/pod-product-compliance
Lightning Source LLC
Chambersburg PA
CBHW050152120726
47903CB00002B/587